THE ARAB FALL

A James Acton Thriller

By
J. Robert Kennedy

James Acton Thrillers

The Protocol
Brass Monkey
Broken Dove
The Templar's Relic
Flags of Sin
The Arab Fall

Detective Shakespeare Mysteries

Depraved Difference
Tick Tock
The Redeemer

Special Agent Dylan Kane Thrillers

Rogue Operator

Zander Varga, Vampire Detective

The Turned

THE ARAB FALL

A James Acton Thriller

J. ROBERT KENNEDY

ISBN-10: 1490509968

ISBN-13: 978-1490509969

First Edition

10 9 8 7 6 5 4 3 2 1

For our dear Harriet Richards, whose mind was taken from us long before her death. You will be missed.

THE ARAB FALL

A James Acton Thriller

"All Muslims are charged with applying the teachings of Islam to remove such idols, as we did in Afghanistan when we destroyed the Buddha statues. God ordered Prophet Mohammed to destroy idols. When I was with the Taliban we destroyed the statue of Buddha, something the government failed to do."

Sheikh Murgan Salem al-Gohary, Dream TV 2 Interview
Nov 10, 2012

"Egypt's Justice and Development for Human Rights warned against the ongoing incitements from a large number of men of the Islamic religion to destroy the Pyramids and other Pharaonic antiquities, deeming them pagan symbols of pre-Islamic Egypt…. these calls have greatly increased after the victory of the Muslim Brotherhood candidate, Dr. Muhammad Morsi."

El-Balad Newspaper
July 17, 2012

PREFACE

One of the most famous figures in history is Cleopatra. Much is known of her as she was the last Pharaoh to lead her kingdom, and died at a time where Roman culture kept written records of events that shed much light upon her.

We know much. She was born Cleopatra VII Philopator in Alexandria, Egypt, in 69 BC. She was married three times, the first two times to her brothers, as was Egyptian custom, then finally to the Roman Mark Antony, a romance that inspires to this day. Before Antony, she famously consummated a relationship with Julius Caesar himself, producing a son Ptolemy Caesar, nicknamed Caesarion (literally translated as Little Caesar). She also had three children with Antony.

Cleopatra was not truly Egyptian. Alexander the Great, a Greek, conquered Egypt, and after his death, Egypt was ruled by the Ptolemaic dynasty. This dynasty famously refused to learn Egyptian, speaking only Greek. Cleopatra changed that however. She learned Egyptian, embraced its ancient culture, and declared herself the reincarnation of the goddess Isis, a popular figure throughout Egyptian history. After her death, her son Caesarion was named Pharaoh by his supporters, but he was promptly put to death on Octavian's orders, Egypt subsequently becoming a Roman province.

There are several versions of Cleopatra's death claimed by history, however whether or not it was one snake or two, or whether she was bitten on the arm or the breast, are irrelevant. She died by her own doing, willingly. One misconception is that she was killed by an asp. Asps were not indigenous to Egypt, however the belief today is that all poisonous snakes, including king cobras, were called asps. It would make sense that a king cobra was used, as this creature held an important place in Egyptian culture.

1

The famous death masks we are so used to seeing, the most recognizable perhaps the blue and gold mask of King Tutankhamen, actually represents a king cobra, the ridge of gold and blue surrounding the face the hood of the snake.

Cleopatra's death is documented, the date, August 12, 30 BC is known, and it is accepted she was entombed with her beloved Antony.

What is not known is where they were buried, and why we have been unable to find the tomb of the most famous, and most recent, of all the Pharaohs.

Liberty Island, New York, New York
Today

Randy Douglas sipped his Diet Coke through the too narrow straw that seemed to turn every drag into a fizzy mess of bubbles rather than the cool treat it should have been. It was always disappointing when that happened, and he never went back to a place a second time if it did. But here he had no choice. This was where he worked, and every time he bought his lunch with fountain drink, he'd comment to the staff member about the straws to no avail.

Maybe someday they'll listen.

He popped the top off the drink, setting the plastic rim and offending straw to the side, instead drinking directly from the cup as he finished his cheeseburger and fries. Sitting at the far corner of the patio overlooking the bay, he watched the Liberty Island ferry approach, a sight he had seen hundreds of times before, over hundreds of lunches.

Lunches that were none too healthy.

He patted his paunch, something he never thought he would let happen, but since retiring from the New York Police Department after thirty years of service, he had gone shack whacky at home with his wife, so decided he had to work in order to stay sane and save his marriage. A friend had hooked him up in this cushy gig as a security guard with the US Park Police.

He eyeballed four men walking off the ferry, his cop instincts kicking in. They appeared Middle Eastern, their faces cleanly shaven, and wearing the latest Western fashions, they shouldn't have stuck out. But they did. Perhaps it was the fact they weren't smiling, but that wasn't it.

Randy took a sip from his open cup, and watched as the four men stepped off the dock and onto the red stone walkway that ringed the island. The four turned to the right, walking along the edge of the seawall, and it wasn't until he saw the group break away from the throng that he realized what had made him single them out.

And no, it wasn't their assumed religion.

It was that they were four single men, all with the same ethnicity, not smiling, and walking separately. He had seen enough crimes go down in his career to know to look for groups of people who were together, but weren't. Those not good at it were too obvious. They kept checking their speed so they wouldn't catch up, they'd stop when another would stop. It could be quite comical sometimes, if it weren't for the fact you knew they were about to commit a crime, but couldn't do anything about it until they had actually begun.

What a screwed up justice system we have.

Catch them on the way to the act, with paraphernalia, weapons and tools of the trade, they get a slap on the wrist so they can go off and do it again. Catch them in the act, they could go away for life. Why not treat the two crimes equally? If they've got the plans to the bank, the equipment to crack the vault, and the guns to hold the hostages, charge them as if they had robbed the bank rather than the intent to rob.

But he was just a cop.

Emphasis on *was*.

He stood up and tossed his trash into the bin, holding onto his half-full cup, the ice cold beverage still cooling him on this hot spring day. It was gorgeous, perfectly blue skies, only a slight haze from the polluted city today, the air smelling fresh and crisp, everything in bloom with new life all over the island. Walking past the stark white gift shop, he slowly closed the distance between him and the four men, four men who seemed to have no interest in Lady Liberty. Where almost every head was turned up to gape at the 151 foot high statue atop its nearly equally high base, theirs were all turned to the right, looking out at the bay.

He looked as well, but noticed nothing out of the ordinary. Pleasure craft, commercial vessels, ferries. Nothing that seemed odd to him. He looked back at the group, and nearly froze, his mind fighting its natural instinct to flee. But he pushed through it, his pace barely slowing at the sight of a group of four men leaning on the railing that surrounded the island, and a third group of four men slowly approaching from the opposite direction. All Middle Eastern, all well dressed, all cleanly shaven.

These two new groups were *not* on the ferry he had just watched arrive with the first group, so must have come in on earlier arrivals before his lunch.

Twelve men, all, in his mind, acting suspicious.

But was it just his cynical cop mind assuming crimes where none were? Life on Liberty Island was boring, the biggest thing he had to deal with was tourists angry about line ups.

No, this was different.

Twelve men, all converged on the south side of the massive structure, all pretending to not be together, not one of them within five feet of another, all leaning on the railing, looking casually out at the bay.

I'm calling this in.

He pulled his radio off his belt and clicked the Push-to-talk button.

"This is Douglas, I've got a possible situation in Sector Six, on the south side walkway, requesting backup, over."

The mike squawked, then he heard his asshole supervisor's voice come over the radio. *Great, here we go again.* Randy couldn't stand this guy, and the feeling was mutual. Pete Yakovski seemed to hate anyone who had been on the force, and after some digging, Randy had found out why. Yakovski had applied, and been rejected, numerous times, once even making it into training which he failed.

But somehow the United States Park Police had hired him at arguably one of the most significant national monuments in the country. And he had worked his way up to shift supervisor.

His shift.

"What is it this time, somebody littering, over?"

Randy felt his blood boil as his face and ears burned red. He sucked in a deep breath, all the way to the bottom of his stomach, then slowly exhaled.

"I have twelve, say again, twelve, Middle Eastern men acting in a suspicious manner, over."

There was a pause, and Yakovski's voice seemed a little more muted. In fact, if Randy didn't know any better, he'd say the bastard was scared.

"How are they acting suspiciously, over."

"They didn't arrive together, but are now all congregated in the same spot. Those that did arrive together are pretending to not know each other, and none of them are looking at the statue, they're all looking out at the bay, over."

"Are you kidding me? A group of tourists decide to look at the city instead of the statue for a few minutes, and you want us to arrest them? Get back to your post, you're wasting my time, out."

The mike went silent and Randy pressed it to his mouth. "Fuck you, you arrogant, ignorant asshole, I'm still on my lunch break."

But he hadn't pressed the button, instead remaining content to know Yakovski was an asshole, and always would be, and that unlike Yakovski, Randy could quit at any time, this merely a hobby job.

So fuck orders.

He hooked his radio on his belt, took a sip of his Diet Coke, then continued his observation of the twelve men, who he was now close enough to see were anywhere from late teens to late thirties. All in good shape.

If something does go down, you don't stand a chance.

His finger absentmindedly flicked open the snap securing the holster of his Heckler & Koch P7M13 pistol as he drained the last of his drink, nothing left but ice in the bottom of his cup. He tossed it into a nearby garbage bin, then took position up the branch in the path leading to the northern entrance of the monument, about two hundred feet from where the first man stood. Tucked nearly out of sight, and in the shade of a large little-leaf linden tree, he waited, for what he did not know, but with the pace his heart was pumping at, he knew his subconscious was telling him it couldn't be anything good.

And finally it began.

One of the men suddenly stood erect, then another, both looking at a specific point in the bay. Their counterparts joined them, and Randy looked to see if he could spot what they were looking at. And a good chunk of bravery was cleaved from his stomach, a pit forming that he had felt innumerous times when things were about to go down.

And he fought through it, as he did every time.

Use the fear. Let the adrenaline flow.

He knew it would heighten his senses, make him more alert, if he could only control the fuel surging through his body. He immediately began his tactical breathing techniques, sucking the air in through his nose, forcing it into his stomach, then slowly exhaling through the mouth, and repeating this several times until he had his heart rate down to near normal.

Shakey hands can't shoot straight.

He flipped the buckle to his holster aside, lifting his weapon slightly as the sight before him unfolded.

Two boats, their sleek white hulls skipping above the waves, any safety measures useless, were racing toward the seawall that stood not fifty feet from where he was. All twelve men were standing tall now, staring at the boats as they rapidly closed the gap.

Randy activated his mike.

"This is Douglas, I've got two high speed boats heading toward the island, directly toward my twelve suspects. Something's going down, we need to sound the alert, now! Over!"

"This is Yakovski. I thought I told you to return to——"

"Listen you ignorant bastard, I'm telling you a terrorist attack is about to go down. Now get your thumb out of your ass, and sound the alarm!"

The screaming engines of the boats began to ease as they powered down for the approach. Randy knew if they made the island, they wouldn't stand a chance at stopping any attack.

So he made the decision that cops, soldiers, and everyday heroes do.

He ran toward the danger.

Rushing from his position, he raced to the seawall, drawing his weapon. He hit the guardrail and saw the two boats cutting in opposite directions, as they slid toward the wall. Each held four men, one at the helm, the rest already lifting what looked like ladders, assembling them into lengths that would easily reach the top of the fifteen foot seawall.

Randy grabbed his mike that Yakovski had been screaming threats over and pressed the button. "Two boats are now at the seawall. Eight men are assembling ladders to come ashore. I am engaging, whether your cowardly ass sends me backup or not. Over and out."

He switched off the radio, flicked off his safety, and took aim at the closest boat. He sucked in a deep breath, and eased it out as he squeezed the trigger. The report was loud, and the ricochet off the hull told him he

8

had found his target. He rapidly began to squeeze off rounds at the first boat, sending the tourists in the vicinity into a panic.

Screams filled his ears as his peripheral vision monitored the hundreds of people around him scrambling to get out of the area. A quick glance at the twelve men had them turning toward him, but not drawing weapons, the security checkpoints before getting on the ferry preventing them from bringing any firearms.

He had to stop the boats. They were obviously bringing the weapons for the group. A crackle of gunfire from the second boat sent him ducking as the seawall took several hits from the return fire. He popped up but another burst of gunfire kept him pinned.

Where the hell is the backup?

He heard someone screaming in what he assumed was Arabic, it familiar enough to his ears from the newscasts and movies. He leaned out and saw two of the men from the ferry charging his position. He took aim and squeezed twice. The first man dropped, two rounds in his chest, the other jumping over his fallen comrade's corpse, screaming "Allahu Akbar" at the top of his lungs, his right fist raised in the air, his eyes burning embers of hate.

Randy squeezed off two more rounds, ending the charge.

He reloaded, and peered back over the edge. Ladders from both boats were against the walls, and gear was being tossed in what looked like backpacks from the boats to the top of the wall. He opened fire again, this time taking out the pilot in the first boat who had been yelling "Yalla! Yalla! Yalla!"

Randy was rewarded with another hail of gunfire that sustained itself until he heard several single shots from further down the path. The weapon assaulting his position didn't stop, but did change direction. He popped his head up and saw the light blue uniform of one of his fellow guards drop behind the seawall as bullets tore into the stone.

Carrie!

He recognized her blonde hair immediately. He switched his radio back on and heard the chatter as his report was finally being taken seriously. He reloaded and peered over the edge. It looked like they were finished transferring their equipment as the men from the boats began to climb the ladders. He looked at the group that had already been on the island and they were pulling weapons from the backpacks, then racing for the base of the massive statue.

And with a sickening feeling in his stomach, he knew what they were trying to do.

He activated his mike.

"They're going to blow up the statue!"

"Who is that? Is that you Randy? Are you okay?"

It was Yakovski, his voice actually one of believable concern.

Maybe he's not such an asshole after all?

He pressed the button. "I'm okay. Carrie is taking fire opposite my position, two hundred yards east of me. Two boats have off-loaded a bunch of equipment. Weapons confirmed, perhaps explosives. They're already heading for the base of the monument. I've taken out two of the original twelve, one of the eight new arrivals. We need the Marine Patrol Unit for the boats and SWAT now! Over!"

He squeezed off several more rounds, taking out one of the climbers, then shifted slightly and took out the gunman raining bullets on Carrie. She immediately responded by jumping up and emptying her clip at those climbing the ladder closest to her. One went down, but a burst of gunfire from the pathway was met with a cry from her and she fell out of sight.

"Carrie!" cried Randy, his chest gripping his heart tight as the young woman, full of so much promise, went down. He grabbed his mike. "Carrie's been hit! I repeat, officer down, over!"

"Is your position secure, over?"

Randy took a look. Now that the boats were empty and the equipment transferred, he seemed to have been forgotten, all the terrorists, for that's what they were, racial profiling be damned, were either at the star shaped base of the monument, or running toward it. He loaded his last clip and emptied it at the men, taking three down permanently, wounding two who continued toward the wall, one limping, the other gripping his shoulder. He ejected the clip and sat down, the little alcove he was hidden in the only thing between him and certain death as bullets tore at the stone pathway, ricochets coming uncomfortably close.

"I'm out of ammo!" he yelled into his mike. "I've taken out three more hostiles, wounded two. By my count that's nine down, eleven still a threat. My position is secure unless they decide to rush it. I need ammo! Over!"

"Help is on its way. Sit tight! Over and out."

Randy peered around the corner and saw the last man clearing the top of the ladder, the two he had wounded lying on the ground, their weapons swinging back and forth as they looked for threats.

"Randy!"

Randy looked over to where the voice had come from, and saw three of his comrades on their bellies, lying on the pathway leading to the entrance to the statue.

"Ammo!" he yelled.

Dick Vance, an old timer like him from the force, waved then tossed a clip that clattered toward him, but was ten feet short. He tossed another one, harder, and this one landed within two feet of him. He reached out and grabbed the clip as bullets tore through the pathway, a shard of stone slicing through the fleshy part of his hand between his thumb and forefinger.

He loaded the clip then looked at the three men across from him.

"Ready?"

Vance gave him the thumbs up.

"On three!" Randy flipped himself over on his knees then pushed himself to one, his kneecap protesting. "One, two, three!" He leaned out as the others jumped up, and began squeezing off rounds at the two men guarding the ladders. Within seconds it was over, the four weapons against two weakened men no match.

Randy ran toward the ladders as Vance and the other two youngsters as he liked to call them ran to join him. Screams from above told them all they needed to know as the cracks of small arms fire was met with the heavy bursts of fully automatic weapons.

Randy looked at Vance.

"Status?"

Vance handed him several clips.

"Harbor Patrol is on the way, the ferry has been recalled, and we're setting up evac points at the dock and on the north side of the island. Tourists are being moved from the monument now, but we haven't had time to get them out. That jackass Yakovski wasted several minutes ranting about you. The damned stairwell is still full, all the way to the torch."

"We may only have minutes." Randy pointed at the two young men who had accompanied Vance. "Jones? Ferrero?" The men nodded. "You two ready to be heroes?"

Jones grinned. "Absofuckinlutely."

"Then get up those ladders and shoot anything that has a gun and isn't wearing a uniform. We'll be right behind you."

The two men charged up the ladders, their weapons slung across their backs, as Randy and Vance followed. Shots rang out in their direction, and Randy heard one of the young men cry out, as the other returned fire. Jones fell past them and Randy reached out, grabbing him and swinging him into the ladder. The young kid grabbed on as Randy's shoulder screamed for relief.

"You alright, kid?"

"I've got it," he winced as he grabbed the rungs. Randy let go and resumed his climb, Vance already over the top. Randy reached the lip of the base and looked over. Ferrero was on his belly, firing at a group near the temporary construction stairs leading to the third level, the rest already either up the stairs or just about to be. Vance was squeezing off rounds from his pistol when Randy dropped beside him, opening fire. A burst shattered the stone in front of them, and Vance cried out, rolling over, his face bloodied where the shards had torn open the skin.

"Fuck this!" cursed Ferrero as he jumped up and ran toward the position, but to the left, pouring bullets on the two terrorists, and drawing their gunfire. Randy got to his knees and took careful aim, squeezing the trigger and taking out one of the men. Lining up for his second shot, he heard Ferrero cry out, and from the corner of his eye saw him stumble and fall.

He squeezed.

The final target was down.

He grabbed his mike and pressed the switch.

"I've got three men down, two on the second level, south side, one at the bottom of the base, south side. Four more terrorists are dead, but the remaining have made it to the third level. You need to empty the monument, now!"

He grabbed Vance by the jacket. "Are you okay?"

13

The man nodded through the blood. "I think so, just hurts like a mother fucker. How's it look?"

"Could be an improvement. I've gotta check on Ferrero."

"Forget it. I'll do it. You go after those bastards."

Randy grimaced, then nodded. He pulled two clips from Vance's vest, then ran toward the steps as his friend, grunting behind him, rose to his feet. Randy reached the steps leading up the side of the monument to the next level, the shouts in Arabic distinct, the gunfire unfortunately stopped, indicating they were meeting no resistance.

And he knew his old legs weren't going to get him up two levels of these steps in time. Sirens had his head spinning to his right and he could see several boats of the harbor patrol arriving at least giving Randy the satisfaction that these men weren't going to get away with what they had planned. They'd be caught.

Unless.

The thought sickened him, but he knew he was right. They had no intention of getting away with it. They intended to die for their cause, martyr themselves for entry into a twisted sexual paradise designed to urge young horny males living in repressed societies to die young for their god so they could access some booty.

Where do the female martyrs go?

He pushed himself up the last few steps, but there was no one there to engage, the last man clearing the second level and disappearing from sight. Finally a burst of gunfire, but it was short-lived, and he had no doubt one of his comrades was now dead.

Randy gasped with each step he took toward the next set of steps, his thighs screaming in agony as he pushed himself to continue. He hit the first step, cursing his age, cursing the sedentary lifestyle he had pretty much adopted since retirement, and swore when he got home today, he would hug his wife, call his daughter as he did every Thursday night, then hit the treadmill.

He heard shouts behind him and a quick glance showed a SWAT team rushing down the path, too far behind to be of any help.

If only that asshole Yakovski had called it in.

As he pushed himself up the steps, one at a time, his hands on his legs, pushing with them, he took a glance up at the most gorgeous woman in his life, save his wife and daughter—Lady Liberty. She stood proudly, arm raised in the air proclaiming the ideals of her country. Made in France by French artisans over a nine year period, then transported in pieces across the ocean, it took two additional years to raise the money to build the base she now stood on, and once erected, she became the symbol, the beacon, that tugged on the heartstrings of every modern American, and drew every immigrant who graced her shores with dreams of those ideals.

Freedom and democracy for all. A place where dreams could come true with hard work, where no man could blame his country for his failures, only himself, a beacon to the world of what could be accomplished if men and women were given the freedom to do what they wanted, when the wanted, with whom they wanted.

And proof of this philosophy stood over his right shoulder, one of the richest, freest cities in the world, in a country that in just two centuries had surpassed all others despite many with histories in the thousands of years.

And this beacon that soared above him in her own adopted home, had inspired him every day of his life growing up and working in New York City, and there was no way in Hell he was going to let her fall.

He pushed the last few steps, and saw the entrance that stood at her south side, unguarded, the shouts inside echoing up and down her copper structure, the screams of trapped tourists inside heart wrenching as the high pitched cries of women and children sometimes drowned out the shouts in Arabic.

He nearly crawled toward the entrance, his legs flaming piles of meat that barely functioned, his hands barely off the ground as he gasped for breath, his weapon, still gripped tightly in his hand, dragging on the stone. Stumbling the last few feet, he willed himself upright, taking a deep breath and pushing the pain to the back of his mind, instead focusing on the job ahead.

The shouts behind him told him the young legs of the SWAT team were closing in quickly, but they were still too far behind. He was the only one here, the only one who could stop what was about to happen. He stepped into the doorway, and he heard the most chilling two words he would ever hear in person shouted by one, then echoed by many.

"Allahu Akbar!"

God is great!

Randy felt his chest tighten as a rumbling sound rolled from the structure, his feet beginning to shake as the entire edifice began to vibrate, then a screeching sound, like a beast from the seventh level of Hell had escaped its confines, tore open his ears as at least a dozen deafening blasts followed each other in rapid succession, and as Randy continued into the entrance, he saw a wall of dust and fire rush toward him. He squeezed his eyes shut, raising his hands to protect himself, and began to turn.

But it was futile.

The blast wave, augmented by the confined space, shoved him off his feet, sending his body soaring through the air, the feeling oddly curious. He should be terrified, he should be in pain, but he felt nothing, his vision filled with the rapidly shrinking monument, her torch held high, her face looking down at him with an expression of pride in what he had tried to do for her, and sympathy for what was to become of him.

16

Tears filled his eyes as he saw the dust and debris from the blast exploding from every opening in the base and the old lady herself. He hit the water hard, his breath knocked from him. Quickly he began to sink and it took him a few moments to realize what was happening. Kicking with his legs, he slowly worked his way to the surface, but something was wrong. He was reaching up with his arms to help, but he wasn't seeing his right hand. Looking over at his shoulder, he gasped. His right arm was gone, nothing but a bloody stump remained. He shouted in panic, expending his air, then stopped, kicking even harder, his still exhausted legs working on the last bit of adrenaline his body could muster.

He broke the surface and sucked in a deep breath, trying to stabilize himself as he strained to reacquire Lady Liberty in his sights. He turned around and saw her, still standing, hand defiantly in the air, and he smiled.

Then frowned.

Something was wrong. She didn't look like she should, she didn't look like she had for the fifty plus years he had been looking at her from every angle imaginable.

She was leaning to the left. His left, her right. And she continued to lean. He gasped as the elaborate stone pedestal she stood on crumbled on its western side, and she tumbled over, the cries of the metal and stonework painstakingly constructed by stonemasons and metalworkers over a century ago failing under the awesome power of modern explosives, carried by fanatics hell bent on destroying the very way of life she represented.

And they had succeeded in their mission.

To destroy the symbol that most truly represented America.

He sobbed as the mighty lady crashed into the ground in a pile of dust, her defiant torch, held to light the way of millions who had come to our shores, disappearing as Randy sank beneath the waves, his attempt to save her a failure, and his will to live, gone.

Alexandria, Egypt
11 August, 30 BC

She gripped her pillow tightly, sobbing as she had never sobbed before, the heartache she felt all-consuming, the thought of going on without her beloved Antony unimaginable. She knew now how he had felt when she had lied, sending word to him that she had died. It had been a desperate act, one born from fear after their forces had deserted them and joined Octavian's forces against her darling Antony, fear that her beloved would think that she, Cleopatra, had betrayed him, and would have her killed.

What a fool she had been.

Her dear Antony, upon hearing the lie repeated by her messenger, overcome by grief, stabbed himself in the stomach with his own sword. And if her messenger was to be believed, he lay on his couch, crying out her name, praying to the gods to deliver him from this wretched place and back into her loving arms in the afterlife. And when his prayers went unanswered, and he continued to slowly bleed out, death escaping him still, he begged his servants and friends to finish him off, but none had the courage nor the will.

Her messenger had fled, bringing her word of his actions, and she had immediately returned him with orders to bring her dying Antony to her sanctuary. She smiled at the remembrance recounted to her by her messenger, of how Antony had apparently reacted to the news she was alive. Smiles and laughter, thanks to the gods, then demands he be taken to her immediately.

But with Octavian's treacherous forces so close, she hadn't trusted the party that had arrived, and rather than welcome him with open arms,

18

ordered her handmaidens to lower ropes to him through the window of her bedchamber so that if it were a ruse, the ropes could be cut, and the perpetrator's skull cracked open upon the rocks below. The act of being hauled up the side of the building had nearly killed her love, but her warrior had hung on, long enough for them to kiss once again, and as she saw how horribly mutilated he was, she had torn her clothes off, covering his shivering body, then tore at her own in anger, for she knew she was the one to blame.

"Stop, my love," he had said.

"But why? It is my fault you have done this to yourself. It was my lie, from my lips, repeated by *my* messenger, that caused you the grief you suffered. The grief that caused you to do *this*!" she cried, pointing at his wound.

"But it is my grief no longer. To know you are alive, to know you will survive, is all this man's heart needs to go on. I may die here today, but our love is eternal, a flame never to be snuffed by the treacheries of others, a bond that will continue after our deaths and into the afterlife, forever at each other's side, forever as one, I Caesar, you my Queen, for eternity."

He winced, and she rushed to his side, her tirade of self-pity over.

"Wine," he gasped, and she motioned for one of her handmaidens to fulfill the request. Cleopatra sat on the couch, lifting his head gently into her lap, tears rolling down her cheeks and onto her bosom, dignity no longer something she cared about, her grief overtaking her, for she knew her lover was about to die.

The wine arrived, she held it to his lips, and he drank it thirstily at first, then with each sip, slightly weaker, until finally his lips drew no more, and he sighed one final time, looking into her eyes, his own filled with tears, as a weak smile looked up at her. She caressed his cheek, wiping away a tear that had escaped, and returned his smile.

"I love you, my darling."

"And I you," he whispered, his eyes closing, his smile waning, and his body going slack in her arms.

"No!" she screamed, dropping her face to his, pressing her lips against his forehead, holding him tighter than she could remember doing before, as her handmaidens rushed to her side, comforting her and urging her away from the corpse that now lay in her lap. She fought them off, refusing to let go, and it was hours before she finally could be convinced to release him.

And with one last kiss, she whispered in his ear, "I shall be with you soon, my love."

But it wasn't to be. The treacherous Octavian had captured her in her mausoleum in the middle of her grief, and ordered his freedman Epaphroditus to guard her lest she should attempt suicide. It was her final defeat. Her armies were wiped out or had deserted her, her lover was gone, dead by her own words, and now she, in a final act of humiliation, was being denied her right to suicide, her right to reunite with her lover, and instead, if she knew Octavian, would be paraded through the streets of Rome, humiliated before the masses, then condemned to either a life of isolation, or worse, torture.

And she was determined not to let that happen.

She let go of her pillow and sat up in her bed, causing the ever alert Epaphroditus to rise as well.

"Can I get you anything?" he asked, always the model of politeness.

"My handmaidens."

He nodded, exiting the room and whispering something to the Roman Centurion standing outside. Within moments her handmaidens arrived, rushing to her side, one brushing her hair, another wiping her face of her tears, another straightening her clothes.

20

It was her trusted confidante, touching up her face, that she whispered her orders to. And as she hoped, the young girl gave no indication she had even heard the horrific directions, other than to make momentary eye contact.

Cleopatra stood up, her entourage scurrying with a flick of her wrist, her plan set in motion.

Residence of Queen's Preferred Goldsman, Alexandria
11 August, 30 BC

"Your Queen needs you."

Tarik's eyebrows shot up, the hooded man who stood in the doorway at first thought to be a beggar, was anything but, the quality of his robes dismissing the very idea. He stepped over the threshold and into the luxurious home of one of Alexandria's greatest goldsmen, and one of several personal jewelers to the Queen.

Tarik regarded the man skeptically. *How can I possibly help the Queen? She's a prisoner of that pile of camel dung Octavian!* He looked at the man again, but all details were hidden by the robes that covered him from head to toe.

Suddenly the man flipped the hood back, and all doubt was removed, the royal markings painted on his face, the necklace that adorned his neck made by Tarik himself.

He bowed, deeply, to this stranger.

"How may I be of assistance to my Queen?"

"Her majesty requires two king cobras to be delivered to her chambers tomorrow morning."

Two king cobras?

Tarik's mind raced as he tried to imagine what she could possibly want them for. They were deadly, terribly deadly, just one bite would kill a man. It would be a slow death, but painless, the venom first paralyzing the eyes, then the body, so nothing would be felt as the heart stopped beating, and the body slowly starved itself of oxygen.

Then he smiled.

A fitting way to strike back at Octavian, who no doubt entered her chambers unannounced, unwanted, to gloat at his victory over her and the great Antony.

If she could have one of the cobras strike him, he would be dead, and even if she were killed, she would have the satisfaction of knowing her enemy died first.

It was an incredible plan, but how he could possibly help her execute it eluded him. He said as much to the messenger.

"Your brothers are farmers?"

"Indeed."

"Suppliers of the royal household?"

Tarik nodded.

"Each day you deliver, among other things, a basket of figs to her majesty?"

"Yes, yes I believe they do."

Tarik wasn't involved in the deliveries, but he remembered his brothers mentioning it once that the Queen had a love of the chewy treat when in season.

"Place the snakes in the basket, pile the figs on top. Once delivered, we will take care of the rest."

Tarik nodded, and before he could ask any further questions, the man had flipped the hood back up, covering his face, and departed into the night, leaving Tarik to tremble in the doorway at what he was about to take part in.

He grabbed a nearby robe, tossing it over his shoulders to protect himself from the chill outside, then stepped from his house to help strike the final blow against their oppressor.

Nubian Desert, Egypt, University College London Dig Site
Two Days Before the Liberty Island Attack

Professor James Acton looked up slightly, spotting a pair of brand new boots, covered in dirt, with pant legs to match. He needn't look any higher to know it was his friend, Hugh Reading, a man who was quickly discovering that an archeological dig site in the desert was *not* his cup of tea.

"Bloody hell! Look at these trousers!"

Laura Palmer, Acton's fiancée and love of his life, leaned over and playfully flicked some of the dirt away with her brush.

"Better?"

The former Scotland Yard Detective Chief Inspector harrumphed and walked away, muttering about getting some fresh air, which Acton knew meant the tent he and Laura slept in. Reading had questioned why they were the only two blessed with air conditioning in the desert, and Laura had tried to explain it was a communal tent during the day, and at night in the desert, you didn't need air conditioning.

Reading had done his best Iceman "Bullshit" cough, which Acton was impressed he knew what with the cultural and partial generational divide. The next morning a shivering Reading had asked how the hell they slept in such bloody cold.

"Didn't bring any warm clothes, did you?" Acton had jibed.

Reading had glared at him. "It's the bloody desert. Of course I didn't bring *warm* clothes."

Warm clothes were donated by Acton and several of the students, along with his former partner at Scotland Yard, Detective Inspector Martin Chaney. Chaney had been eager to accept the invitation, Reading not as much, but with enough cajoling from his friends had agreed. After all the four of them had been through over the past several years, a bond had formed. Reading and Chaney the bond formed between police partners; Acton and Laura the bond of a love forged under fire, and the sharing of those experiences binding them all.

Reading was Interpol now, which had proven convenient for them during recent events in Rome. Chaney's work for the Triarii, a two thousand year old organization founded from the ruins of a Roman legion tasked with protecting the crystal skulls by their Emperor Nero, allowed him the freedom to travel anywhere if it were on Triarii business, and after what Professors James Acton and Laura Palmer had done for them when they all first met, favors were owed.

Which meant Chaney was able to follow his friends into the middle of nowhere and play archeologist, but with a purpose that he had alluded to, but hadn't mentioned to Acton yet. It was driving Acton a little nuts, because he was certain it was Triarii related, and every time they entered the picture, bullets started flying.

All Acton wanted was a nice, peaceful two weeks in the Egyptian desert with his fiancée and friends.

Gunfire erupted to Acton's left, but he ignored it.

"Is it that time already?"

Laura looked at her watch.

"No, not for another five minutes." She looked around then sighed. "Must be Terrence again, I don't see him anywhere. I'm going to have to have a talk with him. The self-defense training is encouraged, but not at the expense of his studies."

Terrence Mitchel was a young university doctoral candidate from the University College of London where Laura taught. He was eager, brilliant, and had discovered recently he loved shooting things. After the events in

London and elsewhere around the globe, Laura had used her considerable inherited wealth to provide both her dig site in Egypt and Acton's in Peru with exceptional security, provided mostly by ex-SAS British Special Forces.

Acton knew they both slept at night a little more secure knowing these guys were around, but also because they were taking the opportunity to be trained in self-defense techniques, along with how to handle pretty much every weapon imaginable. This training had saved their asses on more than one occasion, and allowed them to contribute meaningfully to several operations they had been mixed up in.

After the recent turmoil in Egypt, Laura had thought it might be a good idea if the students, at least those interested, were taught some basic self-defense and survival skills.

They had both been stunned when every single student requested the training.

So at ten each morning the camp would gather for one hour and train with the SAS guards. Much of it was straight physical fitness, but at least half of every session was basic hand-to-hand combat and weapons training, along with a five to ten minute lecture on surviving a hostage situation, tricks on how to break out of zip ties, how to kick down doors, and a myriad of other things that Acton wished he had known years ago. His training with the National Guard and his tour during Desert Storm hadn't prepared him for much of what he'd been through. Straight combat, sure, but escape and evade, recon, hostage rescue, sniper tactics, etc., were all Special Forces type training that he had never been exposed to.

He and Laura took these training sessions seriously, discussing each lesson amongst themselves, and now the students, while working the site. They all found talking about what had just been taught reinforced it in their minds, and they all knew it just might save their lives one day.

Reading's head poked out from the air conditioned tent.

"What the bloody hell was that?"

"Self-defense training starts in five. Want to join us?" asked Laura, still on her knees, chipping away hundreds of years of caked dirt from what they had determined to be the foundation of a house, probably from around two thousand years ago.

"Between the Falklands War and you two, I've heard enough gunfire for a lifetime."

He disappeared back into the tent as Chaney roared with laughter at his former boss. "He just wants to get back to the air conditioning." Chaney turned to the professors, hands on his hips. "Rather than shoot at paper targets, I think I'll go for my morning constitutional."

"Huh?"

"'Walk', dear," explained Laura.

"Oh."

"See you soon," said Chaney who then strode away from the camp and the dig site.

"Where do you think he goes?" asked Acton.

Laura shrugged. "Probably nowhere in particular. There's not much to see around here, we *are* kind of in the middle of nowhere."

Acton stretched his back then wiped his brow with a handkerchief he had fished from his pocket.

"If he finds an ice cream stand, let me know."

"At ten in the morning? You'll lose your figure," teased Laura.

Acton dropped his head, raising his eyebrows, and gave her a look.

"Exsqueeze me? I'll have you know my stomach is still flat after all these years, despite your cooking."

Laura feigned hurt.

"Are you insulting my cooking?"

Acton grinned and wrapped his arm across her shoulders, drawing her into him.

"Not at all, my dear, I love your cooking." He lowered his voice. "Especially your *home* cookin'."

"Is that another American euphemism?"

Acton laughed as he led them toward the training area and the ever increasing gunfire.

Alexandria, Egypt
12 August, 30 BC

Cleopatra stirred at the sound of her door opening, and immediately fought to contain her excitement as her servants entered, bringing her usual supplies for her morning ablutions. Scented hot water, cold water, soaps and perfumes, a basket of assorted fruits, and another of her favorite figs, the basket larger than normal.

But she successfully contained her glee, and instead simply stood, stance wide, arms outstretched, as she was attended to by her servants. Their ministrations seemed impossibly slow today, and her trusted handmaiden looked her in the eye, then glanced at the basket of figs, and she knew her orders had been fulfilled.

She would have her revenge on Octavian, the traitorous heathen who would dare to usurp a Pharaoh. She knew she had lost, she knew it was over for her, and there was no way Octavian would get close enough to her for her to exact the revenge she truly wanted.

Her thoughts turned to her children. Her first son, with Caesar, before Antony, would be named Pharaoh. But Caesarion she knew wouldn't be allowed to live. Her heart ached as she thought of her beautiful boy and the pain he was about to endure after she was dead.

But at least it would be short lived.

There was no glory in parading a seventeen year old boy through Rome, and no reason to torture him, for he had done nothing to Octavian.

He would die, swiftly, before the notice of his ascension to the throne reached the outer edges of the kingdom.

And what of her other children, those she had with her beloved Antony? Ptolemy, and the twins Alexander and Cleopatra Selene? Would they too be killed, or would mercy be shown? She closed her eyes, praying to the gods to spare her children, to let them live, even if in obscurity, the life of a Pharaoh, or royalty, no life at all.

She waved off her handmaiden who tried to wrap her robe around her shoulders, instead letting it hang around the tie at her waist, her breasts exposed to the cool morning breeze making its way through the windows. It was a perfect day. A beautiful day. And on any other day she would have sailed the Nile were she permitted, but no more. No more could she rule her people. No more could she gaze upon her kingdom.

And no more could she make love to her dearest Antony.

She walked over to the table where the supplies had been placed, and took a drink of water. She selected a fig, and chewed on it absentmindedly, staring at the basket, looking for the king cobras that should be at the bottom. She had requested two, should the first escape, but only one was needed to do the deed.

She felt a hand on her shoulder. It was her trusted handmaiden, who had arranged the delivery. Her eyes were glassed over, but her face strong. Cleopatra gave her a smile of thanks, then motioned for her to distract the alert eyes of Octavian, Epaphroditus. Her servant slinked over to the man, her lithe body irresistible to most, but Epaphroditus ignored her.

What is he, a eunuch?

She bent down in front of him, and Cleopatra smiled as the man's eyes were irresistibly drawn to the remarkable example of womanhood being displayed. He shifted in his chair.

Cleopatra began removing the figs from the basket, and before Epaphroditus noticed, she had nearly reached the bottom. Sinking her hand into the remaining figs, she felt something move. She grabbed it tightly, and the basket shook in protest, drawing the attention of Epaphroditus, who pushed her handmaiden away with a brush of his large hand.

Cleopatra pulled her hand from the basket, revealing the king cobra, a young one, less than an arm's length long, but as deadly the day it was born as any adult. She spun toward Epaphroditus, holding the menacing creature out. With her free hand, she reached for its head, grabbing it tightly, it now under her control, but the creature now writhing in anger.

"Stay back!" she ordered, Epaphroditus still advancing. She rushed a step forward, the cobra's hooded head facing her captor, and he stopped, retreating several paces, shouting for help. She rounded her bed, placing it between her and him, her handmaidens huddled in the corner, cowering in fear of the vicious, deadly creature. The door sprung open, several Roman Centurions rushing inside.

"If you take one step toward me, if anybody takes one step toward me, you won't live beyond the morning!"

The creature writhing in her hand flared its hood, the "brave" Roman troops jumping back at the famous hiss, it so low it was easily mistaken as a growl. *Who's in control now?* She smiled as she felt the rush surge through her veins, the feeling of control she hadn't had for days suddenly restored. This was *her* chamber, *her* city, *her* kingdom, once again, and she was a Queen, a Pharaoh, to once again be listened to and respected.

The snake slithered in her hand, its head squirming in protest, but she merely squeezed tighter, controlling it as she had once controlled an empire with her Antony. And now she would strike one final blow in their name against their enemy, by denying him his greatest prize.

She looked at Epaphroditus who stood the closest, but too far to interfere with her plans, even his loyalty to Octavian not great enough to risk the bite of a king cobra.

"You will deliver a message for me to your master."

Epaphroditus bristled at her words.

"I am a freedman," he said, his voice cold, a hint of anger at having to define himself to her creeping into his voice. "I have *no* master, but I serve, by my choice, Octavian."

Cleopatra bowed her head slightly with a smile.

"And at his pleasure, I am sure."

Epaphroditus returned the bow.

"Of course."

"And you will deliver my message?"

"Of course."

"Then tell Octavian that I, Cleopatra the Seventh, daughter of Ptolemy the Twelfth, the reincarnation of the goddess Isis, and rightful ruler of this land, deny him his prize. He will not be permitted to parade me through the streets of Rome as a slave, a humiliated former ruler of a far off land Romans are too ignorant of to realize predated their pathetic empire by thousands of years, with monuments greater than the greatest ever built by their hands, that will last until the end of time as symbols of our power.

"I deny him his prize. Forever shall Romans' memories of me be that of the Pharaoh of Egypt, arriving in Rome, their mighty Julius Caesar my puppet, my entourage so massive and elaborate, it rivaled the entrance of anyone before or since, proving the wealth and superiority of the Egyptian people. Forever will he be forced to remember that it was *my* statue that Caesar erected in his famous temple of Venus, as I am Isis, reincarnated once again to shepherd my children to safety.

"And though I have failed this time, I shall be back, in another form, to deliver the masses from the evil that is Rome, and once again, as I suckled my son Horus, the god of war and protection, at the beginning of time, I shall return, to suckle man's savior from Rome. Remember the words I speak here today, for though they may be forgotten to history, when I

32

return, the world shall shudder in relief as I deliver them their savior, their protector, their warrior against evil and those who would serve it.

"For today I do not die, I merely return to my throne in the heavens, leaving Octavian without his prize, his legacy the humiliation of his failure at preventing a lone woman from taking her own life."

She looked up, through the ceiling, and into the heavens, her heart hammering in her chest.

"I do this for you, my beloved."

She turned the head of the cobra toward her, and plunged it into her bare chest. She felt the creature writhe against her skin as Epaphroditus leapt toward her, her handmaidens and the other guards watching in horror.

Then she felt the bite, the creature finally fed up with her controlling it, it lashing out in the only way it knew how. Its fangs sank into her soft skin, and she cried out in pain as the poison pumped into her blood, then through her system, the warmth, the numbness, flowing through her, spreading rapidly. As her strength waned, she dropped the snake, and Epaphroditus sliced it in half with his sword, catching her near naked form as she collapsed to the floor.

Swinging her into his arms, he placed her gently on the bed, calling for a doctor, but she knew there was no cure for her, no helping her. The bite of a king cobra, even from birth, is deadly, and this one had been angry and scared, pumping her with enough venom that she was certain it would be a quick death. Already she could feel her eyes beginning to lock into place, the toxins paralyzing them.

Her handmaidens came into view, pushing Epaphroditus aside, tears streaking their faces as they praised her for her courage and strength, swearing to repeat the story to all who would listen. Their voices faded, and soon all she could hear was her own heartbeat, each beat seeming a little slower, each beat a little weaker. She had no idea how she long she lay there. Minutes, hours, days, she did not know. All she did know was that as she stared at the heavens above, she could hear her beloved Antony calling to her, welcoming her to his side once again, as her final sigh escaped the smile on her face.

I'm coming, my love!

Nubian Desert, Egypt, University College London Dig Site
Two Days Before the Liberty Island Attack

Chaney marched over the rise to the south of the camp, then across the flat plateau, scanning the horizon for anything of interest, but seeing nothing.

We truly are in the middle of nowhere.

The vegetation was sparse, but there. It wasn't a desert, not here, not this close to the coast, and several ancient river beds, though dried up on the surface, still seemed to have enough water below to feed a remarkable amount of flora.

But the fauna was almost nonexistent. He couldn't actually remember seeing even a bird since he'd arrived. He scanned the horizon again, and saw something flicker in the distance. Shading his eyes with his hand, he took another look, but could see nothing, whatever it was, gone.

Probably just the sun reflecting off water or some crystal in the rocks.

The thought of crystals had him wondering if he'd get the chance to discover something. The idea thrilled him, and he began scouring the ground as he walked. To find something, something ancient, something that hadn't been touched in thousands of years would be an experience he would remember the rest of his life.

And it would drive Hugh nuts.

He grinned at the thought of his former partner holed up in the air conditioned tent. If he were to find something himself, he'd forget the heat and sand, and lack of a telly, and instead get caught up in the excitement of what everyone here was doing.

Exploring the past.

Chaney had always loved history, and excelled at it in school, but with his career, and the Triarii, he barely had time to read anymore. Buying an eReader had solved that somewhat. At least now he had a tiny device with tons of books on it that didn't take up much luggage space.

The Triarii!

The thought of them tore at his heart. An organization he had been a member of for as long as he could remember, that had determined most of his decisions in life, and now once again demanded his time. He had hinted to Professor Acton that there was something he needed to talk to him about, and he could tell by the Professor's voice he knew it was Triarii related.

Before he had left for Egypt the Proconsul had called him in and dictated the message he wanted delivered to the Professor. When he had asked why, he was directed to a chair, and brought up to date on events he had had no idea about, and they chilled him to the bone.

A civil war?

His thought process was interrupted by a grouping of rocks that seemed out of place in that they were the only rocks on the entire plateau. He strode toward them, his eyes scanning the ground, and when he arrived, a quick examination revealed nothing except one of the stones was invitingly flat.

He sat down, removing his canteen from his belt. He took several swigs, then absentmindedly kicked at the dirt as he swished the last sip around his mouth, making certain every nook and cranny was moistened.

His foot hit something and his heart raced as he dropped to his knees and began digging.

Outside Alexandria, Egypt
22 August, 30 BC

Tarik wept silently, his head turned from his brothers in shame as he knelt, looking down at the valley below. It was the end of an era, and the beginning of a new one, and despite the knowledge his Pharaoh, his leader, his master, his god, was not dead, but merely in another place, living in paradise above with the other gods, it tore at him inside. For he had loved his Pharaoh, with all his heart, and had devoted his life to carving the very jewels that adorned the living god.

And it had been he that had arranged delivery of the king cobras to Cleopatra's chambers. When he had heard the news that spread throughout the city, then kingdom, that she had been bitten by a snake and died, he had at first thought the plan had gone wrong, that her attempt to kill Octavian had been a failure, until he had heard the full story.

Suicide.

Intentional suicide.

And when he had heard the story from the mouth of the very messenger who had visited his home that fateful night, he realized how her death was a tragedy, but the method was a celebration. To deny Octavian his prize was the ultimate insult, the ultimate failure on his part.

At first when he heard the story, he had assumed Octavian would take one final act of vengeance, and have her body torn apart and burned, but instead he had allowed the traditional burial to proceed with all the honor and dignity a Pharaoh deserved, save the public displays. She and Antony would be interred with respect, but that was all.

Indeed, Tarik had carved the very necklace that now adorned the fallen divinity in the sarcophagus that would contain the body, now buried in secret, the unforgivable sin of robbing the graves of their dead gods far too common. It was an act so deplorable, so disgusting, that Tarik couldn't fathom the depths of evil and depravity that one must have fallen to in order to even contemplate such an act.

It was an act that should be punished by death. Horrible, agonizing, slow death. No mercy should befall those who would insult their gods, those who would dare touch the final resting places of their corporeal forms in this world.

He felt a rage build in his stomach at the thought of someone stealing from his god, whom he had worshipped since he was first weaned from his mother's teat, and honored with every carving he produced from a little boy. His father, who had fallen to disease six harvests ago, had taught him the art of sculpture and metal works, jewelry crafting and precious stone cutting. It was an honorable trade, a profitable trade, and their family was among the richest in Alexandria, owning many shops and houses, plus farmland outside the city and throughout the kingdom.

His two brothers, with him today, were as equally devoted to their Pharaoh as he was, their own passions taking them to the farms the family owned, rather than the jewelry business. It would be up to Tarik to father a son, and teach him the trade so the family business could continue.

He felt a hand on his shoulder, and he quickly wiped his eyes dry, then rose. His brother Jabari smiled gently at him, his own cheeks stained from tears. Tarik grabbed him and hugged him, the two sobbing as their youngest brother, Fadil, wrapped his arms around them, joining in their sorrow.

He broke away from the hug and held both brothers by the shoulders, looking at Jabari then Fadil. "We must not let our god's final resting place be desecrated. We will stand guard until they have sealed the chamber."

38

Jabari nodded in agreement, but Fadil opened his mouth, then apparently thought better of it, closing it.

"What is it, little brother?" asked Tarik.

Fadil opened his mouth, made a noise as if about to speak, then closed it again, looking at the ground. "It's nothing."

Jabari squeezed Fadil's shoulder. "Speak, we are all brothers here."

Fadil looked up at Jabari, then at Fadil, then down in the valley below at the ceremonial guard. "Well, I mean no disrespect brothers, but isn't that their duty?" he asked, motioning at the troop of soldiers below with his chin.

Tarik grunted. "It may be their duty, but can they be trusted? How many times have we heard of the graves of our ancestors, the graves of our gods, being desecrated, while under guard?"

Fadil nodded slowly. "Yes, I suppose it's true. Anybody can be bought for a price." He looked at his brothers with a smile. "Except us, of course!"

"Of course, little brother!" agreed Jabari, giving him a one armed hug. "We want for nothing, we lust for nothing, we are untouchable by graft and bribery."

"Which is exactly why it should be up to us, up to people like us, to protect the resting places of the gods," said Tarik.

Jabari paused for a moment, studying his brother. "You sound as if you have a greater purpose in mind than simply standing guard until the chamber is sealed at full moon."

Tarik nodded. "Yes, I do. As I think of it more, we have a responsibility to all of our gods. And who better than us to find out who has been robbing these sacred places. I, a gemsman, who has been trained to recognize the craftsmanship of the Pharaoh's jewelers for many dynasty's past. And you two, who also were trained in the trade, but instead decided to get your hands dirty in the soil of the Nile delta"—a grin broke out amongst all three, it an old family joke that Jabari and Fadil moved to the farms to escape the need to bathe daily—"you are both able to recognize the craftsmanship as well, and we as a family frequent the very parties where this wealth would be displayed. It is us that could bring these heathens to justice!"

"But if we did so, brother, would we not expose ourselves to the very element we attempt to find?"

Tarik looked at Jabari then nodded slowly.

"Then we must find them in secret, and bring them to justice in secret."

"You mean murder?"

Tarik looked at his little brother, then placed a hand on his shoulder.

"Justice is never murder." Tarik looked between his brothers, and the burial below. "We three, and others we can trust, will protect our sacred places, and weed out those who would desecrate the final resting places of our gods."

Both Fadil and Jabari smiled, their chests swollen with the pride they all felt in their new sworn task. Tarik broke from the huddle and stepped to the edge of the cliff, staring down at the valley below, hands on his hips, his jaw set, his eyes alive with the prospects before him.

I swear, almighty Cleopatra, we will let you rest in peace. And should we fail, we will bring justice to those who would disturb you.

Nubian Desert, Egypt, University College London Dig Site
Two Days Before the Liberty Island Attack

Acton returned the Glock to Jeffrey, one of the security personnel, and walked away from the shooting range, deciding he had had enough practice for one day. Laura joined him, beginning to limber up for the hand-to-hand combat phase of the training, both of them already crack shots, when Chaney came running into the camp, holding something over his head, a huge smile on his face.

Acton and Laura walked toward their friend and as he neared they could see he was holding a nearly perfectly preserved clay pot. "What do you think?" he asked, breathlessly. "I cleaned it exactly as you showed me."

Acton eyed the pot then took the ancient artifact. As he turned it in his hands, his eyes narrowed. "Where'd you find this?"

"On my morning constitutional, over the ridge, just beyond that rise." Chaney pointed behind the archeologists and both turned their heads to see where he was indicating.

Acton turned to Laura. "Have you done any surveying over there?"

She shook her head. "No, the satellite scans showed this as the center of the town. We decided to start here and work our way out. We won't reach that area for another year at least."

"And everything we've found so far is Fourth Dynasty. Around forty-five hundred years old?"

Laura nodded, her pony tail, tied high to keep her auburn hair out of her face and off her neck, bouncing. "That's right, why?"

He handed her the pot. "What do you make of this?"

She looked it over, her own eyes narrowing. "Interesting!"

"What? What's so interesting?" asked Chaney, his voice sounding frustrated and excited at the same time.

Gunfire, several weapons this time, erupted from behind them as the training continued, but none of them reacted. Laura continued to examine the pot, running her fingers over the painted symbols and figures. She looked up at Chaney.

"This is only two thousand years old. It can't be part of this site, it's far too new."

"Two thousand years old is too *new*?"

She nodded. "By a few thousand years. And these symbols…" Her voice drifted off as her finger tapped on her lower lip, apparently becoming lost in thought.

"What about the symbols?"

This time Chaney just sounded frustrated.

"They're markings indicating they were carved in honor of the death of the last pharaoh."

"Who was that?"

"Cleopatra," whispered Laura, her eyes opened wide in excitement. She looked at Acton who was as equally excited when he suddenly frowned. "Look." He pointed at the one broken part of the pot, near the top lip. Laura looked, as did Chaney, leaning in to see what the professors were looking at.

"Too bad," said Laura, handing the pot back to Chaney.

"What? What's wrong?"

"It was fired in a modern kiln," explained Acton. "It's a replica. A very well done one, still handcrafted, and perhaps several hundred years old, so nothing to be thrown away, simply not what we were hoping for."

"Why, what's so important about finding something made from Cleopatra's time."

"Well, archeologists have been searching for her burial chamber for years."

"How's that possible?" asked Chaney. "They found Tut and a whole bunch of other blokes that are a hell of a lot older than this one," he said, pointing at the female figure on the pot. "How could they not know where she was buried only two thousand years ago?"

Acton shrugged his shoulders.

"Nobody knows. That's the mystery."

Laura nodded at the pot. "Why don't you put that in the tent so we can examine it closer when the sun is at its hottest. We'll do our training, then go take a quick look at the area where you found it."

Chaney nodded, trotting off to the air conditioned tent, as Acton and Laura resumed their stretching.

"Do you think we'll find anything?" Acton asked.

"I doubt it, but he looked so crestfallen I thought I'd throw a little hope his way."

Acton grabbed her by the neck and pulled her toward him, kissing the top of her head.

"That's one of the many reasons I love you."

He glanced over his shoulder and saw Chaney exit the tent, a huge smile on his face.

Sometimes it's the little things.

Alexandria, Egypt
30 BC, Seven Weeks After Cleopatra's Death

Tarik stared at the necklace shown to him by one of his shopkeepers. It was a gorgeous piece, jade and gold with a fistful of sapphires and rubies, in a design meant to elongate the neck, the choker style popular with his beloved Cleopatra, and still very much so in high society since there was no new pharaoh to define their own style, Octavian having killed Cleopatra's son, Caesarian. It was the end of an era. The end of the Pharaoh's. The end of Egypt.

He sighed, returning his attention to the necklace, a necklace that was, in fact, a design he could appreciate, a design he recognized.

For he had made it.

And he knew for a fact it was buried with his late Pharaoh's body, he himself having been brought in to consult on the burial as to what the finest jewels were to bury with their fallen god. He felt a rage build in his heart as he stared at the piece, dumbfounded. His brothers and others they had gathered over the two moons that had passed since the sealing of the burial tomb had watched over it day and night.

Someone had betrayed them.

"Where did you get this?" he asked his shopkeeper, Kontar.

Kontar pointed at the necklace. "It's one of yours, isn't it?"

Tarik nodded.

Kontar frowned, grasping at the narrow goatee he sported in an attempt to appear a higher caste than he actually was. "As soon as I saw it, I knew. Of course I should know it, since I know all your work. But this one. Isn't this…?" He apparently dared not finish the sentence.

Tarik nodded again, running his fingers over the piece, feeling the surge of energy from what was once a living god whose perfect, divine skin it had graced perhaps only days before.

"Where did you get it?" he repeated.

Kontar turned his nose up. "A most disagreeable creature. I've seen him before as he has tried to sell his ill-gotten gains. I've always turned him away before, knowing who and what he was, but this time, when he showed me what he had, I couldn't." Kontar sighed, running his own fingers over the piece. "It is so lovely, and I am certain she would have loved it had she been able to see it."

"She is a god. Of course she was able to see it."

"Yes, of course, I am certain you are right," scrambled Kontar, touching his forehead and looking up in apology. "It is so difficult to think in terms of the divine, that I sometimes forget they are all knowing and all seeing. Forgive me."

"It is not I of whom you must ask forgiveness. Ask it in your prayers tonight." Tarik pointed at the necklace. "Who is this 'disagreeable creature?'"

"His name is Shakir. He lives in the lower quarter, a pickpocket, lowlife. But never before have I seen him with a piece such as this. Usually just trinkets. Small items that locals would wear, not royalty."

"You will take me to him."

"Me? You? You mean you want to go to"—Kontar paused, the look of horror on his face almost comical—"the lower quarter?"

Tarik nodded. "We must get to the bottom of this, and in order to do so, we must go where the answers are."

And right now, those all appeared to be in the lower quarter with a petty thief named Shakir.

Nubian Desert, Egypt, University College London Dig Site
Two Days Before the Liberty Island Attack

"So where did you find it?" asked Laura, her expert eyes scanning the level area for any hint of something of interest. Her beloved James was at her side, his hands on his hips as he too examined the rather plain sight, the sand blown smooth by the wind, not a hint of vegetation, and beyond a grouping of rocks that stretched from left to right for about fifty feet, there was nothing.

"By the rocks," said Chaney, pointing. He rushed over to a spot between two decent sized rocks and jabbed his finger at a spot on the ground. "Right here. There was just a bit of it showing when I found it. I had to dig it out with my hands."

James approached the spot carefully, examining the surroundings, as did Laura. There was nothing obviously special about the spot, except its proximity to the rocks, which might explain why it hadn't been lost to the desert sands, the rocks providing some sort of protection from the wind. Then again, the rocks themselves were just as likely to be buried in a sandstorm, as unburied.

I wonder which it is?

She looked about the area, and there were no other rocks anywhere, just this cluster, which seemed a bit odd, but definitely not out of the realm of possibility. Her expert eye began to examine the rocks more closely as James and their detective friend crawled around on their hands and knees, digging at the dry sand.

There were some high winds two nights ago…

She bit her lip, the pattern of the sand around the rocks suggesting an easterly direction, but not giving her any indication of whether or not these rocks had been buried and out of sight until then, or had stood their lonely vigil for hundreds or thousands of years, undisturbed, their elevated position merely allowing the sand to blow past them and into the depressions surrounding them.

The satellite photos showed that this had once been farmland rather than the barren desert it now was. The bed of an ancient river nearby was clearly visible on the satellite photos, and evidence of irrigation had already been found. This was a rather smooth area, ideal for farming at the time. She crossed her arms, stroking her chin.

"I think these rocks were placed here."

"What's that, Dear?"

"The rocks. I think they were placed here deliberately."

James stopped digging, looking at the rocks surrounding him, Chaney continuing his almost frantic attack at the sand.

"This was farmland, right?"

Laura nodded.

"Perhaps they cleared the rocks from their fields, piling them here?"

Laura scratched her wrist absentmindedly, then brushed some sand off her lap.

"Odd place though to put them. Why not off to the sides, where they would be out of the way? Then this entire area could be plowed without concerning yourself about rocks." It didn't make sense, but only if these were the only rocks. For all she knew there could be dozens if not hundreds buried under the sand all around them. In two thousand years, land could become unrecognizable.

James stepped into the center of the rocks, then slowly turned around, examining the area.

"You're right, it doesn't make sense. Unless this is supposed to mark a spot?"

Laura's eyebrows shot up. "Something ritualistic, perhaps?"

James pursed his lips, then slowly shook his head. "I don't think so. The rocks would be more uniform in size, more perfectly laid out. These seem to be intentionally different, as if to disguise their purpose." He sighed. "Assuming they have a purpose." He dropped to a knee, rolling aside one of the smaller stones. He glanced under it, then at the other rocks, then back at her.

"Perhaps we've been at this too long."

Laura chuckled, rolling the stone nearest her away from the circle and looking under it, finding nothing.

"You mean we're seeing what we want to see?"

Chaney stopped his mad digging. "Are you saying I'm wasting my time?"

The look on his face, that of a disappointed child, made her laugh. "No, you're not wasting your time. It's never a waste to explore an area where an artifact has been found. Sometimes you find nothing, sometimes you find everything. If James hadn't had his team dig out the cave in Peru, he would never have found the crystal skull that the Triarii were searching almost a thousand years for."

"And my students would be alive today if I hadn't had them dig it out."

James pushed another stone, this one larger, out of the way, his anger and sadness at the memories still too raw.

"Sorry, Dear, I shouldn't have mentioned it."

James flashed her a weak smile, then pushed another stone out of the way. "Don't worry about it, it's something I need to deal with. Eventually I'll be able to talk about it, but not yet."

Laura rose and stepped into the center of the rocks, holding out her hands. James rose and she hugged him, squeezing him tightly, willing some of her strength to him as she felt him hold on, his chest heaving a single time as he fought for control of his emotions.

"Hello, what's this?"

They both turned to look at Chaney, who had just rolled another of the larger rocks away. As he wiped the sweat from his brow with the back of his left hand, his right had hold of something and was tugging at it none too gently.

Suddenly whatever he had was torn from his hand and jumped toward her several inches.

"Stay perfectly still," said James, still holding her from behind.

"What is it?" she whispered, afraid to breathe, Chaney's curious expression as he looked at them adding a few extra beats as her heart began to pound harder in her chest.

"We're sinking."

Her immediate instinct was to try and scramble out of what must be quicksand, but she knew that was wrong, it would simply cause them to sink further.

But she also knew this wasn't quicksand. It couldn't be. Not here, not at the top of this plateau, with these rocks, with whatever it was Chaney had been gripping inching toward her slowly.

This was something else entirely.

"Chaney, stay where you are, and get ready to catch Laura."

Chaney stood up, bending slightly at his knees, his arms stretched out.

"But—"

Laura didn't have a chance to voice her objections. She felt James drop suddenly, his hands on her bum, then a terrific shove as he pushed her up and toward Chaney. She felt Chaney's arms around her, pulling her from whatever it was she had been standing in, and as he spun her away from the danger, she looked on with horror as her beloved rapidly sunk, his eyes locked on hers, his hand outstretched, as he disappeared from sight.

"James!"

Alexandria, Lower Quarter, Egypt
30 BC, Seven Weeks After Cleopatra's Death

Tarik stood at the edge of an alleyway with his shopkeeper, Kontar, and watched as the petty thief, Shakir, worked the crowd. Tarik had to admit, watching the elderly man work was like watching a master artist paint, or perhaps more appropriately, a dancer, each movement he made choreographed with precision, executed with the practiced hand of decades of experience.

He was indeed a master thief.

In the twenty minutes they had observed him, he had relieved six people of their purses, and three of bracelets that had yet to be missed. Tarik shook his head in disgust. To him there was nothing worse than thieves. Men and women worked long and hard to earn their money, then thieves simply took it from them, as if they had some sort of entitlement to possess that which they did not earn.

His blood boiled.

He pushed back his robes, revealing his belt, and the money purse hooked to it, then stepped into the marketplace, strolling amongst the stalls, toward Shakir. And he noticed with satisfaction, that Shakir almost immediately spotted him.

Or rather his purse.

Within seconds it seemed Shakir was at his side, and with barely a bump, Tarik had been relieved of his purse.

But not the dagger he pulled from its sheath. Turning, he pressed the blade into Shakir's back, causing him to stop. Tarik leaned in and whispered in his ear.

"Remain silent and walk to the alleyway on the right. Make a sound, and I will run you through."

Shakir thankfully remained silent, only nodding. His arms began to rise and Tarik pushed the tip of the dagger a little harder against the man's back.

"Hands down, act natural."

Again Shakir nodded, his arms quickly coming down, and they began to weave their way through the busy market, Shakir's hands twitching every time a purse made an appearance. Tarik found it remarkable how many people exposed their money to the world without a second thought, some so blatantly he at times felt they deserved to have it stolen, so they could learn a lesson for next time.

But this market not only sold luxuries, it also sold basic food. And a stolen purse here could mean a starving family elsewhere. He pushed the dagger a little harder as his anger boiled at the thought, and he made a promise to himself to donate more at the temple so they could administer to the starving wretches.

They entered the alleyway and his shopkeeper, Kontar, grabbed Shakir and pulled him into the shadows, pushing him face-first against the wall. Tarik flipped their prisoner around and pressed the dagger to the man's throat.

"I'll have my purse."

Shakir's head shook up and down, his old, leathery skin swaying with the effort like a gizzard. The purse quickly made an appearance, and Tarik took it, hooking it back on his belt. He turned to Kontar.

"Show him."

Kontar pulled the necklace out and held it up as Tarik leaned in closer.

"You sold this to my friend yesterday. Do you remember?"

Shakir trembled out a nod.

"Where did you get it?"

Shakir shook his head. "I-I don't know."

"In Ra's name, if you don't tell us, I'll slit your belly open myself and leave you here to stain this filthy place," hissed Kontar, his own dagger making an appearance.

Shakir's eyes were wide with fear, and the sound of water hitting the dirt of the alleyway caused Tarik to look down then step back as a puddle of urine formed at their thief's feet. The old man looked up and away, his face one of shame at the lack of courage his bladder had shown.

What could make an old man steal like this?

But Tarik checked his sympathy, realizing the practiced hand he had watched came from decades of plying his trade as a young man, a young man who had simply grown old by the unfortunate fact he had never been killed.

A tribute to his skill.

"The name."

Shakir shook his head. "I don't know it, but I know the face."

Kontar beamed a quick grin at Tarik, he having a hard time containing his excitement as well

"Where is he?"

"It isn't a he, it's a she."

Tarik wasn't prepared for that answer, but as he thought about it, it did make sense. After all, it was a necklace, one meant for a queen, not a king, its delicate design feminine. Voices near the alleyway caused all their heads to spin as a trio of Roman Centurions paused, their backs to them. Tarik cupped his hand over the old thief's mouth, but the man didn't make a sound, probably no more eager to meet the soldiers than Tarik was.

The Romans moved on, as did Tarik's heart as he slowly removed his hand. He and Kontar both breathed sighs of relief, as did their captive.

Tarik pointed at him, his narrowed eyes and turned down lips meant to elicit as much fear as possible.

"Who is she?"

"I have no idea."

"Where did you steal it?"

Shakir pointed to the marketplace with a shaky finger. "There."

"In this market?"

"Yes."

"Is she a regular?"

Shakir shook his head. "No. At least, she wasn't."

Tarik's eyes narrowed further. "What do you mean?"

"I mean, every day since the necklace was stolen, she has come to the market."

"What does she do?" asked Kontar, apparently unable to contain his excitement any further.

"I don't know. As soon as I see her, I leave."

"Have you seen her today?"

"No, but she should be arriving any moment now. She comes the same time every day."

"Let me guess. The same time you stole the necklace from her."

Shakir nodded.

Tarik felt a twinge of pity for the woman. The necklace was obviously important to her, and this piece of garbage had stolen it with no regard to how it might impact her. But then he remembered why they were there. The necklace itself was stolen, stolen from their god. *She* was a thief as well, or at least associated with thieves.

He had to know who it was. He pushed Shakir toward the entrance of the alleyway, and all three stood in the shadows, looking out. "You will point her out to us. If you try to run, you will find my dagger in your back. It should fetch a good price in the afterlife."

Shakir said nothing, instead his eyes, trained on the crowd, narrowed as he searched the throngs. Tarik spotted a sundial indicating midday when Shakir pointed.

"There."

He pointed at a thick mass of people, and Tarik was about to ask who, when he spotted her. A woman out of place, her face too clean and pampered to fit in, despite the ragged robes she wore as a disguise. The expression on her face was one of worry as her head darted from left to right, then back again, searching not the vendors, but the customers undulating through the stalls and past the carts.

It was a beautiful face, a regal face.

And it was a face he knew well.

For it was the face of his sister-in-law, the wife of his beloved youngest brother, Fadil.

Nubian Desert, Egypt, University College London Dig Site
Two Days Before the Liberty Island Attack

Special Agent Hugh Reading, Interpol, had decided he hated the heat. How he had allowed himself to be convinced to join this dig on his vacation was something he'd need to closely examine, to make certain whatever pressure points had been used on him could never be used again. But at this particular moment, he was quite content. His chair, positioned in front of the air conditioner, he himself slouched in it, his feet propped up on either side of the blessed machine, he now positioned perfectly to enjoy the frigid air that poured from the belly of the beast, running up his legs, over the boys, up his stomach and chest, to his sunburnt neck and face.

Simply put, it was heavenly, if not a little obscene.

And with his eyes closed, he knew why he was here.

Protection.

It was a miracle James and Laura had made it out of China alive during the incident there a few months back. At least this time they had successfully avoided the news, their contribution to go down in some secret files opened to the public in twenty five years when no one cared. But here in Egypt, with the Muslim Brotherhood, whose name belied their true nature as rabid Islamic fundamentalists, now in control since the ouster of Mubarak, Egypt was no longer safe.

Not that it had ever truly been safe.

But now there was an entirely different level of extremism out there, endorsed by the government, tacitly endorsed by a police force that was content to sit idly by, and ignored by a military that was simply waiting for the country to fall into chaos before they stepped back in and took control, with the blessing of the international community, and the average non-political citizen.

Egypt was turning into the prime example of how Islam and democracy were fundamentally incompatible. Democracy demanded a separation of Church and State. Islam was not only a religious belief system, it was a legal and judicial system.

Reading sighed, debating whether or not opening his fly to let the cool air gain access would be taking things too far. Deciding against it, he recalled his friend Rahim phoning him at the office during the overthrow of the longtime military dictator, and the excitement in his voice.

Reading had been excited too, watching the protests on the television, cheering as victory after victory was won, he too caught up in the naiveté of the average Westerner who had no clue about the true underpinnings of Arab politics.

And when the first election results had come in, he realized the Arab world's most populous country was in trouble. And he hadn't heard from Rahim since.

Reading shifted and sighed as the cool air reached a nether region it hadn't before, his smile growing. *Why the hell did we fight a war down here?* He tried to remember his history, and decided it must have been the Suez Canal that had been the objective, but of that he couldn't be certain, since World War Two had spread across the entire of North Africa. His brief stint in the Falklands as a young man had been nothing compared to what those poor bastards had endured during WWII.

And it had dragged for years.

Speaking of dragging.

He squeezed his butt cheeks, discovering they still ached from the drive here from Cairo. *I'm getting too old for this.* He was on the wrong side of fifty, and after the events in London a couple of years ago he had left for

Interpol to avoid the publicity, but it wasn't just that. He was getting old. He was feeling old. The joints didn't hold up like they used to, and chasing down a suspect was murder in itself.

He patted his stomach, his eyes still closed, and felt the soft layer that had developed over the past few years, his flat stomach long since having gone into hiding.

Washboard abs for delicates.

He smiled at the phrase he had heard from Acton once. Acton was barely on the wrong side of forty, and was still in remarkable shape. Reading envied him sometimes, and always felt a touch of chagrin when he did. He was attractive, successful, loved by his students, had friends who would give their lives for him, and a spectacular younger woman who not only was rich, but worshipped the ground he walked on.

That might be pushing it.

He chuckled, then opened his eyes to make sure he was still alone. Satisfied, he closed his eyes again.

Laura Palmer worships no one.

But there was no denying she loved him, and was absolutely devoted to him. And he to her.

Reading remembered feeling that way about his wife years ago when they had first met, but the feeling had been fleeting, and if it weren't for her being pregnant, they would have gone their separate ways. Instead, they stayed together for as long as they could stand each other, then separated, and eventually divorced, his own son becoming estranged from him. They had recently begun to patch things up, as it had never truly been the typical estrangement where former spouses used the child as a proxy in their war with each other.

It had been his fear of being a father.

He had failed as a husband.

Miserably.

And he had feared failing his son, so had found excuses to avoid him, the job usually providing an excuse for him, and when not hearing from his dad had become the norm, Reading merely kept the expectations low. Christmas gifts and birthday gifts were always on time, the occasional phone call, but little contact, and almost none for the poor kid's teenage years when he could have really used a father.

You ran away from your problems.

Reading frowned, shifting slightly to see if he could work the breeze a little further up. *Is that what you're doing now? Running away?* He could honestly say he wasn't contemplating retirement out of fear. He had never been a coward. And his job now was mostly behind a desk, so the physical aspect shouldn't be an issue anymore.

Maybe you're afraid of letting your friends down when they need you.

Reading bit his lip. *Could that be it?* Could he be afraid of failing his friends? As he thought about it, he realized that this could very well be the reason he was in a funk. He hadn't been able to help them in China, but then he hadn't even known it was happening until it was too late. He had helped them on several occasions, successfully he thought, but Laura had still been shot and almost killed.

He shook his head. *You can't be everywhere at once.*

Something from outside the tent yanked Reading from his reverie and he bolted upright, his eyes shooting open as he strained to hear again what he thought he had just heard. A woman's cry. He heard nothing, but struggled from his seat nonetheless and was soon outside, several of the students pointing and beginning to run toward a ridge south of the camp.

"What's going on?" he yelled.

Terrence Mitchell, the senior grad student, turned and waved for him to follow.

"We just heard Professor Palmer yelling!" he said, his uncoordinated feet nearly tripping him up as he looked behind him.

Reading pointed at two of the ex-SAS guards. "You're with us. The rest stay and guard the camp."

The two men nodded, sprinting ahead of the group, their weapons at the ready, as Reading labored through the sand, then up the embankment. As he cleared the ridge, he saw the guards followed by several of the students approaching a group of rocks where his former partner Chaney stood, holding Laura as she cried, both looking down at the ground.

Where's Jim?

As he arrived he found a circle of students blocking his view, witnesses to a crime impeding his police investigation.

"Step aside," he ordered, his old training kicking in, and the authority in his voice parted them like the staff of Moses did the Red Sea, and he stepped through, only to gasp at the hole that greeted him. "Did he fall in there?" he asked, looking at his partner.

Chaney nodded.

Reading sucked in a breath, then took command of the situation. He pointed at Terrence. "You, get as much rope as you can carry. Take someone to help you." Terrence nodded, tapping the shoulder of the boy beside him, and they both sprinted toward the camp. He pointed at the next student in line. "You, go get flashlights and glow sticks if you have them. As many as you can carry. Go!" She nodded, chasing her friends. He picked two more. "You two, get shovels and pickaxes. You two, water. Go!"

With most of the students now busy with jobs, he was able to survey the area a little closer. He pointed to Chaney. "You two get out of there, on this side of the rocks. Chaney nodded, guiding Laura out of the danger area. Reading dropped to his knees, and crawled as close to the edge of the hole as he dared.

"Hello!" he yelled. "Jim! Can you hear me?"

His voice echoed into the hollow, and he breathed a sigh of relief that it wasn't quicksand that had swallowed up his friend. He turned his head to listen for a reply, but heard nothing.

"Jim!" he yelled, louder this time. "Can you hear me?"

"Yes!" came the faint reply. Laura yelped in joy, breaking free from Chaney's grasp as she dropped beside Reading.

"James, it's me, are you okay?"

"Excuse me, sir."

Reading looked up to see Lt. Colonel Leather, Retired, beckoning him to stand up. Reading looked at Chaney and pointed Laura, who continued to talk excitedly to her fiancé, then climbed to his feet.

"What is it?"

Leather casually looked back toward the camp, positioning himself between Reading and the hole.

"Over my right shoulder, sir."

"What is it?" asked Reading, looking over Leather's shoulder, but seeing nothing.

"We're being watched, sir."

Then Reading saw it, a glint of light off glass.

Binoculars!

He successfully hid his surprise, and casually turned his head to the side.

"How many do you figure?"

"I've spotted two distinct positions manned, but there could be more."

"Recommendation?"

"If this were a military op, I'd send out a team to flank them and recce the area, capture them if possible, eliminate them if necessary."

"But since this isn't a military operation?"

"Recce it is."

Reading nodded. "Do it, but keep it quiet. We don't want to panic the civilians."

Leather nodded, walking away and getting on his radio.

Reading dropped to a knee, pretending to look at the pit containing his friend, but instead scanning the horizon without moving his head.

And this time saw at least two different flashes, separated enough to know it was more than one person.

Who the hell could be watching us out here? And why?

Then he looked at the pit and his heart slammed into his chest as the adrenaline of realization surged through his body.

They're not watching us, they're watching this hole!

Tarik's Residence, Alexandria

30 BC, Seven Weeks After Cleopatra's Death

Tarik sat on the step overlooking the Nile, the view from the back of his estate breathtaking on any other day, but today it went unnoticed, the hundreds of vessels plying its waters mere shadows on an equally dark canvas that was his soul.

My own brother!

He couldn't believe it. As soon as he had realized who it was, he had sent Shakir and Kontar off, hoping his shopkeeper Kontar hadn't spotted her, and if he had, hadn't recognized her. But there was no doubting who she was. He had seen her face a thousand times, had seen it laugh, had seen it smile, had seen it admire the jewelry worn by others richer than him, had seen the envy in those green eyes.

Footsteps behind him echoed across the marble and stone, but he didn't look. He recognized the step. It was his brother Jabari, whom he had sent for immediately upon arriving home.

"Brother, what is it? Your messenger said it was urgent!"

Jabari walked down several of the steps, then turned to face his eldest brother. Tarik didn't say anything, instead pointing at a nearby table where the necklace sat. Jabari stepped over to look.

"Why, isn't this the necklace you crafted for our Pharaoh?" asked Jabari, his voice barely a whisper, as his hand reached out, tracing the jewels without touching, the object revered the moment it had graced the skin of their beloved Cleopatra.

"Yes, it is."

"But where, how, I mean—" Jabari stopped, unable to find the words, then sat down in a nearby chair, grabbing his hair. "Why do you have it? How? We've been guarding the burial site. It should be impossible!"

"Yes, it should be, unless…"

Tarik let the statement drift, waiting for Jabari to come to his own conclusions.

"Unless what?" demanded Jabari. "Unless…" And he too let his voice drift as his jaw dropped. "Unless one of our own has betrayed us!" he hissed, looking about. "Do you know who?"

Tarik nodded. "The answer lies in who had the necklace."

Jabari rose then took a knee at Tarik's feet, looking up at him as they both kept their voices low lest the servants be listening.

"One of my shopkeepers, Kontar, was approached by a petty thief, a pickpocket, with the necklace yesterday. He brought it to me as he recognized it, then we apprehended the thief, a wretched old creature named Shakir—very skilled, very old. He pointed out the woman from whom he had stolen it."

"Did you have her arrested?"

Tarik shook his head.

"No."

"Why not?"

"It was Dalila, Fadil's wife."

Tarik felt his stomach flip as he said the words, the very idea of it still not having sunk in, and he could see the horror on his younger brother's face as he too processed what he had just heard. It was simply too fantastic to believe, that their own family, their own brother, could be involved.

"Are we sure it's him?"

Tarik looked at his brother. "Of course, what other explanation could there be? She's his wife, how else would she have obtained it?"

Jabari covered his face with his hands, his shoulders shaking for several moments, then he sucked in a deep breath and looked up at his brother, tears streaking down his cheeks.

"You realize what this means?"

Tarik knew exactly what it meant, which was why he had been sick since the moment he had seen her face in the market. Desecration of a god's tomb was sacrilege. It was an unforgivable sin.

And there was only one punishment for it.

Death.

Nubian Desert, Egypt, University College London Dig Site
Two Days Before the Liberty Island Attack

Lt. Colonel Cameron Leather expertly guided the jeep down the road to what some might call the main motorway. He didn't. It was a strip of pavement that was at times barely visible due to drifting sand. But that didn't matter, he wasn't going to the road. He cranked the wheel to the right, gunning the engine as he crested a hill, sending the butterflies in his stomach into action, that feeling of near weightlessness he loved so much as the upward g-force equaled with that of Mother Nature herself, then the jolt as the jeep came crashing back to the ground.

I love this shit!

He had retired young in his mind, mid-forties. When he had been promoted to a desk after being wounded on a mission in Afghanistan, he had labored long and hard to recover fully so he could return to active duty, but it wasn't to be. He had gone crazy with paperwork before he could return himself to the physical condition a soldier in the Special Air Service needed to be. They were Britain's elite soldiers, the best of the best, and there was no way he would let himself return to them unless he was in top form.

It would put the rest at risk.

So he had retired, and taken the gig as Professor Laura Palmer's head of security. When he had first heard of the position, he had laughed, then cried a little inside at the thought of what had become of his life. One day he was a super soldier, killing the enemy and protecting his country, and the next, he was a babysitter to some woman and her children in Egypt.

66

But he had recruited a few of the lads from the unit that had rotated out for various reasons, or followed him out, and created his own firm, with four of them here in Egypt now, another four in Peru at Professor Acton's dig site.

When he had heard what had happened to the professors—and even that was through the news and through friends in the know since the Profs never talked about it—he had been gobsmacked. And after working with them for a couple of years, he had come to respect them, and even admire them.

And he had quickly decided they needed to be trained if they were going to survive the ordeals they continually found themselves in. Professor Acton already had a fair amount of training from his days in the National Guard and his time in theatre during Desert Storm, and with Leather's guidance, Acton's old training quickly came back, and he excelled at the advanced self-defense techniques Leather and his men would teach. Professor Palmer had come green, but had no fear. The woman was remarkable in Leather's mind, not afraid to try anything, and would insist on continuing until she got it right.

They were ideal students who were appreciative of his efforts, and he took some pride in hearing about some of their exploits, and how his training had saved their asses on more than one occasion.

Which was why when they had suggested the students be trained as well, he had jumped at it. These kids were going to be working in hotspots all around the world, and living in cities that were becoming more and more violent. Knowing how to take care of yourself not only gave confidence, but it allowed you to not only help yourself when needed, but others too.

And with the disaster Egypt was turning into, these students may need the skills sooner than he hoped.

"Look."

He followed the outstretched arm of Sergeant Hewlett and saw a puff of dust on the horizon, then a second. He gunned the engine and sped along the top of a ridge, closing the distance then skidded to a halt, jumping up onto the driver's seat, his binoculars already at his eyes.

"Two men on horseback, armed. AK's most likely."

Hewlett, also standing on his seat, nodded.

"Dressed like Bedouins. What do you think?"

"I think we're being watched. We'll do a loop around the camp, just to see if there are others, then I think it's time to increase security."

They both dropped into their seats and Leather gunned the engine, the jeep surging forward as they made their round. Two curious Bedouins didn't concern him too much, but his encounters with them in the past showed them to be bold warriors, who wouldn't have run just because two white guys showed up in a jeep.

This was something different.

And Leather knew from the tingling running up and down his spine that this was more than what it appeared.

Tarik's Residence, Alexandria, Egypt
30 BC, Seven Weeks After Cleopatra's Death

Tarik and Jabari sat quietly on the veranda overlooking the Nile, it now evening, the sun having just set behind them. The banks of the river were now lit with torches, as the commerce never ceased, hundreds of craft continuing their voyages up and down the Nile, the only evidence of their existence tiny lights on their bows and sterns, and the occasional shout from one of the crew.

Fadil! How could you have done such a thing?

Tarik had sent a messenger to have his brother and his wife join them for dinner, but no dinner would be served tonight. Though Tarik's stomach growled on occasion for attention, he feared he would immediately reject anything he ate, and throw it up.

Instead he nursed a glass of wine, a Roman vintage he had grown to love over the years, acquiring it whenever he could manage, all his contacts having standing orders to notify him immediately when new stock arrived on the shores of Egypt. But tonight it was merely a beverage, and brought no joy or pleasure, other than to dull the nerves slightly at what must be done.

Sounds from within, then voices, announced the arrival of his youngest brother and his wife who Tarik was certain had forced him into this. He looked at Jabari, who looked as pale as he felt, then rose with his brother to face their duty. Fadil rounded the corner, Dalila on his arm, both draped in the latest fashions, Dalila adorned with remarkable jewelry of which Tarik had to question how they could afford such luxury, the youngest brother's position affording him only a small portion of the family fortune.

"What's wrong, brothers?" asked Fadil as he saw their faces. "You both look as if you've seen Apep himself!"

Tarik pointed to two chairs, specially arranged for the two of them.

"Sit."

Fadil chuckled, looking at Dalila. "Okay, but we are not beasts to be ordered around, brother."

They both sat, and Tarik motioned for Jabari to bring the necklace. Jabari retrieved it from the table, and held it out for their two thieves to see as Tarik scrutinized them both.

Dalila gasped, immediately turning pale, her guilt obvious, but Fadil's reaction had Tarik confused. His jaw dropped, and he paled in what Tarik could only describe as horror. He looked up at Jabari, then at Tarik.

"What are you doing with that?" he whispered. "Isn't that the necklace you made for our beloved Pharaoh?"

Tarik nodded. "Indeed it is."

"Then I ask again, what are you doing with it? This is sacrilege!"

Tarik glanced at Jabari, who appeared equally confused.

"You claim you don't know how we have come into possession of this?"

"Of course not, only you can know how."

"And your wife?"

"How could she possible know?" He looked at his wife who had turned away, gripping the back of her chair for support. "Dear, what is it?"

Dalila shook her head, it having dropped to her chest as she began to shake with sobs. Fadil was confused, looking between her and his brothers, then kneeling in front of her, taking her hands.

"What is it, my love, please tell me."

"I-I'm so sorry," she whispered.

"For what? What could you possibly have to do with this?"

"It was me. I took it."

Fadil gasped and fell backward, landing on his backside. Tarik's eyes shot up as his jaw dropped, this turn of events completely unexpected, but at once welcome and unwelcome. It meant his beloved younger brother was innocent, but his wife, whom he loved as well, was guilty, with only one sentence permissible.

Tarik looked at Jabari and saw the conflicting emotions he too was experiencing written all over his face. Tears filled his eyes as a smile kept invading the expression of horror, and when realized, was wiped away just as quickly. Though they both were clearly elated their brother was innocent, the situation was still horrifying. A woman they both knew and loved, who was loved desperately by their young brother, had betrayed their most sacred laws.

"How did you come into possession of the necklace?" asked Tarik, his voice slightly gentler. "Did you buy it from someone?"

She shook her head. "No."

"Then how did you get it?" asked Fadil, still on the floor, having pushed himself to a sitting position, but apparently not trusting his legs to keep him afoot.

"I stole it."

Fadil laughed, and even Tarik had to admit it sounded absurd. *How could she have possibly stolen it?* He looked at her, and she at him, and he could see immediately that she was serious.

"How?" he asked. "When?" It didn't make any sense. If she stole it, then that meant she had entered the tomb, but the tomb was guarded by one of The Brotherhood at all times. He looked at his brother, Fadil, who had named their small organization The Brotherhood just last week, thinking it appropriate since it had been founded by three brothers, and now consisted of trusted men who were devout believers in the gods, and refused to abide by the false gods the Romans would have them worship. They were traditionalists, all of them, and The Brotherhood had sworn to protect the ancient artifacts, the ancient tombs, from those who would loot or destroy them.

The Brotherhood.

It sounded so lonely to him now, and as he looked at Dalila, he suddenly realized it was Fadil himself who had said women shouldn't be allowed in the organization, as they couldn't be trusted. Both Tarik and Jabari had thought the notion ridiculous, after all, the entire idea was inspired by wanting to protect their *Queen's* final resting place.

He sighed, looking again at Dalila.

"Please explain it to us."

She nodded, staring at her hands as they clasped and unclasped in her lap. "One night, a week ago, Fadil was guarding the tomb, and I went with him. My darling husband was tired, so I told him to sleep, told him that I would watch in his stead." She looked at her husband, her eyes pleading with him to forgive her, but he could only stare at her in horror, his wide eyes and slightly open mouth revealing only the shock of betrayal.

"I was restless, so I went for a walk, then heard voices. I came upon two men coming out of a crevice. Too afraid to confront them, for I only had a dagger, I hid amongst the stones, then waited for them to leave, their horse loaded with goods. But—" Her voice faltered.

"But?" encouraged Tarik.

"But instead of getting my husband, my curiosity won out, and I slipped into the crevice they had emerged from, and followed the path. It opened into a large array of underground caves, carved out by the gods eons ago. I followed the footprints on the cave floor, and found they had dug a hole deeper inside. I climbed through and found our Pharaoh's tomb. It had been ransacked"—all three brothers exchanged shocked looks at this statement—"and I immediately checked her sarcophagus. It had been pried open, but not completely. Apparently they planned on coming back. I remembered the necklace you, my sweet brother-in-law, had crafted with your own hands, and needed to know if it was still inside. I reached in, and felt it, but instead of leaving it, I for some reason pulled it off her body, and ran with it. I couldn't help it! I don't know why I did it, but I felt I had to have it! To possess it! It was something so much more beautiful than we could ever afford!"

"But you would never be able to wear it!"

"Oh, but I did! I wore it all the time when alone, and when I did, I felt like a queen." Her voice had become full of life again, the Dalila they had all known and loved, revealed as the greedy, wealth obsessed desecrator she was.

"You knew I was improving our position, it would just take time," cried Fadil, finally pushing himself to his feet. "You wanted for nothing. I gave you everything I could, including jewels I could barely afford, yet, yet—!"

He couldn't bring himself to finish the sentence, instead spinning on his heel and walking away.

Tarik stepped forward as Jabari went to comfort their brother. "You must have realized the punishment if caught."

She nodded, her pride once again in check as her eyes and chin lowered. "I did. I do."

"Is the necklace all you took?"

She nodded.

"These two thieves, would you recognize them?"

She shook her head. "But they said they would be back tonight."

Tarik felt his heart leap. "Are you certain?"

She nodded.

A chance at catching the thieves was almost unhoped for, but if they could not only protect the tomb from further desecration, and capture those responsible, they might be able to recover the goods stolen.

He heard the scrape of feet behind him, and he turned to see Jabari with Fadil under his arm, standing nearby.

"You will show us the entrance," said Fadil to his wife, and she nodded. "Then we will deal with your treachery."

He turned and walked toward the front of the house, leaving the rest on the veranda, his shoulders squared, then shaking as he rounded the corner, out of sight.

Tarik motioned for Dalila to stand, then looked at Jabari and pointed at a nearby basket.

"Take that, we'll need it later."

Jabari grimaced, but nodded. As he picked it up, the contents hissed, and Tarik felt the same shiver he was certain they all felt as he pictured what lay inside.

Justice.

Nubian Desert, Egypt, University College London Dig Site
Two Days Before the Liberty Island Attack

Acton stared up at the ring of light above his head as he dangled from what, he did not know, suspended an unknown distance above a surface below. And he slipped some more. He tried to calm his pounding heart, the roar in his ears deafening. As he focused on his breathing, he thanked God he was able to get Laura to safety. If he died now, at least he'd die knowing she was safe.

"Jim! Can you hear me?"

Acton's heart leapt as he recognized Reading's voice, and he wondered how long he had just hung on, ignoring calls from above in his panic. *If he was able to get here from the camp, it had to be several minutes.*

"Yes!" he yelled, but it was weak, his mouth dried from the sand he had swallowed while falling.

"James, it's me, are you okay?"

Laura! Her voice renewed him with determination, his will to survive surging forth.

"Yes, I'm fine." *Are you?* "Sort of. I'm hanging from something, I don't know what. And I can't see how far down the ground is!"

"We're getting ropes and flashlights. Hang tight, you'll be okay."

As if to object to her statement, he felt himself begin to slip again.

"I'm slipping!"

He heard shouts, and talking above, but nothing he could make out, then suddenly he stopped sliding.

"Are you okay?" yelled Laura.

"I've stopped slipping. What happened?"

"It looks like you're holding onto some sort of cloth. Canvas maybe. I think the stones were holding it in place, then when we started moving them, you fell through."

Deliberate. Which made him think if it were, then what lay below may not be that far, and may be worth finding.

He felt his fingers slipping, and he wrapped himself tighter against the canvas, wondering how long his already shaking muscles might last before he'd be forced to let go.

More noise above had him looking at the circle of light he figured must be about ten feet above him, then a head blocked the light. "Tossing some glow sticks down now. Watch your head," said Reading. Acton closed his eyes and dropped his chin to his chest. He heard something hit the ground below him, then another clicking sound and yet another.

"Okay, it's safe. What do you see?"

Acton opened his eyes and laughed. He saw three glow sticks, sitting on the ground, about three inches from his heels. He let himself slide down the canvas and touch the floor, his pounding heart quickly beginning to calm as he stretched.

"I'm okay, I'm on the ground now. Can you lower a bucket with a flashlight and some water?"

"Coming right up!" he heard Reading yell, then orders being barked. He picked up one of the glow sticks and held it out in front of him, but it was useless, the eerie green glow merely revealing shadows. "Heads up!"

Acton looked up and saw a bucket being lowered and moments later it was on the ground beside him.

"Got it!"

He pulled out the flashlight and flicked it on, playing the beam about him, and gasped.

"You're not going to believe what I'm looking at!" he yelled, his heart again pounding, but this time with excitement.

"What is it?" asked Laura.

Acton dropped to his knees as he played the beam across the stone wall in front of him.

"It's the mother lode."

Outskirts, Alexandria, Egypt
30 BC, Seven Weeks After Cleopatra's Death

"There, just behind that outcropping."

Dalila pointed with a shaking hand and Tarik held up the torch, lighting the way. At first he didn't see it, merely more shadows, but as he neared, he began to see a deep shadow the light didn't seem to penetrate. He stepped next to the shadow, and pushed the torch inside, followed by his head, and gasped. There was indeed a passageway, leading deeper into the cliff side.

"I found it!" he whispered. He felt a hand on his shoulder and turned. It was Jabari.

"Wait, I hear something," he said. They all froze, then Jabari stepped back, allowing Tarik to exit the crevice.

"What is it?"

Jabari shook his head, then pointed to where he had heard the sound. Tarik drew his dagger, as did Jabari, and they both rounded the outcropping, Tarik now hearing the sound. He couldn't describe it over the pounding of his heart in his chest, his ears flooded with panic, but as he rounded the stone mass, he knew he had to calm himself for the battle he might be about to step into.

He regretted not bringing a sword.

Next time you come prepared!

It had been a mad rush in the dark of night to get here, all of them stunned by the revelation that Dalila was the desecrator, the betrayer of their trust. None had thought about what they were doing, instead rushing headlong here, and it wasn't until their arrival that he remembered why they were here.

78

Dalila had said the thieves were returning tonight.

And that meant their weaponry was woefully inadequate.

They rounded the outcropping and he heard Jabari, in the lead, breathe a sigh of relief, and moments later Tarik saw why. It was a horse, munching quietly on a pile of hay left by its owner to keep it in place. The docile beast looked up at them, then returned to its feeding, unperturbed.

"They must be here," said Dalila behind them.

Tarik nodded. "We must be careful. They may be better armed than us."

Jabari pointed at the supplies loaded on the camel.

"Perhaps not."

Draped over the back of the beast were several leather straps, bags attached, and two swords, tucked into their sheaths.

Tarik smiled.

"It would appear they aren't expecting company."

He stepped up to the animal, then lay a hand on its neck, patting it gently. "That's it, you've nothing to fear from me. Your master sent me to get his swords, that's all," he whispered, soothing the unpredictable creature. He didn't want to get in the way of a startled or panicked horse. Having been kicked by one when he was younger, he had learned his lesson well.

The animal continued to eat, and Tarik gripped the first sword, drawing it slowly, continuing to whisper to the animal. Successful, he handed the first weapon to Jabari, then slowly withdrew the second. With it freed, he stepped back and examined the weapon. It felt like a good weight, well balanced. A quality weapon. His brother had already decided he liked his, the smile he was displaying telling Tarik all he needed to know.

"Let's hurry," said Tarik. "Perhaps we can surprise them." He quickly led them back to the crevice, and he stepped inside. It was tight, and after a few steps, he prayed it opened up soon, otherwise the mild claustrophobia he suffered from might kick in, and he'd need to be rescued.

He also decided then and there to lay off the dates. His stomach had been slowly expanding over the past few years, and if this was to now be his life, he would need to get himself trim again so he could fight if necessary, and squeeze into tight places should the need arise.

The torch whipped in his outstretched hand, and he saw the passage open up. He pushed himself the final few paces, then gasped in relief as he was able to breathe normally again, the cave he now found himself in large enough to easily fit a dozen men. He waited for the others as he caught his breath, and the tightness in his chest eased with the appearance of each torch, shedding additional light on the still enclosed space.

Fadil finally appeared with Dalila, and the hollowed out space was now well lit, though beginning to feel a bit cramped again. Tarik closed his eyes and took a deep breath, a comforting hand on his shoulder from Jabari helping ease his tension slightly.

"You okay?"

Tarik nodded at his brother's voice, but didn't open his eyes. "You know how I don't like tight spaces."

"It will soon be over," said Jabari gently, and Tarik felt his brother turn to the others. "Which way?"

"Down here," Tarik heard Dalila say as he opened his eyes.

"I will go first this time," said Jabari, leading the way down another opening in the wall, Tarik following closely behind so he could keep an eye on his brother, or more accurately, his back, rather than the cave walls. He knew if his brother could fit, he most likely could as well, though his brother was blessed with a physique that put his own to shame, life on a farm much more active than that at a store designing jewelry on one's backside.

Moments later they emerged into a massive hollow, the ceiling tall enough for the tallest ship's mast to easily clear, the breadth wide enough for their torches to not reach the other wall.

Tarik smiled.

His tension eased, completely, and he stepped aside for Dalila and Fadil.

"Where now?" asked her husband.

Dalila pointed at the ground. "Follow the footprints. They will lead the way."

"How far?"

"Not far, a couple of hundred paces maybe."

Jabari continued to lead the way, his torch held out in front, but lower, his own head hunched over, as he followed the faint prints in the dusting of sand on the cave floor. Tarik followed, torch in his left hand, held up high, sword in the other. As they rounded a sharp bend, he saw something move in the shadows, then a glint of light reflecting off something, then his jaw dropped in horror as a form merged from the dark, charging at his brother, sword held high in the air.

Tarik yelled, kicking his brother in the ass, sending him flying forward as Tarik thrust his sword out to prevent the attacker's blade from opening up his brother's back. The two blades clashed, the shudder from the impact rippling up the metal and into his arms, a feeling he was unused to, his practice usually just that, the thrusts and parries from his partners weak compared to this man's all-out attack.

Another yell from the darkness had Tarik spinning toward it as he stepped to his left, covering Jabari who still lay on the ground. Fadil rushed past him on his right, into the darkness, tossing the torch ahead of him, revealing a second man, armed with a sword far finer that those left on the camel outside.

Tarik's man swung his sword at Tarik's shoulder. Tarik raised his sword, dropping the blade to the left, blocking the attack, then stepped forward and kicked the man in the stomach. As he doubled over in pain, Tarik raised his sword and dropped it, fast, cleaving the man's head in half, the sword stuck in the bone of the skull.

Pushing on the man's shoulder with his foot, he yanked the blade free as he watched Fadil battle the second man. Jabari rushed past, torch in one hand, sword in the other as Fadil was knocked to the ground.

"Fadil!" yelled Tarik as he finally worked his weapon free, pushing hard against the ground as he raced to save his youngest family member. The attacker's blade was coming down, hard and fast, the double handed attack leaving no chance Fadil would survive. Fadil raised his hands, covering his head, raising his legs as he did so in an attempt to kick at his attacker, but it was too late.

Jabari lunged forward, his sword held out in front of him as far as his arm could stretch as he dropped the torch, but even his blade was too far. Suddenly there was a scream to his right, Dalila's horror echoing through the cavern, but it was the blur of motion that caught his eye as she pulled something from the bun of hair atop her head. It glinted in the torchlight, then her arm whipped out, and a heartbeat later Fadil's attacker gasped, his swing aborted, the blade falling atop Fadil but, the momentum gone, the man instead gripping a dagger now embedded in his chest.

Jabari reached the man and finished him off with a single thrust of his sword, followed by a twist of the blade. Tarik pulled Fadil away from the collapsing corpse, and examined his brother's arm where the blade had fallen. It was cut, but his brother's tunic and heavy bracelets seemed to have absorbed much of the blow.

Dalila pushed him aside and quickly began to administer to her husband. Tarik stepped back, then retrieved his torch, he and Jabari covering both sides of their fallen brother, searching the shadows for other foes, but finding none.

"Are these the same two men you saw when you were here before?" asked Jabari.

Dalila looked at the nearest one. "I believe so, but it was dark."

"And you are certain there were only two?"

"Again, it was dark. Perhaps there were others who had left earlier, but when I saw them, there were only two."

She tied a scarf around her husband's arm, stemming the light bleeding, then rose, helping Fadil to his feet. Fadil retrieved his sword and Dalila carried the torch, leading the way. They followed her through the darkness, and quickly found themselves at an opening in the wall, several tools lying about that had obviously been used to break through the cavern wall.

Tarik wondered how they had known to dig here, and was about to wonder aloud, when he saw every five paces a small hole in the wall, where it appeared a spike had been driven, apparently to discover where the wall was hollow on the other side. Indeed, he spotted the long spike lying to his right, discarded in the excitement by their attackers when they had finally found an opening.

Jabari stuck the flame inside and knelt down on one knee to look. His hand darted to his heart, covering it as if to protect it, then he rose, looking at Tarik.

"As the eldest, I think it is your duty to go first."

Tarik nodded, having no doubt there wasn't a trace of cowardice in Jabari's conclusion. It *was* his duty as the eldest, and it *was* his duty due to the fact this entire endeavor was his idea. The irony wasn't lost on him that if they hadn't been watching the tomb, the necklace wouldn't have been stolen by Dalila, but if the necklace hadn't been stolen, they would not have known of the thieves who now lay dead behind them, never to plunder again.

But thieves usually had masters, and as he crawled through the small opening and emerged into the large burial chamber, he realized what must be done. As his hand ran across the sarcophagus of his beloved Cleopatra, then that of her beloved Antony, dead barely a week before she committed suicide. His chest tightened as he imagined each of their final thoughts, filled with love and heartbreak, two lovers as the world had never before seen, and he doubted would again.

"We have to move them," he said to his brothers who stood respectfully aside. Jabari's jaw was the first to drop, followed by Fadil's.

"Are you mad? That's sacrilege!" exclaimed Jabari.

Tarik shook his head slowly, his hand resting on the sarcophagus of his Pharaoh. "No, it would be sacrilege to leave it here, unprotected, where thieves could loot it at any time."

"But that's why we are guarding it!" Fadil stepped forward, then back as he came too near Antony's sarcophagus. "*We* will protect them!"

"But what if something happens to us?" asked Tarik. "What if we are all killed somehow, or what of when we get old and grey? Who will protect her then?"

Fadil had no answer, his jaw clamped shut as his eyes sought a solution, darting about the room uselessly. His eyes finally rested upon Jabari, it clear to Tarik that his youngest brother hoped for some sanity from the middle-brother.

Jabari looked at Fadil, smiling slightly, suggesting he understood Fadil's concerns, then stepped forward, placing his hand respectfully on Cleopatra's sarcophagus.

"What do you propose, brother?"

Tarik smiled at Jabari, knowing he would see the reasoning behind his argument, then motioned for Fadil to join them. He did, reluctantly, and he too placed a hand on the sarcophagus. Tarik took the hand and placed it atop Jabari's, then placed his own on top of both.

"We, The Brotherhood, shall move this tomb to a place of safety, known only to us, so our beloved Pharaoh may rest in peace for eternity, and we and our children, and our children's children, shall stand guard over her, ensuring her security, and the restful slumber of our Queen."

And with that solemn declaration, their lives changed forever, the weight of the moment lost on none of them.

A scream pierced the chamber, and Fadil broke their huddle first, crying out his wife's name as he dove for the small opening dug by the thieves. Jabari was next, followed by Tarik, who when he emerged, gasped as he found Fadil cradling his wife in his arms, her face pale, covered in sweat.

"Why? Why did you do it?" he cried, holding her cheek against his.

"To save you from having to," she whispered, raising her hand to touch her husband's. "To save my darling husband the pain of having to execute his own wife for her crimes."

Fadil's eyes poured tears, the clang of a sword on stone going unnoticed as Jabari killed the king cobra that had been in the basket brought with them for this very purpose. As Tarik watched, joined quietly by Jabari, his mind reeled with the duty he had just committed them to. They had already killed two tonight, a third life was in the process of being claimed, the price for violating the tomb

He only prayed that the gods would forgive them their desecration, and grant them the wisdom, the courage, and the permission, to protect them in the afterlife.

And with a sigh, Dalila's last breath echoed through the cave, followed by the heart wrenching cry of her devoted husband.

Nubian Desert, Egypt, University College London Dig Site
Two Days Before the Liberty Island Attack

Acton held his hands up, mentally guiding the rope that held his most precious treasure, Laura. The rope swung slightly from side to side, but not too badly and in just another foot or so, he'd be able to touch her boot to steady her.

"Almost there," he called, his voice reassuring, the cavern now well lit, several powerful LED lanterns passed down via bucket before Laura insisted she be lowered. He had objected, silently, but realized this was her dig site, and most other weeks he wouldn't have been here to object regardless of how he felt.

This was their job, to dangle from ropes, climb into caves, brave spiders and snakes, outsmart ancient booby traps, and battle boredom, the most common enemy of a dig going badly. But he couldn't recall a dig where he had been bored. Pick your site well, do your research, then follow the grid pattern, reevaluating as you go along.

How could you ever get bored doing this?

He grabbed his fiancée and carefully guided her to the floor. With her feet on the ground, she gave him a kiss, then untied herself, tossing the rope aside.

"I'm clear!" she called to those above, and immediately the rope was pulled up.

"Hugh! You wanna come and join us?" asked Acton with a wink to Laura, knowing full well what the answer would be.

"No, I'll coordinate things from up here."

"Martin?"

"Thought you'd never bloody ask!"

Moments later a set of boots appeared, and Acton waited for their friend to be lowered as Laura began to examine the find. As she circled the large cavern they had stumbled upon, it was quite obvious that the place had been chosen carefully to hide a secret so precious, so important, it was clearly never meant to be found.

But they had found it.

And he immediately began to wonder if the Curse of the Pharaoh's would plague their dig now that they had.

Suddenly his nose stung and his eyes watered as he took a boot from Chaney to the head, cursing himself for not paying attention.

"Sorry, Professor, didn't see you there."

"Don't worry about it, my fault," replied Acton as he guided Chaney to the ground.

Has the Curse already begun?

He smiled and shook his head.

If a boot to the head is the best they can do, I think we'll be okay.

Nubian Desert, Egypt

30 BC, Five Months After Cleopatra's Death

The three brothers lay exhausted on the ground, soaked in sweat, covered in dirt, their clothes nearly in tatters. But they all had smiles on their faces, staring up at their handiwork. It had taken months of painstaking, laborious work, but it was done. The first thing they had to accomplish, and it had been done quickly, was to find a new location, out of the way, hidden from prying eyes.

That had turned out to be easy.

Jabari had discovered a deep crevice on newly purchased land that was easily passable, yet had probably not seen a visitor in hundreds if not thousands of moons, and his own explorations had revealed caverns carved into the rock face by whatever force of the gods had created the crevice in the first place.

A specific location was chosen, then every night they would journey to the tomb, load their carts, then transport them to Tarik's house, where they would then be carefully packaged by trusted servants, then moved to their new home. No suspicions were raised as it was their land they were travelling to, and with no one the wiser, this part of their plan was merely laborious.

But the third and final part, thought of that first night by Fadil, was the most difficult.

The decoy.

They knew if the tomb was discovered with the bodies of their revered Pharaoh and her husband missing, a hunt, far and wide, would ensue, and three brothers, out at all hours of the night, transporting goods to newly acquired land, may be looked upon with enough suspicion to cause problems.

So Fadil made a suggestion that Tarik thought beyond his years.

A brilliant suggestion.

The tomb could be left emptied, the victim of tomb raiders, but the bodies had to remain behind. Which was exactly what they did. A funeral had to be held for Dalila, and Fadil paid to have her embalmed in the traditional way, and with a large additional payment, the body of one of the slain thieves was also embalmed with no questions asked, a vague reference to a despised cousin provided.

A lavish funeral was held, hundreds in attendance, the body of their beloved Dalila entombed in the family crypt. But when night fell, it and the embalmed body of the thief were moved to Cleopatra and Antony's former resting place, and left for future generations to find.

Tarik wondered what questions would be raised if those bodies were actually found. Would they be what they expected, or completely different? Would history be rewritten, Antony's legacy of suicide changed to death in battle due to the sword wound that had cleaved open the man's head who now took his place?

He knew the job of those bodies was merely to take the place of their revered counterparts long enough for memories to forget the months long labors of three brothers in the night, and if fortunate, long enough for their duties to have been inherited by the next generation of The Brotherhood.

Nubian Desert, Egypt, University College London Dig Site
Two Days Before the Liberty Island Attack

Reading ignored the now organized activity about him, and instead scanned the horizon for the telltale signs of their observers, but could see nothing. He walked over to one of the guards providing security for the new site, his sunglass covered eyes slowly casing the area.

Or providing cover while he stared at the female students' arses.

Who knew?

It was one of the reasons he always had a suspect remove their sunglasses before interrogation. The key were the eyes. You could tell if they were lying, scared, hiding something.

Or completely psychotic.

Those were the ones who sent a chill up your spine. The calm ones, the collected ones, the ones whose eyes revealed nothing, who could look at a hacked up corpse as if it were a Christmas dinner.

I miss it.

It had been a tough choice to go Interpol, a choice more or less forced on him due to the incident with the Triarii and the inquiries that had occurred later. He was too high profile after that, and knew he'd be hounded by his colleagues and by witnesses, victims and suspects if they recognized him from the newscasts.

Then the offer had come out of nowhere.

And after twenty-four long hours of procrastination, he had decided to take it. He had to admit to himself that certain aspects he enjoyed. The intel he had on hand was incredible, knowing what was going on around the world, that the average citizen had no clue of, was at once exhilarating as it was terrifying. It also allowed him the flexibility to travel almost anywhere in the world, and on occasion, help out his friends Jim and Laura, who seemed to be magnets for trouble.

Which was why the flashes on the horizon had concerned him so much. He knew they were a foreshadowing of things to come if this pair's history was any indication. But what it might mean, who it might be, and what they might do, were mysteries.

"Any word?" he asked the man.

"They're on their way back. ETA two minutes."

"Did they find anything?"

"There was some chatter. The colonel said he'd fill you in when he returned."

Reading nodded, knowing there was no point in pressing the former soldier. He'd obey his chain of command, and about the only people who could perhaps convince him otherwise were twenty feet below them, playing in the sand.

That's not fair.

He mentally slapped himself for insulting his friends' profession as he returned to the hole. As he watched the pulley system erected by the students in no time, and the organized effort that was a credit to their teacher, he realized that these were professionals, doing a serious job, in a deliberate way. There was a process, there were rules. He could respect that. And though they weren't out saving lives as part of their job—that part was merely coincidental—they were teaching kids, something he could respect, and with the character these two had displayed over the couple of years he had known them, he couldn't imagine two other people he'd want more to mold the hearts and minds of his own son.

These are good people.

And he knew he was lucky to have them in his life. After a near lifetime of seeing the dark side of society, socializing with fellow cops who only saw that side as well, they were a welcome relief despite their penchant for getting into trouble.

Reading looked over as a jeep pulled up. Former Lieutenant Colonel Leather was everything his name implied. Well-worn but tough. He exited the jeep and strode over to Reading.

"Sir, are the professors available?"

"Negative, they're in the pit right now. Is it urgent?"

"It's got potential, hard to say." Leather looked toward the horizon where the flashes had been seen earlier. "When we arrived we saw two men already departing on horseback, far enough from their original position to tell me that they had been tipped off we were coming."

"From one of us?"

Leather shook his head.

"Doubt it, but it is possible one of the helpers isn't playing for the home team. I'm guessing however they have other lookouts and simply spotted us leaving."

"And now they know we know."

Leather nodded.

"Which is what could make this situation escalate should their intentions be hostile."

Reading sighed.

"We have to assume their intentions aren't good. If they were just curious, why run?"

"We did have guns prominently displayed, so we can't rule out that we just scared them."

Reading looked at the sunglasses, his own concerned visage looking back.

"You don't sound convinced."

"No, sir, not at all. I think the prudent thing to do would be to shut this operation down until we can ascertain who is watching us."

Reading grunted.

"You'll never get them to agree to that," he said, his head nodding toward the pit where the two professors were working.

Leather's face revealed no emotion.

"Agreed."

"Recommendations?"

"Firm policy on leaving the camp, I call for some reinforcements—they can be here in two days—we watch for hostiles, monitor the help, and you try to convince them it's time to leave, at least for a little while."

Reading wasn't sure about calling in reinforcements. It would turn the dig into an armed camp, was bound to attract more attention, and he wasn't sure they could win any gunfight should one happen. But this was Islamic Egypt, where what semblance of law and order it had under the military dictatorship, was now gone, replaced by near anarchy, with little to no protection for infidels like the millions of resident Christians, and isolated foreigners.

He looked at the excited university students, students that reminded him of his son, a son he would trust would have professors concerned enough to have him sent home should they be in this situation.

If only we knew for sure what was going on.

There was a shout from the pit and he turned to see Acton's head poke out of the hole, a huge smile etched across his sand covered face. He was helped to the ground by several students, one of whom handed him a canteen. He took a drink, swished out his mouth, then spit the water on the ground. Taking another swig which he swallowed, he poured much of the remaining water over his face and head, ridding himself of most of the caked-on sand and sweat.

"What did you find, Professor?"

Acton grinned, looking at the gathered students, saying nothing, causing the suspense to rise amongst the anxious youngsters. Even Reading found his pulse picking up as he too couldn't wait to hear the news.

"Perhaps the greatest find in archeological history."

"Bigger than Tut?"

Acton's grin stretched even further.

"After the world reads about this, they'll be saying, 'Tut who?'"

Reading's shoulders dropped.

We'll never get them out of here now.

Valley of the Kings, Egypt
November 25, 1922 AD

It was a disaster. There was no other way to describe it. Basel and several fellow members of The Brotherhood watch in horror at the activity in the valley below, powerless to stop it. Word of the discovery of an ancient tomb, long unknown to all, including The Brotherhood, had reached them only hours before, and a rushed expedition was assembled, racing to the site on horseback, but to no avail.

The tomb had been opened, and desecrated.

If they had found it themselves, they might have moved it to their secret, and sacred, valley in the desert, the cave system housing over a dozen fallen Pharaohs and their treasures, their tombs staged as robberies by generations past of The Brotherhood.

But this tomb no one knew about.

They had over the centuries rescued several of the tombs in the Valley of the Kings, or as it was more properly known, the Valley of the Gates of the Kings, but had clearly failed in this case. Basel felt rage fill his chest as he saw Europeans scrambling over the sacred ground in excitement, their modern equipment leaving nothing undiscovered. This tomb had been lost, but a plan was already formulating as to how to prevent it from being a completely wasted moment.

His brother, Nadeem, arrived, jumping off his horse and racing to their position, dropping to his stomach and scurrying the last few feet.

"What have you found out?"

"The leader is named Carter. From the markings I saw, it appears to be the tomb of Tutankhamen."

"Tutankhamen?" Basel scratched his beard. "I don't recall the name. Are you sure?"

Nadeem shook his head. "No, I am just telling you what I read before I was kicked out."

"And this man, Carter, what of him?"

"Seems excited, friendly, seems to care about preserving everything as much as possible, but also doesn't understand our ways, and is blundering inside, desecrating the fallen king with every step, with every word spoken in the chamber."

"A warning must be sent," muttered Fadi, Basel's second in command of The Brotherhood.

Basel nodded. "Agreed. Have a cobra delivered to this man's house immediately, hopefully if he is at all learned in our ways, he will understand the meaning, that the Egyptian Monarch he has disturbed is angry, and the Royal Cobra is striking back."

"At once," said Fadi, scrambling backward from the edge of the cliff, then mounting his horse, galloping away.

Basel turned to Nadeem. "Go back down there and point at some hieroglyphs, tell them it is the Curse of the Pharaohs."

"But won't they know it isn't? We haven't written the curse on a tomb in over a millennia."

"These fools have no idea what they're looking at."

Nadeem's eyes narrowed and he turned his attention to the valley below, as he muttered the curse The Brotherhood had inscribed on every tomb they had protected, "Death shall come on swift wings to him that toucheth the tomb of a Pharaoh."

Basel nodded. "Those words alone should be enough to scare away the laborers, and perhaps after we are finished with them, make some people think twice."

"Why? What else do you have planned?"

"The members of this expedition must die, but it must not appear to be us that has done it, it must be the curse."

Nadeem grinned then scurried back to his horse to deliver the "curse" as Basel rolled back on his stomach, watching the proceedings below.

If enough die, perhaps future desecrations can be prevented.

al-Hirak, Syria

One Day Before the Liberty Island Attack

Command Master Sergeant Burt "Big Dog" Dawson, BD for short to his men, stared through his binoculars, the hazy green of the night vision setting all too familiar. There was very little movement, the sentries clearly amateur, having taken their posts at their appointed hour when dusk hit, then all slowly migrating to a fire and a game of craps which had preoccupied them for the better part of the past hour.

A tank could roll through without these guys noticing.

He activated his comm.

"Bravo Two, this is Bravo One. Status, over?"

The voice of his second in command, Mike "Red" Belme, squawked through the earpiece.

"Bravo One, Bravo Two. We're in position, all quiet here, over."

"Bravo One to Bravo team. Remember we're dealing with sarin gas and amateurs, both dangerous things. Our contact will give us the location of the crate. We go in, locate it, confirm the gas is inside and intact, plant your explosives, notify the team, everyone put your gas masks on, and get the hell out of there. And don't forget your atropine shots. If you're exposed, it's the only damned thing that will save your ass."

Dawson felt Spock elbow him.

"What is it?"

"We've got movement. Two o'clock."

Dawson looked through his binoculars and quickly spotted the target heading directly for their position. The infrared marker on his chest indicated he was a friendly, obviously their contact, or someone who had borrowed his clothes, so Dawson shifted his focus to the sentries and their game.

No movement.

In fact, none at all.

Spock apparently had picked up on the same thing.

"When the hell did he take them out?"

"You mean all *eight* of them?"

Who the hell is this guy?

Dawson knew he was CIA and that was it. He'd met dozens of their Special Activities Division men before, in fact some had even come from his own Delta Force command. They were tough bastards, their training picking up where his left off. But they were a different breed as well. Dawson didn't have a death wish. He hoped to live a long, full life, and retire to some beach in some country where he hadn't killed anybody.

But these agents seemed to feel they were already dead. Dawson of course knew of the Memorial Wall at CIA Headquarters in Langley, where there were over one hundred stars, each representing a dead agent, many of whom weren't named due to national security, but to go through life expecting your name to be recorded in a leather book if you were lucky, a star on a wall all that remained of your life?

That wasn't for him.

If he died, he died. That was part of the job. If he wanted a cushy job, he would have become an officer and a gentleman. Instead, he chose the life of a noncommissioned officer, an NCO, who got dirty, killed people with his bare hands, and got shit-faced drunk with the boys at the end of a mission.

The figure was close now and jumped over a small rise and into the hands of Jimmy and Niner.

"Thunder!" the man hissed.

"Flash!" replied Niner, everyone visibly relaxing.

"Who's in command?"

"I am," replied Dawson, waving the man over. Jimmy and Niner helped him up and as he neared, a smile spread across Dawson's face. He was about to blurt out Dylan Kane's name when he caught himself. He may know who this was, but the rest of his men didn't, and for Kane's safety, and his family's, he held his tongue.

Kane dropped beside him and smiled, smacking Dawson on the shoulder.

"Good to see you again, Sergeant."

"Good to see you too. I see my training paid off."

Kane grinned with a chuckle. "You have *no* idea."

I'm sure I don't.

Dawson nodded toward the compound.

"Sit rep."

Kane pulled out a satellite photo of the compound less than twenty-four hours old. He motioned to Spock for his head gear, and Spock complied, handing him the night vision gear. Dawson flicked his night vision lenses down and the specially printed map jumped at him, bright as day.

"Unfortunately their craps game was blocking my only means of egress. If they're discovered, you'll lose the element of surprise, so let's make this quick. The perimeter now has nobody guarding it. Inside there's a mix, at least twenty armed hostiles, but there's also women and children, so aim high and go for the headshots. These are fanatics, so expect the women to act as meat shields. The gas is here"—he circled a building in the center of the compound—"and is heavily guarded; fourteen by my count. It's amateur hour though, with them all in plain sight. They're arrogant enough to think the Syrian government won't dare touch them."

"And they're right."

Kane nodded with a smile. "They didn't count on Delta though."

Dawson grunted. "No, they didn't."

"I recommend we set up covering positions here, here and here," he said, indicating three positions surrounding the compound that would provide cover for the team going in.

Dawson looked up at Red, his second-in-command. "You concur?"

"That's exactly where I'd put us. It's almost like we trained this guy," said Red with a wink.

Dawson allowed himself a chuckle, then motioned for Red to leave. "Get your men in position, radio when ready."

"Yes, sergeant."

Red motioned to his squad and after a quick huddle over his own copy of the map, they split into three teams of two for their assigned positions. Kane pointed at the map.

"We should head in the same way I came out. There's lots of cover from here to the compound, go in the way I came"—he indicated where he had killed the guards—"then around the south side of this main building which is where most of the civilians are, then a direct assault on the storage building where the sarin gas is. We can have your sniper teams take out most of the opposition before they even know what hit them. Verify the target, plant the explosives, evac and light it. No problems."

"And the civilians?"

Kane shook his head. "The explosives you're packing are designed to consume the gas in the blast. They should be okay."

Dawson nodded, then motioned for his team to gather around, Kane returning the night vision glasses to Spock. Dawson outlined the plan, as Red's teams radioed their readiness.

"Okay, let's go."

Dawson motioned with his hands for the team to move forward as he activated his comm. "Bravo Two, Bravo One. We're moving in now, over."

"Roger that, Bravo One."

Dawson took up the rear, Kane already far out ahead, the rest of his team hot on his heels. The terrain was rough, countless holes and rocks eager to swallow a foot or turn a heel, but the experienced operators cleared it quickly, and in less than a minute were safely under cover of the rebel encampment.

Though they called themselves rebels, fighting the Syrian dictatorship, the reality was never as black and white as most in the West believed. We are so blinded by our democratic ideals thinking that anything is better than a dictatorship. While true democracy is absolutely better, the fundamental incompatibility between democracy and Islamic fundamentalism was lost on many. And what the Western media portrayed as a civil war pitting the evil military dictatorship against the brave freedom fighters was far more complex than a thirty second news clip would suggest.

The war had always been sectarian, the Alawite Muslims of the ruling class, versus the Sunni Muslims of the subjugated majority. But the rebels had been joined by Islamic fundamentalists from around the world, whose only aim was the establishment of another theocracy like Iran, with Sharia law to rule the day, and chemical weapons to protect its borders.

Which was why they were here. The Syrian government had lost one of their bases only temporarily, and an Israeli Mossad team had tracked the gas, and called in the intel to her American allies. It was considered far better politically to have an American team discovered with boots on the ground rather than an Israeli team, which might lead to a wider war.

As they rushed past the dead perimeter guards, they silently entered a small building guarding the entrance of the walled compound, then emerged into a courtyard. It appeared to have once been a large house with a six foot high stone wall surrounding it on all sides, much of that however now knocked down from the months of fighting. The main building covered much of the south side. Kane sprinted for the cover it provided, their position currently exposed, the rest of the Bravo team following.

As Dawson neared the position a figure suddenly emerged from a doorway, stretching, his eyes closed. Dawson swung his hand flat at the man's throat, crushing his windpipe so he couldn't make a sound, then buried a knife deep into his kidney, twisting it then dragging the man to the rear of the building.

He tossed the gurgling mass against the stone wall and continued after the rest. Using hand signals, Kane indicated twelve guards. Dawson signaled an acknowledgement, then activated his comm.

"Bravo Two, Bravo One. Twelve targets at the building in the center of the compound. Engage, over."

"Roger that."

Dawson moved forward so he could get eyeballs on the target, and as he rounded the corner where Kane was crouched, he saw the first target drop. Two more quickly followed, then another three before their companions finally realized what was happening.

"Let's move," ordered Dawson in a harsh whisper as he stepped out from behind the wall, raising his weapon and taking aim. Kane surged forward and to his right, .40 caliber Glock 23 in hand, squeezing off several rounds as Dawson did the same, and within less than twenty seconds all dozen guards had been eliminated.

"Masks," ordered Dawson as he and Kane took up positions on either side of the door holding the sarin gas, the rest covering the compound. Kane nodded to Dawson who then grabbed the handle and turned, shoving the door open. They were greeted with a burst of gunfire, and an "Allahu Akbar!"

Dawson tossed in a flash-bang, not willing to risk a shrapnel grenade with the gas. There was a muffled explosion and a bright flash, followed by screams from inside. Dawson pushed through the door, knife in hand, and silenced the screams. Spock rushed past him with Atlas, who yanked the top off the crate sitting in the middle of the room as Spock planted the explosives.

Atlas gave a thumbs up. "It's all here."

Spock stood up, tossing the remote detonator to Dawson. "All set."

"Evac."

Spock and Atlas rushed from the building, followed by Kane and Dawson. What greeted them outside however was chaos. Women and children were pouring out of the main building, screaming in anger and anguish. Their wails were loud, loud enough Dawson knew to attract the attention of other fighters in the area, and though they might not be the same fundamentalist faction as they had just eliminated, they were definitely not on the side of a group of infidels.

Kane stepped forward, his hands raised, motioning for them to back up, yelling in Arabic, "Move back, or you will get hurt!" His voice was muffled, Dawson barely able to understand him, the gas mask still snugly attached to his face.

"Let's get out of here!" ordered Dawson. "Grab the kids, the women will follow. Once we're behind the main building, I'll blow the charges."

He rushed forward and grabbed two girls who couldn't be more than five, one under each arm, and rushed toward the rear of the building. Their wails and kicks went unnoticed, the swatting by two female relatives making more of an impression.

But they followed him.

He heard more screams as other children were grabbed. He rounded the rear of the building, rushing toward the far end, a quick glance over his shoulder showing the rest of his team, including Kane, with kids under arms or over shoulders, mothers and grandmothers chasing the men.

"All clear," came Red's voice over the comm. Dawson placed his precious load on the ground, then flipped the cover protecting the switch from accidental activation, and flicked it. A terrific explosion rocked the compound, the high explosives hopefully doing their job.

"Spock, Atlas, report!"

Spock and Atlas rushed around the corner and out of sight, and a moment later Spock's voice crackled over the comm.

"Crate confirmed destroyed, contents vaporized. And we've got a lot of company coming our way, over."

"Bravo Two, Bravo One. Your team covers us, then rendezvous at evac point Alpha, over."

"Roger that, Bravo One."

Dawson and his team raced from the compound, rushing across the craggy landscape toward their former position, as a growing chorus of shouts and sporadic gunfire broke out behind them. Dawson cleared the berm first and hit the deck, immediately flipping over and scrambling up the embankment to assess their situation as another half dozen bodies thudded to the ground behind him. He could see over a hundred hostiles through the night vision goggles, and several technicals moving through the streets, gathering rebels in the rear of their improvised tactical vehicles.

"Let's go!" he said, motioning for them to take a line along the berm that should keep them out of sight for a good portion of their egress. Dawson led the way at a crouch, the rest of the men following, when he heard Red's voice over the comm.

"You've got two technicals coming straight for you, over."

"Take them out, over."

"Roger that, engaging."

Dawson could hear the engines approaching, then suddenly a loud bang, followed by a cracking sound then the shouts of the occupants as their transportation was brought to a standstill. Seconds later this repeated itself on the second vehicle.

"Both vehicles out of commission. You're in the clear, over."

"Roger that, Bravo Two. Begin your evac, over."

Red gave orders to his teams as Dawson continued the crouched sprint for another half mile, rounding a series of large rocks and feeling a sense of relief at the sight of the two Gen-3 Ghost Hawk "Jedi Ride" choppers waiting for them. He loaded his team on the first chopper, himself waiting for Red's team as the helicopters pushed to full power, their remarkably quiet engines still a thrill to Dawson's ears, having grown up with the thumping of Hueys and worse.

Red's team rounded the same rocks and he directed them to the second chopper, climbing aboard his own. Seconds later the skids were off the ground, and they were pushing south toward the Israeli border and clear of Syrian airspace.

"Bravo Two, Bravo One. Sit rep, over."

"All present and accounted for, no casualties, over."

"Roger that, same for us. Over and out."

The helicopter banked sharply to the right as they entered Israeli territory on their Israeli approved course, rushing toward the sea and the USS Arleigh Burke. Within minutes they'd be safely aboard, leaving the blame for the poor Israelis, who he was certain were used to it by now.

I wonder what it's like to live surrounded by millions of people who want to wipe you off the face of the earth.

Dawson thanked God he lived in the United States, where to the south you had a country of people desperate to live where you did, and to the north a country of people so polite, if it weren't for terrorist paranoia, the border could be left pretty much unguarded. Red and his family were going to Niagara Falls in a few weeks and had invited him along. He hadn't decided one way or the other, but perhaps a vacation somewhere peaceful might be nice, and he had always wanted to see the falls, and besides, Red's son Bryson was also Dawson's godson, and he knew with his lifestyle, at his age, the chances of him ever finding somebody to settle down with besides the unit were next to nothing.

His mind drifted to the two professors who had caused him so much grief over the past few years, and on occasion had proved capable warriors when necessary. Jim was older than him, and he had found Laura. Under fire of all places. Dawson pictured the women he had encountered over the past few years under fire. Most were dead, or the enemy. In fact, he couldn't think of one eligible woman he had met while on duty except for Laura Palmer.

The Chinese girl had been cute.

But she was dead.

Dawson sighed. *Dead or enemies.* He pictured his Xbox, 3D TV and beer fridge at home, and the unit where his team met, trained and socialized. His eyes rounded the chopper, remembering how he had met each of his team, then rested on Kane.

What would I do without these guys?

"You look a million miles away."

It took a moment for him to realize Kane had spoken.

"What's that?"

"A piastre for your thoughts."

"Huh?"

"Piastre. It's a Syrian penny."

"Oh." Dawson pursed his lips, then shook his head. "Nothing, just thinking about home."

Kane's head bobbed slowly, his eyes glassing over as he looked out the window. "Home. Sometimes I wonder if I even have a home anymore."

"We all have a home."

"I have an apartment outside of Langley that I barely see."

The life of a spy.

"Forget what's on your driver's license. Where's your heart?"

Kane looked at his old instructor. "I guess home is where I grew up. Where my parents still live." He shook his head. "But that means *home* is where I have to lie to the ones I love about what I do."

Dawson nodded knowingly. His family had no idea what he did, but at least knew he was in the military. He looked at Kane. "What do they think you do?"

"Insurance investigator."

Dawson chuckled at the thought, then started to laugh out loud, Kane joining in.

"Ridiculous, isn't it?"

Dawson covered his mouth and bit his forefinger, trying to stifle his laughter.

"I'm logistics, so I guess it's not that much better."

"At least you're armed forces. I'm a fucking glorified insurance salesman." Kane scratched his chin. "Do you know last Christmas I spent most of my time giving my family advice on their property and life insurance?"

Dawson grinned. "Must have been a good test of your cover."

"Thank God I represent Shaw's of London, otherwise I'd probably have to sell them some policies."

Dawson leaned back and closed his eyes. "My mom takes credit for my supposed logistics capabilities. She says, 'Keeping a family clothed and fed is the same as keeping an army clothed and fed, just a bigger family.'"

"Sounds like a strong woman."

"You have no idea."

Kane became silent, looking out the window again.

"Perhaps you're right."

"How so?"

"Home *is* where the heart is, no matter how corny it sounds."

As Dawson nodded, he looked at the water rushing past below, his mind thousands of miles away at a dining room table set for Christmas dinner. His mouth watered at the thought of a turkey dinner with all the trimmings.

And his stomach grumbled.

I think it's time for a visit home.

The comm squawked, yanking him from his reverie.

"ETA two minutes. CAG wants to see you all for a debrief."

Dawson activated his comm.

"Acknowledged."

He sat back, crossing his arms over his chest as he tried to regain the image of a family dinner, instead his mind insisting on showing images of sarin gas victims.

I definitely need a vacation.

Lord Carnarvon's Room, Continental-Savoy Hotel, Cairo, Egypt
March 25th, 1923

George Herbert, the 5th Earl of Carnarvon, stroked his moustache in the mirror with satisfaction. It had been a good day. The dig at the Valley of the Kings continued to surprise, King Tutankhamen's tomb, or Tut's as some of the men had taken to calling him, proving more valuable than any had expected. The treasures were spectacular, this one of the few finds that hadn't been at least partially looted. With the burial chamber completely intact, they were finding treasures like nothing ever seen before. Every day was an adventure that kept his aging, crippled bones alive.

"Another wise investment," he mumbled to himself, clipping a stray whisker, then returning the tiny scissors to their case. A final inspection of his moustache in the mirror, and he returned to his bed chamber, climbing into the lonely bed, his beloved wife Almina visiting family back in England. "Yes, another wise investment."

But it was more to him. He justified the expense publicly as an investment, but in truth he could care less. They were discovering ancient treasures, ancient secrets, that could now be shared with the world. With his money this forgotten king that the professor had said appeared to be barely a boy, would now be known to the world.

If only we could find Cleopatra's tomb! Now that would be something!

He turned down the light, then rolled to his side, tucking his arm under the pillow, closing his eyes, breathing deeply to calm himself as the day's excitement played across his eyelids like one of those motion pictures he had seen in London last year. He tossed and turned, the excitement of the day simply too much, finally sitting up and turning up the light.

He gasped.

Two men stood at the foot of the bed. One with a pistol aimed directly at him, the other holding what appeared to be a syringe. Both wore masks that resembled snake heads, much like that found entombing the child king. His heart hammered in his chest, fear gripping him like nothing he had experienced since his near fatal car accident years ago, a foolish incident he regretted every day since. But this was a terror that he knew would haunt him until the end of his days, his fear now that those days would be few, or none.

George was about to call out for help when the gun was cocked. He bit his lip, his racing heart refusing to obey his wishes of calming down to let him think.

"What is it you want?" he finally managed, his wavering voice not the model of British courage he would have preferred to portray.

"You are Lord Carnarvon? The funder of the King Tutankhamen expedition?"

George nodded to the one who had spoken, the one with the syringe, noting the accent was thick with the local Egyptian dialect.

"And what of it?"

"You have desecrated the final resting place of a Pharaoh, a crime punishable by death," replied the one with the gun. His English was Oxford, but there was a hint of something else, probably Egyptian.

And pure, unmitigated hatred.

And it terrified him to his very core.

But he was British, and he'd be damned if he'd let his enemy know his fear. He took a deep breath, filling his stomach with courage, then slowly let it out, staring down the man in the Royal Cobra death mask.

"I apologize unreservedly if our expedition offended you in some way. We are merely explorers, archeologists who want to share history with the people of the world, so they can learn better about history—both theirs and yours. This King Tutankhamen had been forgotten by time, and now, thanks to our expedition, he will be forever remembered, perhaps more so than any that have come before or will come again. Surely you must see that we are not grave robbers, but preservers of the past. We have painstakingly documented the chambers, where every artifact, every speck of dust was, so that nothing will be forgotten." He took another deep breath, slowing down his speech. "We have done everything we can to honor your Pharaoh."

The man with the needle rounded the bedside, and George's muscles tensed to scramble away, then relaxed, knowing there was no escape. He was an old man, an invalid by some accounts due to his accident, and would have no hope of fighting off two young, healthy men.

But they couldn't take away his dignity.

The other man spoke, remaining at the foot of the bed.

"If you wanted to honor our Pharaoh, there was only one thing you needed to do."

"Name it, we'll do it."

"Leave him to rest in peace."

The man sporting the needle darted forward, plunging the device into his cheek. He gritted his teeth, then the needle was removed and the man stepped back.

"The curse of the Pharaoh's has begun," said the Oxford man. "Tell the others it will continue until the Pharaoh's tomb is returned as it was, and all activity stops."

George nodded. "I will deliver the message, but they won't stop"—he pointed at where he had been jabbed—"not over this."

"Perhaps not tomorrow," said the first, his voice almost smiling. "But after your agonizing death, they may feel differently."

And it was an agonizing death.

At first it seemed like nothing, and the next morning he could have been forgiven for thinking the entire episode was a dream, save one thing. The small mark on his face where he had been injected.

Each morning in the mirror it grew. But he felt fine. He tried to ignore it, dabbing his face with shaving cream, covering up the welt, as he performed his morning ritual, and with a hiss and a wince, he realized he had sliced the top off the growing welt.

Blood spilled over the blade and down his cheek, mixing with the foamy white soap. Cursing his stupidity, he finished shaving, then administered to the blemish by holding a handkerchief on the spot until the bleeding stopped. It took some time, but eventually it did, and he was able to depart for the dig site.

It would be the last time he saw it.

His wife was sent for, and she arrived in time to say goodbye, his days filled with fever and cough, pneumonia having set in. And one week later, on the 5th of April, he met his maker, after a week of agonizing pain and hallucinations, all the while crying of the Curse of the Pharaohs, and the king cobras that had visited his bed chamber to deliver a warning.

All who disturb the Pharaohs, shall die.

Nubian Desert, Egypt, University College London Dig Site
One Day Before the Liberty Island Attack

Acton's lungs were sucking air at an alarming rate and he knew if the massive cover stone didn't start to move soon, he would have to call a halt to the operation. The cavern they had found yesterday was a good size, but it seemed crowded now. He and Laura were accompanied by Chaney, half a dozen students, and another half dozen Egyptian laborers. A pulley system had been set up, a massive pile of sand had been transferred in overnight and piled on either side of the stone doorway, and a dozen men were grunting as they pulled on the ropes.

And it wasn't working.

He exchanged a quick glance with Laura who was directing the operations. She nodded as if she read his mind.

I'm going to die if we don't stop!

"One last time, give it everything you've got!" she yelled, one of the Egyptian supervisors screaming it in Arabic.

Everyone eased off on the ropes then snapped them back, hard, pulling with all their might. Acton started to see spots as he pulled with every ounce of strength he could muster, and still nothing.

Then suddenly, something.

It was a scraping sound, stone scraping on stone, and it sent a surge of adrenaline through him, and from the smiles he saw on the other sweat streaked faces surrounding him, the others as well. Everyone was pulling hard, everyone giving it everything they had. They all wanted to see what was inside, to see if what could be the greatest archeological find in

114

centuries was still intact. When Acton's flashlight had first lit the cover stone, he had known immediately what this was.

The lost tomb of Antony and Cleopatra.

Why it was out here in the Nubian Desert, so far from Alexandria, was beyond him. But he didn't care if he was in the middle of Nevada; if the find were genuine, it would be the most exciting, incredible thing he had ever laid eyes upon in his entire career.

But they needed to move this damned stone first.

"Again!" yelled an excited Laura, and they all pulled with renewed vigor, and again the scraping sound, louder and longer. The stone, laying against the cavern wall, at about an 80 degree angle from the ground, was moving, finally, and soon would come the difficult part. The skill part.

"This time both crews! Again!"

And this time the two crews pulled in unison, his crew the brute force crew, the second the guiding crew, tasked with not only preserving any gains made by the first crew, but to guide the stone when it finally came free, which was why the second crew were entirely students and Chaney. They had to be certain the instructions had been understood, and assurances from a translator weren't enough.

The stone began to tip, passing the 90 degree mark, and the momentum they had built had it tipping outward and toward those manning the ropes.

"Everyone toward me!" she yelled, her Arabic echo shouting the same.

Acton dug his heel into the ground and began to pull to his left instead of away from the wall, and he realized immediately that Laura's insistence on the instruction being "toward me" rather than "to the left" was the right choice. He wasn't certain the laborers would know their left from their right, and in his own exhaustion, he couldn't be sure he knew either.

But he knew exactly where the most lovely voice in the world was coming from, even if it were barking orders like a slave driver. He felt the stone start to swing, the grinding sound echoing through the chamber, terrifyingly loud. A glance over his shoulder showed the massive stone now turning away from the cave wall, and toward the huge pile of sand that Laura stood near the top of, on the side away from the stone, and as it continued to swing around, he lost track, his exhaustion taking over, when he heard a shout.

"Let go!"

He tossed his rope and stepped away from the stone as it collapsed slowly toward the mound of sand, Laura stepping back quickly as the enormous stone picked up speed.

It hit with an almost anti-climactic thud, the sand serving its purpose of cushioning the fall, preserving the cover stone bearing the carved symbols indicating whose tomb this was for future generations to enjoy. A smile spread across his face as he collapsed to the ground and the chamber filled with cheers. He felt arms around him as Laura rushed over and hugged him.

"Are you okay, Dear?"

"I'm getting too old for this shit," he moaned.

"Lethal Weapon." She grinned, seemingly pleased with herself that she had picked up the reference to one of his all-time favorite series. "And sorry, Darling, but you're more Riggs than Murtaugh, so you don't have any excuses."

"Ugh, you *are* a slave driver."

"If we had a drum, I think it would have helped."

"Next time I'll be sure to bring one."

She laughed and helped him to his feet.

"Lights!" he called, and several students rushed forward with large lanterns and flashlights as Acton and his fiancée approached the now gaping entranceway into what Acton hoped would be the greatest find in the history of Egyptian archeology.

And as they stepped through the entrance, their lights flickering on the mysterious interior, there was a cry from somebody behind them, then the sound of panic setting in. Acton swung around to see the laborers all scrambling for the rope ladder that led to the surface, pushing and shoving at each other as they competed for the narrow escape route.

"What's wrong?" he asked, stepping out, but as his light played across the back of the cover stone, he didn't bother listen for an answer. The cause for their panic was clear. In the center of the massive stone was a carving of a king cobra, coiled around the hieroglyph representing Death, with an inscription carved in hieroglyphics, Latin, and Arabic. Quickly translating the Latin, he gasped.

"The Curse of the Pharaohs!"

Cairo, Egypt
One Day Before the Liberty Island Attack

Imam Mahmoud Khalil sat cross-legged on the floor, his followers few but devoted, spread throughout the room, similarly seated, devouring his every word. This was what he loved. The rapt attention, the hanging on every word. It was power. The power to inspire, the power to control.

The power to effect change.

Tired of the far too moderate teachings of the Imam he had followed since his youth, he struck out on his own, preaching his own views, far more hardline than most, but in his view, far more true to the Koran than some moderates would have the Infidels believe.

The ultimate goal of the Koran was to lay out the foundation necessary to convert the entire world to Islam. It was plain to anyone who read the Holy words. Peaceful coexistence was not an option. Peaceful subjugation was, in which those of a different religion could live amongst Muslims, but it was every good Muslim's duty to harass them until they converted, or struck out in violence so they could be killed in the name of Allah.

Those who wanted to live in peace would convert to the religion of peace. It was very simple. Why so many pussyfooted around the true message was beyond him. The Infidels had already lost, they just didn't realize it yet. Their economies were collapsing in a frenzy of security spending brought on by the glorious successes of Osama bin Laden, their populations were scared, and when just two young men bombing a marathon could bring a city of almost five million to a halt for a day, and distract a nation for days, costing untold billions in lost productivity, imagine what sustained, small attacks could do.

But Khalil wanted to inspire, and his plan, in the making for years, would not only uphold one of the tenets of Islam, but stab a dagger of fear throughout the Western world when those countries decided what monuments to decadence to build; it would encourage the nation of Islam, spread throughout every country, to rise up, and commit the small acts of terror necessary to bring the Western economies to a grinding halt, thus destroying their ability to strike back.

For tomorrow, the world would change forever, and the idol, worshipped by an entire nation, and the huddled masses around the world, would be no more.

The Arab Spring had been a glorious triumph, but not in the way the ignorant West thought. The countries that had overthrown their leaders had overthrown secularist leaders and replaced them with "democratically" elected Islamist governments. And as each domino fell, more and more of the caliphate was being restored. Eventually these countries would unite in common purpose and eliminate the plague that was Israel, then push all Western influence from their lands.

And tomorrow's inspiration would enflame the passions of today's youth for generations, demonstrating the superiority of those who followed the true religion.

Khalil turned to the monitors facing him, his much larger base of followers spread throughout the world awaiting their final instructions before chaos was unleashed. He smiled as he looked at each screen, the true believers, willing to die for their god and his prophet, staring back with expressions ranging from fear to excitement, but without exception, devotion burning in their eyes.

He held out his hands, encompassing those watching remotely, and those in the room ready for their domestic assault, and turned his eyes upward.

"Rejoice today in the gifts granted you by Allah, enjoy yourselves, then purify your souls, for tomorrow your brave sacrifice will see you in Jannah, with Allah's perpetual blessing in Paradise, for helping fulfill his Word brought to us by the prophet Mohammad, peace be upon him." His head lowered, his eyes opening as he looked at his flock, then with a surge of fury in his heart as he thought of those who would dare try to stop him, he shouted, "Allahu Akbar!", and was quickly drowned out by those around him as they lost themselves in the rapture of true belief.

And with that belief, that devotion, the restoration of the Caliphate would begin tomorrow as the false idols were destroyed.

Nubian Desert, Egypt, University College London Dig Site
One Day Before the Liberty Island Attack

Laura stepped forward, her expert hands running over the inscription carved into the stone. She read the words several times, then finally said them out loud, confirming Acton's translation.

"Death shall come on swift wings to him that toucheth the tomb of a Pharaoh."

"Good thing you're a woman otherwise I'd be scared for you."

He received an elbow to the gut.

He grunted then chuckled as she stepped back.

"I always thought that the curse was a myth created by the newspapers during the King Tut excavations. There were no actual glyphs with those words, it was made up by someone."

"A joke?"

She shook her head. "These look like they were carved here long before the Tut expedition. And judging from what I saw inside, no grave robbers have touched this place."

Acton turned back toward the opening, holding up his lantern and sighed again. It was breathtaking. The amount of gold, silver and precious gems was spectacular, but the two sarcophagi, side by side, touching as if the arms of two lovers were forever together. He stepped inside, Laura at his side, several students following with their own lights.

"Bloody hell, it's incredible."

Acton smiled at Chaney's outburst, then remembered where he was and the importance of it.

"I'm sure I don't need to remind anybody not to touch anything." He glanced over at Chaney whose hand hovered in midair, about to touch a sculpture of a scarab. His hand darted back to his side, then his chest, then his stomach, Chaney apparently desperate to find a place where it would be under control.

He stuffed it in his pocket.

Acton chuckled as Laura turned to the students.

"Two at a time. Five minutes, then switch off. Don't worry, when we start to catalog everything, you'll get plenty of chances to enjoy this." She turned back to the sarcophagi, then looked at Acton.

"What do you think?"

Acton nodded to the one closest him.

"This is obviously Cleopatra."

Laura sighed, placing her hand on the other sarcophagus.

"And this must be Antony." She looked up at Acton. "Isn't it romantic, buried side by side for eternity, together forever."

Acton smiled. "Don't you think you'd get tired of me after two thousand years?"

Laura's hand continued to travel along Antony's sarcophagus, reaching his head.

"I suppose so."

"What?"

She looked up at him and winked.

"Har har."

Suddenly gunfire from above echoed through the chamber.

"What the hell—"

"Professors, you better get up here!" yelled a voice from the surface. Laura and Acton exchanged concerned glances, then hurried everyone from the room. Laura pointed at Terrence Mitchel and another student.

"You two guard this entrance, make sure no one goes inside." She turned to the remaining students. "Everyone else out. We'll organize shifts tomorrow."

Chaney held the rope ladder steady as Laura climbed it, followed by Acton. As he pushed through the hole at the top, he gasped at the heat of the late afternoon sun, it so cool below. As soon as he recovered from the shock, he heard shouting and another burst of gunfire from the camp.

He and Laura ran toward the commotion, the camp coming into view below as they began their descent. The workers were all clamoring to board a truck, two of the security team holding them at bay with weapons, Reading with them trying to calm them down, despite the fact few spoke little if any English.

"What's going on here?" Laura asked in Arabic.

The foreman, who spoke English, spun toward them and rapid fired the situation.

"We must leave! We cannot disturb the tomb of Cleopatra, otherwise we and our families will be cursed for eternity!"

"Nonsense. It's just words on a wall. You know there is no such thing as curses."

Acton's words seemed to have no effect.

"You must let us leave. Now! We will work here no longer."

Acton sighed, looking at Laura.

"What about just here, at the camp. Forget the tomb."

The man shook his head emphatically.

"No! We must go!"

Acton looked at Laura, who shrugged her shoulders.

"They refuse to work; they're scared of the curse. I don't think there's any reasoning with them."

"Agreed," sighed Acton. "Might as well let them go."

Laura nodded, motioning the guards and Reading out of the way, and the truck was stormed, rolling away within seconds as bodies continued to be hauled into the back of those not fortunate enough to get aboard in the first wave.

"Now we have a problem."

"What's that?" asked Reading.

Acton motioned at the departing truck with his chin.

"Now the world's about to find out what we discovered."

Cairo, Egypt

Night Before the Liberty Island Attack

"They found it."

Colonel Soliman frowned, scratching his thick but trimmed beard. They had known it was a possibility, ever since that damned professor from London had received a permit to dig. How she had done it, he didn't know. His people had tried to block it at every turn, but she seemed to have connections even better than his.

"You're certain?"

His friend of over thirty years, Mansoor, nodded. "There's no doubt."

"And of course the curse didn't work?"

"It worked on the hired help, but not the professor and her students."

Soliman sighed. He hadn't expected it to work. After all, no educated person believed in curses any more. About all they had accomplished with the curse was to slow them down. Without their manual labor, they'd have to do everything themselves. But it didn't matter. In the end the result was the same.

Desecration.

The ruse had lasted for two millennia. Archeologists for years had theorized the tomb was underwater, a victim of Alexandria's partial collapse into the sea, but the truth was the remains of Cleopatra and her husband, Antony, had been moved to a secret site almost a thousand miles away, along with several other Pharaohs' remains over the years.

But now the site had been compromised and something had to be done.

Mansoor looked at him. "What do we do? We can't scare them away."

Soliman shook his head. "No, we can't scare them away."

Mansoor looked out the window at the rooftops spread across Cairo, a clash of ancient buildings and construction techniques, stabbed with antennae and satellite dishes, electrical and telephone wires dangling in an unorganized tangle in a desperate attempt to modernize a city never meant to be modernized.

"There's only one thing these Westerners believe in," he said.

Soliman's eyebrows rose slightly. "What's that?"

"Violence."

"Is that what you believe?"

Mansoor nodded.

"So what do you propose? We kill them all?"

Mansoor frowned.

"I don't like it any more than you do, but they have desecrated the tomb of a Pharaoh. Isn't that punishable by death?"

Soliman bit his lip as he closed his eyes, leaning his head against the back of his chair.

"Yes, normally it would be. But consider their intent. Do they intend to steal what's inside?"

Mansoor shrugged. "I guess not. They're legitimate archeologists."

"And with the current laws, anything they find has to be turned over to the authorities. Nothing can leave Egypt."

"True." Mansoor's eyes narrowed. "You're not defending this, are you?"

Soliman smiled. "Not at all. But before we go and kill them all, I think we need to examine the situation."

Suddenly the door burst open and young Ahmed rushed in, his face flushed, his brow covered in sweat, his chest heaving as his lungs sucked in precious oxygen.

Both Soliman and Mansoor jumped from their chairs, rushing over to him.

"What is it, Ahmed?" asked Soliman, placing a hand on his shoulder.

But Ahmed couldn't answer, his lungs still desperate for oxygen. Instead he shoved a tablet computer he had been gripping toward Soliman. Soliman took it, holding it up for them all to see. Mansoor gasped at the headline.

British Archeologist Team Locates Cleopatra's Tomb.

"We're too late!" cried Mansoor, spinning around and booting his chair across the room.

Soliman quickly scanned the article, noting the sources quoted were workers from the dig site. Mansoor was right. They were too late if killing them were the only option.

But there's one other thing Westerners believe in, perhaps even more than violence.

Nubian Desert, Egypt, University College London Dig Site

Acton poked a stick at the fire, mesmerized by the dancing flames. They were all there, it a nightly ritual missed by none. Gathered by the open fire, the wood collected from the surrounding area, and never taken from a live plant, was used sparingly—artificial logs flown in at Laura's personal expense added to the flame, along with a healthy helping of camel dung supplied by their laborers who in their rush had left their beasts behind. It wasn't a roaring fire as they might have at his dig site in Peru, but it was beautiful nonetheless.

"So what exactly have we stumbled upon," asked Reading. "Is it really Cleopatra's tomb?"

Acton nodded, his eyes still on the flames.

"It would appear so."

"What the devil is it doing out here in the middle of nowhere?"

Laura chuckled and waved her arm toward the dig site sitting nearby.

"Two thousand years ago this wasn't the middle of nowhere. There was a thriving community here."

"But no city."

She dropped her head slightly in acknowledgement.

"But no city. Why the tomb is here, I have no idea, I'm just pointing out that what is now barren and abandoned wasn't always so. There is obviously a reason her remains are here."

"What can you tell us about Cleopatra that the movie didn't tell us?" asked Chaney.

Reading's eyebrows shot up. "You've seen the movie?"

Chaney shrugged. "I like the classics."

128

Reading looked at Acton. "I worked with him for years and never knew that."

Acton winked and then looked at Chaney. "Let's ignore the movie. First, her name wasn't officially Cleopatra, it was actually Cleopatra the Seventh Philopator, as she was the seventh to use that name. As well, she wasn't Egyptian. She was actually Greek, her family lineage descendant from when Alexander the Great conquered Egypt."

"She wasn't Egyptian?" exclaimed Reading. "I've always wondered about that. I would have expected a Roman at the time to not publicly be involved with an African, even North African, but if she was Macedonian, she was probably as white as he was."

"True. They were more similar than many realize from a cultural standpoint."

"That coin that showed her certainly had her looking pretty beastly," piped in one of the students, which resulted in a round of laughter.

"Hard to tell from the coin what she really looked like, and our definition of beauty was probably quite different from theirs back then. The stories speak of her beauty and her power over men. It could simply be the way she dressed which may have been more provocative than what European men were used to at the time, or her confidence in her sexuality that made her so alluring. We don't really know, but whatever it was, Mark Antony fell for her head over heels, much to the objections of the Roman aristocracy."

"Wasn't he responsible for the destruction of the Library of Alexandria?" asked Chaney.

"No, that's the movie confusing things," replied Laura. "In fact when the Romans set fire to the ships in the harbor, it ignited fires in nearby buildings, but the Library was nowhere near the docks. History records the destruction of thousands of scrolls, but these were most likely just paperwork."

"Then how was it destroyed?"

"There are several theories, one of which Laura just debunked," began Acton. "The attack of Aurelian, the decree of a Coptic Pope, or after the conquest by the Muslims."

"Which do you think it is, Professor?" asked Terrence.

"I think they're all true in their own way."

Reading's eyebrows shot up. "Huh?"

"During the attack of Emperor Aurelian, it is recorded that the main library was destroyed, but a smaller part of the library, in a separate building, survived. This was nearly three hundred years after the death of Cleopatra. Then, over a hundred years later, the Coptic Pope Theophilus declared paganism illegal, and ordered the destruction of all pagan artifacts, including documents. This resulted in the destruction of much if not all of what remained of the library in my opinion."

Chaney raised a hand, then dropped it quickly as if realizing he weren't in school. "What about the Muslims?"

"Several Muslim texts refer to the destruction of the Library at their hands after their conquest due to it containing information that contradicted the Koran. But these accounts were written over five hundred years later. Modern scholars think that these were stories spread by Saladin to justify his own destruction of a collection of heretical texts."

"It would make sense though, if you think about it," said Terrence. "What with what they did to the Buddhas in Afghanistan, and what they're doing in Timbuktu right now."

Laura nodded. "There's definitely a pattern, but in this case, I think history has judged them unfairly."

"So what happened to Cleopatra?" asked Chaney. "How did she die?"

Acton poked the fire, eliciting a shower of sparks that drifted over their heads. "There was a civil war in Rome, between Octavian and Antony. Antony and Cleopatra's armies suffered a series of defeats, and they ultimately fled to Egypt, but Octavian's armies pursued them. Nearing defeat, Antony received word that Cleopatra had committed suicide, and rather than go on without her, he ran himself through with his sword. As he lay dying, he received word that she was alive, and he was taken to her, to die in her arms."

"That's so romantic," cooed one of the girls, sniffles given anonymity by the darkness indicating she wasn't alone in her sentiment.

"Probably why Shakespeare wrote about it," mumbled Reading.

"I didn't know you were a Shakespeare fan," said Laura.

Reading shrugged. "School, the occasional play. That's about it."

"Are you sure you're not a closet fan?"

Reading shot her a look that left her giggling.

"So what happened?" asked Chaney, hanging on every word it seemed.

"Octavian captured Cleopatra, but she was permitted to carry out the burial rites, then she too committed suicide."

Chaney gasped. "Why?"

"She knew Octavian planned to parade her in chains in Rome, and she wanted none of it. She killed herself using what was probably a king cobra, to bite her chest. When she died, her son was briefly named Pharaoh, but he was killed by Octavian, ending the rule of the Pharaohs; Egypt becoming a Roman province called Aegyptus."

"So why here? Why bury her in the middle of nowhere"—Chaney raised his hand—"sorry, Professor—in a small town like this?"

Laura smiled at the apology as Acton continued. "I find it highly unlikely she would have been buried here. Most think she is buried near Alexandria, and with much of the ancient parts now underwater after a series of earthquakes, it has always been assumed it had been lost forever. But"—Acton shrugged, looking over his shoulder at the new dig site—"it would appear somebody moved her tomb, probably to protect it from grave robbers. And from what we've seen, I would guess that they were successful."

"Until we came along," laughed Terrence.

"Until we came along," repeated Acton, his voice drifting as he wondered who might have been protecting the tomb, and whether or not they were still around. *It's been two thousand years.* He frowned. *That means nothing.* His own experiences over the past couple of years had proven that two thousand years only meant an organization could grow to immense proportions if needed, or remain a devoted few, still thriving, if the devotion were strong enough.

We need more guards.

"Umm, Professor?"

Laura leaned toward Acton to see the face the timid voice belonged to.

"Yes, Angela?"

"What would happen if they found out about the tomb?"

"Who found out, dear?"

"The fanatics. Like those who destroyed the Buddhas."

"Oh, don't worry about that. We're quite safe here," said Laura, exchanging a glance with Acton who suddenly felt as unconvinced as she sounded.

For he knew when word got out, they might be in serious danger.

En route to Nubian Desert, Egypt, University College London Dig Site
Morning of the Liberty Island Attack

Colonel Soliman hung onto the dash of the truck, eyeballing Mansoor who was behind the wheel, apparently trying to hit every hole in the road he could find. He kept his mouth shut, as he knew time was of the essence. Their two trucks of men, two dozen in total, as well as a third truck for those at the tomb, had departed within an hour of hearing the news. The location was remote, and their observers had been chased off but remained near, and would join them when they reached the camp, which Soliman estimated should be less than five hours away at this point.

The only thing that could stop them now was a checkpoint, more frequent now with the chaos after the so-called elections, which was why Mansoor was taking the back roads to the site. It was a few hours slower, but even the army didn't care about this area.

The real question was whether or not the press would beat them to the dig site. He had had his contacts immediately call the press to claim they were at the site and that it wasn't true, but the feedback had been less than encouraging.

Everyone wanted to confirm the story and were sending out teams.

And they would take the faster main roads, and some would have had a massive head-start since he himself only found out from an advance copy of the paper his connections afforded him.

If they couldn't beat the press to the site, he didn't know what they would do. He glanced over his shoulder at the men crammed into the back, their automatic weapons at the ready, their military uniforms genuine, though those wearing them no longer soldiers defending their country.

They were now soldiers of The Brotherhood.

And what task he would ask of them, he did not know, though he feared the worst.

Safe House, Cairo, Egypt

Imam Khalil lay on his bed, eyes closed, listening to the sounds of the city. Images played across the back of his eyelids like movies, imagining the glory of today's deeds to be carried out by his followers in the name of Allah. He opened his eyes and surveyed the austere room without moving his head.

It will be difficult.

He knew once he went public with his address to the world, he would be the most hunted man in the world, and would eventually die, hopefully years later like Osama, with a gun in his hand, having lived out what remained of his life in relative comfort.

He had followers. He had connections. And he would need them all to survive in the days to come.

And this small room in this small house was only the first of many he would be rotated through over the coming months and years. If, Allah willing, all went perfectly, the Muslim Brotherhood would complete its takeover of Egypt, tossing aside its long alliance with the United States and the Infidels, and organizing a joint Arab invasion of Israel to eliminate the cancer that festered in their region. Push them into the sea; leave what remained for the filthy Palestinians. Empty the refugee camps so they could return to their own "land" and stop leeching of the good people of Egypt, Lebanon, Jordan and elsewhere.

He always enjoyed a good chuckle watching or reading the Western press when they would refer to the Palestinian situation. They quite often seemed to ignore the fact that the Arab nations surrounding Israel were home to millions of Palestinian refugees, and none had been allowed to become citizens of their new homelands, all forced to continue to live in squalor for fifty years as the Arab nations wanted them even less than the Israelis did. The Palestinians throughout most of history never truly had a country, always subjugated by one empire or another, and the idea of a Palestinian nation was a modern construct created by Westerners who had no understanding of how much of the world had worked before they conquered it. Most modern borders throughout the Middle East, Africa and much of Asia were drawn by men in London and Paris, who had a penchant for straight lines, ignoring tribal histories in favor of borders composed of neat lines, rivers and mountain ranges.

And the legacy?

Afghanistan, Pakistan and India. The Kashmir region ignored, not to mention the fact there is no concept of borders amongst Pashtun culture. Then there was Turkey, Iraq, Iran, ignoring the Kurds, and Syria, Jordan, Israel, Egypt, and others, ignoring the Palestinians. It wasn't the Jews who had forced the Palestinians out; it was the ignorant post war leaders who did, by arbitrarily drawing lines on maps to suit their needs, rather than those of the indigenous peoples.

And in the end the Palestinians were forgotten, the Arabs were insulted, and they immediately went to war with Israel. And that infidel state had continually won the wars, and expanded their territory. All perfectly legal, since they were invaded, and didn't invade to take over territory, but the public relations campaign waged by the Palestinians and the Arabs had confused the issue so much, many if not most in the West thought Israel was the aggressor.

But soon we will be once again.

And with one final push, one concerted effort with the newly restored Islamic fundamentalist states working together, the Jewish question would be solved once and for all, and the single blot on the map of the Arab world would be gone forever, a page in the history books never to be taught to the children who would live there in the future.

Khalil closed his eyes again, a smile on his face as he pictured a world free of the Jews.

If only Hitler had been given more time.

He wasn't one of those naïve holocaust deniers. He knew it had happened. He simply didn't think it was a bad thing. Ridding the world of the Jews, along with the homosexuals, mentally and physically handicapped, was merely the responsible thing to do. By ridding the world of them, Hitler intended to create a purer race, and he had succeeded. Look at Europe today. More peaceful than it ever has been throughout its tumultuous history. And why? What had changed?

Hitler had removed eleven million problems. Six million Jews, along with five million other *problems*.

A glorious achievement.

And his beloved Egypt would soon follow. The Jews were pretty much gone already. Now it was the Christians. With enough pressure, enough violence, those who weren't killed in the streets or their churches, would flee to the West as refugees, and the Islamic State of Egypt would be happy to see them go, leaving behind a purely Islamic nation.

But first to go would be the false idols. And he could think of nothing more egregious than the pyramids and other structures built to honor pagan false gods. These would be eliminated over time, the first of which would be this afternoon.

There was a knock on his door that had him sitting up and swinging his legs from the bed.

"Enter."

The owner of the house he was now staying in, Fadil, entered, holding up a copy of the newspaper, shaking it in the air.

"I thought you should see this."

"What is it?"

Rather than answer, Fadil unfolded the front page and jabbed a finger at the headline.

Khalil's heart leapt as he saw the page, his chest tightening as adrenaline pumped through his veins as he thought of the opportunity this news brought. To think that today they were going to attack the Pyramid of Cheops, most likely in a failed yet heroic battle, when here lay an even better, unprotected opportunity that would enrapture the world with its audacity.

Today they would destroy the Tomb of Cleopatra.

Nubian Desert, Egypt, University College London Dig Site

Professor James Acton looked at the computer screen, the satellite connection he was using nowhere near the speed he was accustomed to, but as the CNN.com site refreshed, he cursed as he saw a link pop up on the left listing the top stories.

Cleopatra Found?

"We've got trouble."

Laura, lying in her cot, looked up from her eReader.

"How's that?"

"The story just broke on CNN."

Laura swung her legs from the cot, putting the eReader under her pillow. "Blast! Already? You'd think they'd at least verify the story before running it."

Acton chuckled. "Not today, hon. Remember 9/11? CNN and the other stations were reporting everything, unverified, so they wouldn't be scooped. I remember watching the coverage, and the outlets were reporting seventeen planes unaccounted for, explosions on Capitol Hill, helicopters being shot down at the Pentagon. It was ridiculous! The news is no longer the news, it's just opinion mixed in with some verified facts now and then. There just isn't twenty-four hours of interesting stuff happening in the world to keep the viewers' attention.

"When I was a kid I would sit on my parents' couch and we would all watch Tom Brokaw, Peter Jennings or Sam Donaldson read the news, depending on who my dad wasn't mad at that week. You'd get the day's news in thirty minutes, and it was the news. You could flip between the channels, and they'd all be reporting the same, verified facts, and occasionally one would scoop the other. But once CNN came along, everything changed for the worse." Acton shook his head. "I love sitting in front of the TV watching news, listening to the commentary, but too many people nowadays think it's *all* news."

He looked at Laura who was grinning.

"What?"

"Done?"

His eyes narrowed as he looked at her puzzled, then it dawned on him what she was talking about.

"Ha ha. Yes, my diatribe is finished."

"You should have the university do a study."

"Remind me when we get back." Acton stood up. "We better get the site ready for the newshounds. They'll probably be here by the end of the day."

Laura rose and they both exited the tent. She stepped over to a pole that had a bell attached to it, and rang the bell several times, signaling the students to assemble at the main tent. Heads poked up from grids, out of tents and one from the port-a-potty, and within minutes everyone had gathered, including the ex-SAS guard.

"May I have everyone's attention please," said Laura, raising her voice over the flapping of the tent behind her, a stiff breeze suddenly blowing. "CNN is reporting our discovery, most likely from one of our laborers who fled yesterday. That means we will probably have company soon."

"Should we be worried?" asked Terrence Mitchell. He had been on this very site when Laura had been kidnapped, and Acton knew full-well how terrified all the students had been based upon Reading's account when he found them. It was a tribute to their courage that they all came back.

"No," said Acton, shaking his head. "We might get a deluge of reporters that will quickly die off as they discover we won't give them access. They'll get bored, might leave some local crews here for a bit, then things will get back to normal. You'll probably all get your fifteen minutes on camera, become social media celebrities, get on all the talk shows when you get home, date famous actors, then when the next big discovery is found, you'll all be dumped like yesterday's King Tut exhibit."

There was laughter from the gathered students, and Laura elbowed him.

"You see I'm clearly not marrying him for his sense of humor."

More laughter, and Acton faked a stab to the heart, dropping to a knee as he looked up at her in mock horror.

"In all seriousness, we will have company. Untrained company, and we need to protect our dig. Luckily I've prepared for this. We'll stake off the site, extending our perimeter to include the new discovery, then set up an area where they can park, set up their own tents if they want, and have access to our latrines and a common area for interviews. Our tents and storage facilities are off limits, the digs and of course the tomb are off limits. Feel free to answer any questions, we're not hiding anything, but if they want to see anything, they have to come through either myself or Professor Acton."

Acton, having already risen to both feet, pointed toward the guards.

"If you discover a security breach, don't try to deal with it yourself, get one of the guards. That's why they're here. We might have some riffraff come in and try to steal some artifacts, which is why we'll need the tomb guarded at all times, twenty-four-seven."

Leather nodded an acknowledgement.

Laura handed a map to Terrence. "I want you to take charge. Stake off everything with one meter high stakes and cord as indicated by the blue line on the map."

Terrence took the map and looked it over along with several other students.

"Questions?"

Head shakes and "no's" rippled through the gathered throng.

"Okay, get to it, we don't have much time."

The students broke, leaving Acton and Laura along with Reading and Chaney and the four guards.

"How can we help?" asked Reading.

"When they get here, having a copper might settle things down a bit, so be prepared for that," said Laura. "I really hate to ask this of you two, but if you could perhaps keep an eye on things when they get here, maybe in shifts, until things die down or we see how it's going, that would be fabulous."

Chaney nodded. "No problem. I'll help the kids with the staking, Hugh, you get some sleep until our visitors get here. You can take the first shift, I'll take the night shift."

"Sounds good to me," said Reading. "I'm going to make a couple of calls first, see if we can get some local crowd control."

"Rahim?"

Reading nodded. "He may be more than he said he was, but he's still an Egyptian cop." Laura handed him the satellite phone and he wandered off to make his call.

"Rahim?" she asked with a whisper.

"Local cop who was actually a plant. He and Reading were first on the scene when you were kidnapped."

"Of course, I forgot his name."

Acton smiled. "If that really is his name."

Laura winked then turned to Leather.

"How do we think we should use your men?"

Leather stepped forward, his shades reflecting both their images.

"There's one thing we're forgetting."

142

"What's that?" asked Acton.

"The observers. We know someone was watching us, in numbers. To ignore that fact invites trouble. I think we should be preparing for the worst. I've called for reinforcements, but they can't be here until late tomorrow."

Acton frowned, remembering Reading's briefing on their uninvited guests after he had fallen in the hole. In all the excitement, he had indeed forgotten about them, and it brought an uneasiness he hadn't felt in some time.

A feeling he had learned to heed.

"What do you suggest?"

"We need to set up several discrete defensive positions, and an evac point."

"We don't want this to look like an armed camp," said Laura, "otherwise the parents back home who watch the report will wonder what I have their children in the middle of."

"Which is why I said discrete." He pointed at the two remaining trucks, one a jeep that could seat a cramped six, and a lorry that could easily hold a dozen. "Those are our lives if things get out of hand. We should reposition them to the rear of the camp. I've already scouted out an escape route to the north that has us on back roads for ten miles then the military checkpoint where we can be safe."

"Are you sure we can be safe with the military?"

Leather nodded. "It's the police you need to worry about. Most of the army is fairly disciplined. They're content to sit back and watch the Muslim Brotherhood lose control of the country so the military can take over again with the support of the people."

"Okay," said Laura, "set up your defensive positions. Just don't make it too obvious. I don't want to alarm the students." Leather nodded then trotted off with his men. "Or myself," she muttered.

Acton put his arm over her shoulder and squeezed.

"It'll be okay."

"Uh huh. It never is, so why assume it now?"

She flashed him a grin and caught the phone tossed to her by Reading as he approached.

"What's up?" asked Acton.

Reading frowned.

"There's a lot of chatter apparently, all around the world. They think something big is being planned somewhere, but they don't know where. They think the Internet is being flooded with false flags to hide the real operation. Otherwise…"

His voice drifted off, which tugged at Acton's alarm bell.

"Otherwise?"

Reading shook his head.

"Otherwise they're hitting pretty much everything imaginable. Which is obviously bollocks."

"Obviously."

Acton felt as unconvinced as Reading sounded.

"Well, there's nothing we can do about the world, we can only take care of ourselves," said Laura, placing her hands on her hips in defiance to all the flags out there, false or otherwise.

"And to that end I managed to contact Rahim. He and a dozen trusted men will be here as soon as they can."

Laura sighed. "Thank goodness. So we just need to keep control of the frenzy until then."

"Here they come!"

It was Terrence who trumpeted the warning and they all turned to the road to see a vehicle race around the final bend and into the "parking lot" as they liked to call it.

One man stepped out, young and greasy from his trip, a camera around his neck, notepad in the other, and a wide-eyed smile at apparently being first.

Acton and Laura walked toward him, their best smiles on their faces. Acton hung slightly behind, letting Laura take the lead since this was her show, content to be the "muscle".

"How do you do, I'm Professor Laura Palmer."

"Nigel Hendricks. Associated Press." He looked around. "Am I the first?"

Laura nodded. "And hopefully last."

Hendricks laughed. "Oh, judging by the lineup at the roadblock I just left, there'll be a lot more any minute now."

Shit!

He looked about.

"So where is she?"

"Who?" asked Laura, playing dumb.

"The lovely lady! The Queen! Cleopatra of course!"

"All in good time. Why don't you get yourself settled over there"— Laura pointed to an area reserved for the media tents—"and when your compatriots arrive, we'll take you all on a tour."

"But I got here first!"

Laura shrugged. "Congratulations. I'll make sure you're in the first group."

And as if to punctuate her statement, an SUV roared around the bend, barreling toward the parking lot, followed quickly by another.

This is going to be a mess very quickly.

Nubian Desert, Egypt, Five miles from University College London Dig Site

Colonel Soliman pointed to the right at a group of men on horseback. One held his hand in the air, his Kalashnikov strapped to his back barely visible save the muzzle projecting over his shoulder. Soliman recognized him immediately.

"There's Rahman!"

Mansoor geared down and came to a stop beside the men, Soliman immediately exiting the truck when he was certain Mansoor had turned it off, vowing never again to trust the man's driving.

Then again, he got us here alive and in record time.

"As-salam alaykum," he said to Rahman, holding out his hands.

"Wa alaykum e-salam," replied Rahman, jumping from his horse. Soliman embraced his old friend with a smile.

"Tell us what you have found."

Rahman nodded at the horizon. "They have found the tomb, as I told you. We were chased off two days ago by some of their guards. I think they think we're thieves."

"They're the thieves," muttered Mansoor who had joined them.

Soliman held up his hand. "Have they taken anything yet?"

Rahman shook his head. "I don't think so. We returned the next day. It looks like they've set up equipment to get in and out easily, but it appears they're only moving stuff in."

Soliman grimaced. "First, like good archeologists, they will catalog and document, disturbing as little as possible. Then they will begin moving things out."

"We must stop them. Kill them all if need be," hissed Rahman. "This is blasphemy!"

Soliman gripped his friend's shoulder.

"There are other ways besides killing, my friend."

Nubian Desert, Egypt, Thirty-three miles from University College London Dig Site

Imam Khalil looked at his watch and, turning to his driver, Ali, smiled. The joy he felt in his heart couldn't be contained. The number of Infidels who died today was irrelevant. He actually predicted the numbers would be far less than what some of his flock were hoping for.

But the psychological damage would be irreversible.

With their icons destroyed, the nations of the world would be reminded daily of the might of Allah and his true believers. The West would cower in fear at the foot of Mohammad's followers, and life would never be the same. Imagine if every day soldiers were hacked to pieces on their way to work. No one would feel safe, and their Western ideals wouldn't allow them to protect themselves the way they should. Sure they'd shut down Muslim immigration, but what of the millions upon millions of Muslims who were already citizens, most of whom were born in the very countries they hated?

The inspiration today's attacks would provide would lead dozens, then hundreds, and eventually thousands, to join the struggle against their adopted homelands, creating chaos, and eventually forcing the Western nations to withdraw their forces from around the world in order to quell a domestic uprising from within.

This would allow the Muslim nations of the world to take their true place, at the forefront of a new revolution, controlling their own resources, without Western interference. And the West, with its pitiable birthrate, would dwindle away, too scared to bring in more immigrants to bolster their failing social systems.

And within a few generations, when there was another billion or two Muslims on the planet, and hundreds of millions fewer Christians, all living in bankrupt countries, at or near retirement age, the Caliphate would no longer be a dream, but just a matter of time.

"Sir, roadblock ahead."

Khalil nodded, grabbing his radio. "Roadblock ahead. You know what to do."

Ali slowed, pulling to the side as two other trucks passed them. Khalil sat back in his seat, AK-47 at the ready, but his heart at ease. If he were to die today, doing Allah's bidding, he would be blessed with eternal ecstasy in Jannah. He smiled as he closed his eyes, the opening bursts of gunfire from directly ahead greeted with panicked shouts as the poorly manned roadblock, in a forgotten south-eastern corner of the massive country, was overrun.

The distinctive rattle of the Kalashnikovs overwhelmed the thunderous response of the more modern American made Mk43's the military forces were equipped with. Though arguably a better weapon, they were simply outmanned.

A lucky round ricocheted off the hood of their truck, causing Ali to yelp, but Khalil continued to meditate to the sound of the gunfire, then the shouts of "Allahu Akbar!" as victory was secured.

He opened his eyes and watched the barrier being hauled aside as the trucks reloaded with the now fired up men, hot off one victory, and ready for the next.

Something flashed on the horizon, causing his head to spin to the right, but whatever it had been, was gone.

But it didn't matter.

Today Allah is on our side.

Nubian Desert, Egypt, Thirty-three miles from University College London Dig Site

Abdel lifted his head, spitting out the sand he had nearly eaten when the gunshots had begun. It was silent now, and he could hear several vehicles' engines roaring as they pulled away. He dropped his head back to the ground, this time on its side, and waited for silence.

That was when he noticed the damp feeling in his pants.

He cursed, then begged Allah's forgiveness, pushing himself to his knees, the danger momentarily forgotten. He looked down at his open fly and dangling member, urine staining his pants, he having dropped to the ground in midstream, his act of relieving himself interrupted by the shots.

Frowning, he again asked for Allah's forgiveness as he touched himself, caging his disgrace, and zipping up his fly. Turning to face the sun, he forced his hips out to try and dry his pants, when he heard a moan, and the reality of the situation returned.

Spinning around, he saw the carnage on the other side of the rise. The roadblock had been decimated, three army vehicles destroyed, the gate open and smoldering, bodies littering the ground. He rushed toward the scene, eying his own car the entire way, hoping, praying—but it wasn't to be.

He circled the car, its hood open, its windows down, to find not a scratch on it. He kicked the piece of junk he had been hired to transport. It had broken down twice on him already, this the third time, and he knew this beautiful piece of garbage would be the death of him if he had to continue.

And he wasn't willing to die for some piece of junk.

He looked around and saw a weapon lying beside one of the soldier's bodies. He picked it up, aimed it at the car, then unloaded the entire clip into the engine compartment, laughing in glee as he did so, praising Allah for bringing some goodness from the tragedy that had befallen the checkpoint.

The weapon spent, he tossed it to the ground, then stared at his handiwork with a smile.

I hate Jaguars.

Nubian Desert, Egypt, University College London Dig Site

Laura pulled at her hair in exasperation. There were at least a dozen reporters, most with crews, all demanding their attention at once. She hadn't dealt with this much press since the London incident, and there she had the luxury of the "no comment" statement.

Here, she did not.

But James, her rock, had rescued her from the frenzy, offering anyone who would follow a blow-by-blow description of how the tomb was found, slowly walking away from her, leaving her alone within seconds.

And she had made her escape to the tent, lying down on her cot and closing her eyes. She heard the outer flap open, then the inner, the dual entry designed to keep the air conditioned coolness inside as much as possible. Whoever it was banged into something, then cursed, and she smiled as she recognized Terrence's clumsiness.

She debated announcing herself, but decided instead to feign sleep, her eyes still closed, and her body almost ready to slip into a deep slumber as her weary muscles collapsed, one by one.

Tapping at a keyboard told her either her ruse was successful, or more likely, Terrence hadn't noticed he wasn't alone.

I really hope he's not in here to 'read a magazine'.

She nearly chuckled out loud to the *How I Met Your Mother* euphemism, but caught herself.

"Oh my God!"

It was a whisper, one that at first had her thinking he really was 'reading a magazine', but then she recognized the horror in it. There was a confusion of sounds as she opened her eyes. Terrence was bolting for the tent door, the chair he had been sitting at was turned over, the computer monitor still open.

She swung herself from the cot and walked over to the monitor.

What she saw had her hand darting to her mouth, her eyes watering with tears.

Oh no!

USS Arleigh Burke, Segregated Common Area

Dawson lay on a faux leather couch, his eyes closed, his hat sitting over his face, as he continued to unwind from the mission. The debriefs had been long and detailed, which was to be expected considering the sensitivity of the region. Every piece of equipment had been inventoried before they left, and every piece checked upon their return.

And as he could have told them, nothing but bullets and sweat had been left behind.

And those bullets were from weapons common to the area, so untraceable to the US military.

It was a completely successful op. No friendlies were hurt, no civilians, and there would be no evidence they had ever been there. But most importantly, the sarin gas had been destroyed, and it wouldn't be harming any innocents in the future.

"What the fuck is that?"

It was Niner's voice that finally brought him out of his stupor.

"Turn it up!" ordered Atlas, and suddenly the television was blaring and the music killed.

"—*seeing live footage of what* was *the Statue of Liberty.*"

Dawson bolted upright. *'Was'?*

His jaw dropped as he saw the screen. The great lady was a smoldering heap, her body, gutted, laying on its side, her head, off to the side, the smoke still drifting up from the base. The camera panned to show her arm, the torch gripped tightly, embedded in the ground, still raised in defiance of her attackers. The sight grabbed his chest as he felt a rage build inside, something he hadn't felt since the first tower had collapsed on 9/11. His home had been attacked again, by the same cowards he had no doubt, the audacity of something like this too bold for domestic terrorism.

His jaw tightened. *It had better not have been 'home grown'.* His teeth gritted at the thought of Americans doing this to America. He couldn't believe it. *She* was America. Even the most crazed anti-government radical worshiped her. She was the true American idol, an icon to everything the great nation of America stood for. She was beyond governments, she was beyond scandals.

She was pure.

She was America.

And she was gone.

"Christ, they hit Paris too."

Dawson glanced at Jimmy, then at the screen his eyes had blurred at. The shot showed the Eiffel Tower, still standing, one of its four struts badly damaged but still mostly intact, hundreds of emergency crew swarming the still volatile area.

The image then flashed to a Breaking News graphic and an image of a building he'd recognize anywhere.

Jesus no!

Nubian Desert, Egypt, University College London Dig Site

"This is the man who actually found the site."

All the cameras and microphones spun to follow Acton's outstretched arm, and an embarrassed Detective Inspector Chaney turned beet red as he was bombarded with questions. He stammered several times, not knowing who to answer, beginning only to be cutoff by the next question.

Finally he had had enough and raised his hands.

"One at a time." He pointed. "You."

Acton smiled as Reading approached, a pleased expression on his face as he watched his former protégé begin to handle the throng.

"I taught him well."

"Indeed you did."

"How long do you think this circus will last?"

Acton shrugged.

"Who knows? I've told them I'd let one pool cameraman into the tomb later to take some footage that they could share, then that was it. My guess is once they've distributed that amongst themselves, and they've all got a few minutes of sound bites, they'll be gone.

"Let's hope."

"Oh my God!" yelled a voice, bursting from the communal tent. Acton looked over to see Terrence stumbling from the full height structure, tripping over one of the cords.

That kid with a gun is terrifying.

"What is it?" asked one of the students closest him.

"They just blew up the Statue of Liberty, and now there's an attack in London!"

Acton felt his chest tighten and the world swim as images of the fallen lady filled his mind. If there was one symbol that was America besides her flag, it was the Statue of Liberty. To think of New York City without her guarding its harbor was unimaginable, to think of her shores unguarded by her arm, raised defiantly in the air, gripping her torch, was unthinkable.

He stood frozen, as they all did, then the reporters suddenly broke from their questioning of Chaney and hit their phones as he felt a hand grip his arm, pulling him toward Terrence.

It was Reading, taking control.

"Who did it?" he managed, as he neared Terrence.

"Early reports say Islamic fundamentalists. It's just happening now. London is still happening!"

"What's happening in London?" asked Reading, but before Terrence had a chance to answer, Laura burst from the tent.

"They're attacking Buckingham Palace!"

Reading and the cadre of British students gasped.

"The Queen!" exclaimed one of the girls, who had to be held up by a classmate.

"Is she there?" asked another.

Laura nodded, her voice cracking.

"They're all there."

Buckingham Palace, London, England

William lay on the bed, one leg crossed over the other, hands clasped behind his head, eyes closed as his wife busied herself in the mirror. He didn't see the need for makeup—he thought she was beautiful just the way she was, but she always insisted on looking her best, especially when seeing Grandmother. There was no arguing with her, not that he would.

Especially with that baby bump growing every day.

Me! A father!

It was shocking how quickly things were happening. He knew nothing was happening fast enough for the public, but that was to be expected. He tried to ignore the pressures from the public, and completely ignored the press, his morning news briefings provided by staff who vetted the papers of anything "Royals" related.

"How do I look?"

He opened his eyes and pushed himself up on his elbows, then smiled.

"Absolutely fab," he said, then added with a wink, "as always."

Kate did a quick curtsey and motioned for him to get off the bed. William swung his feet off the bed and onto the floor, then grabbed her hand, pulling her toward him. Wrapping his arms around her, he rested his ear against her stomach, listening for the tiny heartbeat inside.

"Can you hear him?"

"I think so."

He pulled back slightly then placed his forehead on her stomach.

"Someday, you'll be King."

"Or Queen!"

He kissed his wife's stomach then stood up, giving her a peck on the forehead, not daring mess up her carefully drawn lips. He puffed out his chest, pushed his shoulders back, and stuck his left elbow out, his hand on his hip.

"Shall we, my dear?"

Kate looked at him, desperately trying to keep a straight face, finally losing the battle with a burst of laughter that quickly infected him. Recovered, she took his arm, then he did a walk that would have been worthy of the Ministry of Silly Walks, which had her gasping for breath again.

"Stop, Will, please, or I'll give birth right now!"

William snapped to attention, grabbed the door knob, then looked at her red face, tears threatening to spoil her makeup. He let out the breath he had been holding, and offered her his handkerchief.

"Time to be serious," he said, his smile gentle so as not to elicit any further laughter.

Kate took the handkerchief and dabbed the corners of her eyes, the red quickly subsiding, but her cheeks retaining a healthy glow. He pulled open the door and two palace guards snapped to attention. Having grown up with them all his life, he had long ago stopped wondering how much they heard through the thin doors, but his wife hadn't.

Which had led to the order that at night, the guards were to position themselves down the hall, otherwise the baby the public so desperately wanted, might never have happened.

A loud noise had him immediately thinking of a car crash, but to hear it in here would mean it would be on the palace grounds, which was nearly impossible unless somebody had done something spectacularly stupid.

He rushed to the window, fingers crossed, hoping his brother wasn't about to make the papers again. He gasped at what he saw. Below, it appeared a breakdown lorry with a ramp had run into the east gate, the reinforced barrier holding.

There's no way this is an accident.

And as if to confirm it, three cars that had stopped at the scene suddenly emptied of their occupants, who rushed up the ramp of the wrecked truck, and jumped over the fence to the palace grounds below.

And they were all armed.

He spun on his heel and pointed at one of the guards.

"We're under attack. Get the princess to safety immediately."

"What about you, sir?" asked the guard, readying his weapon.

"I need to get to Her Majesty. They'll be after her."

"Will, no, come with me!"

William shook his head, taking his beloved wife in his arms for what he prayed wouldn't be the last time. He kissed the top of her head. "You need to protect our child. Go with them. I'll be along shortly."

She nodded, and he turned to the guards.

"You have your orders, now go!"

The two guards snapped to attention, then nearly carried Kate away as her reluctant legs refused to cooperate. William turned down the hall and saw his brother Harry poke his head out the door.

"What in blazes is going on?" he asked, wearing nothing but trousers and an undershirt.

"We're under attack!" replied William. He pointed at one of the guards manning his brother's door. "Weapon."

Without hesitation the man tossed his L85A1 rifle to the Prince as Harry grabbed the other guard's weapon.

"Where's Kate?"

"They're taking her to the safe room."

"Plan?"

"Get to Grandmother, then Father."

"Let's do it."

William turned to the guards. "You're with us. Cover our sixes."

The men nodded, their sidearms already out. The foursome rushed forward, soon meeting up with other guards and staff. William recognized one of the senior staff, Reginald Tucker, and waved him over.

"Status?"

"I'm not certain, sir."

"Why has no one raised the alarm?"

"The alarm? Why on Earth would we do that, sir? It's just a car accident, isn't it?"

As if to underline the uninformed character of the question, gunfire erupted outside. Tucker blanched.

Christ, no one is preparing!

"At least one dozen hostiles are over the fence and on the grounds. This is a terrorist attack."

He pointed at a guard standing nearby. "Who has a radio?"

A guard stepped forward, holding his radio out. "Here, sir."

"This is Flight Lieutenant Wales. The palace is under attack by at least twelve armed hostiles. Sound the alarm, protect Her Majesty at all costs. I repeat, this is Flight Lieutenant Wales. We are under attack by at least twelve armed hostiles. Sound the alarm, protect Her Majesty, over."

He tossed the radio back to the guard as a klaxon began to sound through the halls. Shouts and cries began to spread around them as panic set in, and more gunfire was heard outside.

William pointed at Tucker who had blanched considerably more.

"Where is Her Majesty?"

"She's preparing for dinner, sir."

"And father?"

"He and the Duchess are not on the grounds. They left earlier for the Prince's Trust banquet, sir."

Thank the Lord for that.

William's head spun as gunfire, heavy and steady, echoed through the halls from outside. He looked back at Tucker. "Follow your escape plan."

Tucker stood frozen, pale as the marble columns of the entrance.

William grabbed his shoulder and shook. "Reggie! Snap out of it. Go! You know what to do! Your staff are relying on you!"

Tucker suddenly stared at the prince, then nodded his head, a little color returning as he took a breath. William shoved him in the direction of the escape route, then pointed at the guards around him.

"You're with us. We must save Her Majesty. To her chambers!"

Two of the guards took point, racing down the hallway as an explosion erupted behind them. Over the radio there was a squelch then a near panicked voice.

"They've breached the main entrance. I say again, the main entrance has been breach—"

Gunfire erupted over the speaker, and from behind them, and William knew the man delivering the report was most likely dead. More explosions from behind them, and reports of a second breach merely urged them on faster. There were only six of them. He, his brother Harry who ran at his side, and the four guards they had managed to collect. He knew Grandmother would have equivalent to a platoon within earshot. They would be able to protect her from being taken hostage, or shot, but his fear was explosives.

These would most likely be suicide bombers, and if they had enough explosives with them, they could take out an entire section of the palace, killing everyone inside.

As if to punctuate his thoughts, a terrific explosion rocked the palace, bringing everyone to a halt as smoke and debris flew from the front gate. The tow truck that he had seen earlier had pulled away, and now the gate was off its hinges, the entrance now completely clear. A bus roared around the Queen Victoria Memorial and through the gutted gate, surging toward the front entrance of the massive palace, the vehicle's windows filled with faces.

Oh my God!

"Call it in!" he ordered as they resumed their sprint. He heard the guard begin to speak but get cut off as another higher priority signal came through.

"Main entrance has been lost. Concentrate all fire on the bus in the courtyard!"

William looked out the window and saw men, all armed, streaming off the bus. He skidded to a halt and threw open the windows, taking aim and squeezing off controlled bursts of fire, taking out several of the men as windows flew open around him, his brother and the other guards raining fire down on the men as they tried to leave the bus.

Fire was quickly returned from within the bus through smashed out windows, causing William to duck behind the wall separating his window from Harry's. He pointed at the two guards to his right. "You two aim at the bus windows, the rest at the targets. Go!"

The guards to his right opened up, and he spun around, emptying what remained of his clip on the men surging from the vehicle, the rest doing the same. He took cover again.

"Clip!"

"Here, sir!"

A clip was tossed from his left, another to his brother, and he spun back at the window, his weapon at the ready.

But it was too late. All the men were either dead, wounded, or already inside the building.

Bloody hell!

"We've done all we can here, let's get to Her Majesty!"

Their sprint resumed as William reassessed the situation. He knew a dozen had arrived in the initial assault, and the bus could have brought dozens more. At least a dozen, if not a score were taken out by his team, but dozens more could have gained entry.

We don't stand a chance.

His chest tightened at the implications. If the Queen were murdered by terrorists, Middle Eastern terrorists by all appearances, the streets would be drenched in blood. No visible minority, Muslim or otherwise, would be safe. The British people would rise up and avenge the death of their monarch, and his father, who would become King, who he had no doubt would urge the populace to remain calm, would most likely be powerless to stop it. Hundreds if not thousands of innocents could die.

Which was exactly what these maniacs wanted.

They wanted to trigger a reaction exactly as he feared, and then proclaim to an outraged Muslim world that the West was anti-Islamic and to rise up and fight back.

He was sick of the constant fighting, the wars, the bombings, the plots. He knew as a future king he needed to be accepting of all his people, no matter what faith, but why, why must one religion constantly cause all of the problems?

He shook the thought from his head as he glanced out the window he had just passed and noticed the police arriving, pushing the curious public back.

But when will the Armed Response Units arrive?

They rounded the final corner as shots rang out behind them. Harry yelped and fell to the ground. *No!* William grabbed his brother by the collar and pulled him around the corner and to safety, as the four guards they were with split to either side of the corridor and returned fire.

"Where are you hit?"

"Left leg," winced Harry. "I don't think it's too bad, just shocked me, that's all."

William pulled Harry's trousers up and saw the wound. He breathed a sigh of relief as it was barely bleeding. "Just a graze," he said, pulling the pant leg back down. "Now get up, and stop slowing us down," said William with a smile.

Harry mouthed an obscenity and held up his hand. William pulled his brother to his feet, then turned to the guards. "Hold this corridor as long as you can, use your ammo sparingly. We will carry on to Her Majesty's chambers. Fall back to our position should it be necessary."

"Yes, sir!" returned the chorus, and William, with Harry's arm draped over his shoulder, hurried toward the room at the end of the hall. Four guards stood at the ready, their weapons out, concerned but professional expressions etched on their faces.

"Report," ordered William as he handed his brother off to one of the men.

"Her Majesty is secure in her chambers, however we cannot hold this position for long against superior numbers, sir."

"Where are the others?"

"They were sent to investigate what happened."

"What?"

"By Her Majesty's orders, sir."

William frowned, but held his tongue.

"Evacuation?"

"She refuses, sir," replied the guard with a hint of pride and frustration in his voice.

"What?" exclaimed Harry. "Is she daft?"

William's eyes darted at Harry, who mumbled an apology.

"Explain," he said.

"She refuses to flee her home in the face of terrorists. She said she will confront them here, and if it is her time to die, then may God take her as a Queen, and not a coward, fleeing for safety."

William's chest surged with pride then tightened with concern at the words of the fierce monarch he respected and loved. He knocked twice on the door, and the double-doors swung open in response, two servants standing on either side pulling them aside.

"Princes William and Harry, Your Majesty."

William turned as a heavy burst of sustained gunfire echoed down the hall. One of the guards dropped, writhing in pain, his comrade pulling him out of the way.

"Can you hold?" yelled William down the hall.

"Negative, sir, there's too many!"

William looked about, but there was no cover here. Unfortunately the best cover was at the position they had just left. At least there they had walls to take refuge behind. Here was an open corridor with doors, and hiding on the other side of the doors was futile, they would be opened within seconds.

And if he knew his grandmother, she would never agree to the possibility of a gun battle in her chambers.

He squared his jaw, a decision made.

"You, give your sidearm and any clips to Harry," he said to one of the men, who immediately complied. Harry handed over the rifle he had been using. The soldier removed the clip, then tossed the weapon aside. William

166

pointed to another. "Side arm, clips." He exchanged weapons, pocketing the clips, then pointed to the four men still holding the end of the hall. "Reinforce them. Hold them off as long as you can. Conserve your ammo as best as possible. Remember, we just need to delay them until reinforcements arrive. If you need to retreat, then do so, but away from these chambers. We don't want a gun battle in this direction, a stray bullet is liable to hit Her Majesty. Now go!" he said with a wave of his hand.

"Yes, sir!" echoed the men as they charged toward the defensive position that was again taking heavy fire.

William entered the chambers, his brother already sitting on a settee, his leg up, wincing as he examined it. He looked up. "What's the situation?"

"Not good. Their position is about to be overwhelmed, then there'll be nothing between them and us but this door."

"Alternate routes?"

William shook his head, then turned to his grandmother. "Grandmother, there wouldn't happen to be any secret passages out of here?"

She finished fixing her hair then turned in her chair. "None we would want to use, we assure you."

William smiled, her expression one of determination, but not a hint of resignation at their soon to be fate. She was every bit the queen, every bit the monarch, every bit the grandmother he knew and loved, and that the public expected her to be. Dignified. Brave. And kowtowing to no one.

She was Britain.

And Britain would never yield.

William picked up the phone sitting nearby, and dialed his wife's cellphone. It picked up on the second ring.

"Hello?"

He breathed a sigh of relief as he heard her worried voice.

"Kate, darling, are you okay?"

"Oh thank God, William, I'm fine, we're in the shelter. What about you, where are you?"

"We're with Grandmother. Tell them to send armed units to her chambers when they arrive."

He heard her muffled voice yelling the order to someone, the phone momentarily covered. There was a shuffling noise then her intoxicating voice returned.

"I've told them. Will you be okay?"

The truth? Or a white lie? He clenched his jaw tight. *The truth.* It was what he had always been taught to tell as a child, a soldier, and a Prince.

"I don't know. Harry is here with me and several servants. We have eight royal guards holding them off, but they are running out of ammo, and are greatly outnumbered. I just don't know." He could hear her breaths, quick and halted as she sobbed, trying to stifle the sounds for his benefit. "Be brave, my darling. But if something should happen—"

"It won't."

"But if it should, tell our child when he—"

"Or she!"

He smiled. "Or she, is old enough, that her daddy loved her. And Darling?"

"Yes?"

"I will always love you, and be watching over you."

She finally lost control, her sobs wreaking havoc on his own self-control. Sustained gunfire and several cries on the other side of the door ended his moment of self-pity.

"I have to go, my dear. I will call you as soon as it is over. I love you."

"I love you too."

168

He hung up the phone, and looked about the room. The servants, experts at disguising their emotions were looking elsewhere as if nothing were amiss, Harry continued to examine his leg uselessly, and his grandmother looked at him with a slight smile. She held out her hand.

Suddenly there was pounding on the door with shouts in English and Arabic to open it. This got a reaction from the room. The servants looked about, unsure what to do. Harry rose to his feet, readying his weapon, and his grandmother rose, still holding his hand.

"Dignity, everyone, dignity."

She positioned herself at the center of the room, Harry and William on either side of her, their weapons clasped behind their backs. She nodded at the servants.

The doors were opened, and the servants stepped back, positioning themselves in front of their Royal Highness, their bravery not lost on William as they stared down the dozen men, unarmed, guns pointed at them as they surged into the room.

William, closest to the window, took a quick sideways glance outside and saw several black vans race through the gates toward the entrance.

The ARU!

Depending upon resistance, they could be there in as little as two minutes. They needed to stall.

"Who is in charge here?" he demanded, stepping forward, his weapon still gripped tightly behind him. He stared past the three servants and at the half dozen men in the room, another half dozen outside, in the hall.

One man pushed his way forward, shouldering his weapon.

"I am."

The man looked young, perhaps early thirties. He had no accent, was well dressed considering what was happening, and had an air of dignity, of pride in purpose.

And eyes that burned red with rage.

"You know who I am?"

"Of course."

"Then may I ask your name?"

"You may not."

Gunfire in the distance almost made William pause, but he continued, as if it were of no importance, hoping their attackers would treat it the same.

"And why might that be?"

The man sneered at him. "Because I don't answer to false idols."

It would appear to me you just did.

"False idols?"

"All representations of Allah's creation of man, all monstrosities built by man then worshipped by men, must be destroyed. Statues, sculptures, paintings, people."

"People?"

"Those who would pretend to be Allah's representatives on Earth, like the infidel Pope, or the head of the Church of England, for example." The man stared at the Queen over William's shoulder, and William instinctively leaned more to his left to block the view.

"Under what authority do you do this?" But he already knew the answer. It would be some insanity about Allah and Mohammad, and he also knew there would be no rational debate.

Delay, however.

"Under the authority of almighty God! Under the authority of the blessed Koran, written by Mohammad, peace be upon him, guided by the angel Gabriel, who on Allah's behalf provided the Holy words meant to save mankind from the corruption of His will by those who came before, to create a world ruled by the word of Allah, not the word of Man, to create a

Caliphate the world over where all worshipped under a single flag, the flag of Islam."

William debated whether or not to point out the fact that Mohammad was illiterate and didn't write down anything Gabriel had told him, assuming Gabriel had told him anything, which though open minded, William found hard to believe. But he *was* open minded, raised to be so, his people of all faiths, so he had to respect their beliefs.

But I don't have to respect the way they have implemented those beliefs.

"Is Allah not merciful?"

"Blasphemy!" roared the man, his eyes flaring with rage. "How dare an infidel use this form of the almighty's name? Only true Muslims may call God 'Allah'!"

William bowed slightly, his hands still clasped behind his back, his finger sliding along the weapon to see if the safety was off as more gunfire erupted.

That's sounding closer.

"I apologize. I wasn't aware of the restriction. But is not *God* merciful?"

"Of course he is. Allah is merciful to all who believe in him."

"And is not my god the same as your god?"

The man frowned, but nodded. "This is true."

"So would he not be merciful to us as well?"

The man smiled. "Yes, he would. If you are true believers, true followers of him, he will be merciful, even if an infidel such as yourself. Indeed, Allah is merciful."

Footsteps pounded down the hallway causing the terrorists to turn as one. Something was barked in Arabic by their captor, and those guarding the hall opened fire, the flashes from their muzzles causing the dimly lit hall to flicker like a fireworks display. His captor returned to looking at William, failing to see several of his men dropping behind him, the better trained ARU team apparently closing in.

"So then why not show us mercy?"

The man chuckled.

"It is not for me to show you mercy, it is for Allah. I am but a man, who cannot take the place of the Almighty. It is up to Him to be merciful."

And William suddenly understood the logic the man was employing. He flicked his weapon twice, signaling Harry, hoping he would pick up on it.

Two more dropped in the hall, the footfalls closer.

"When you die, Allah may very well be merciful." William saw the man's hand begin to move, then freeze as a throat cleared behind William. He turned to see his grandmother step forward.

"We understand your concerns young man, but if you think you can frighten us, you are sadly mistaken. Should we die here today, we will die free, not under the yoke of oppression that your warping of God's word would have us live under. In England we have freedom of religion, and *from* religion. It is an important distinction, that you and your kind have failed to realize. We are free to worship as we wish, or not at all. We have separated Church and State, which is a concept your religion does not appear to fathom. Mankind needs to be free. We yearn for it instinctively, we were created, by God, to be free. And free men are more powerful than any forced into service, whether it be to their country, or to their God.

"We will prevail in the end, no matter how many of us you kill, as we are free, and freedom is the most important of God's gifts, for it is life, and life without freedom is mere existence, and existence is not what we stand for in our country, in our Britain, or in our church. You may kill us today, but you merely create martyrs to a cause that in the end will ultimately defeat your ignorance and hate for all things different. Just as we learned to look at the Bible figuratively rather than literally, you need to learn the same of your Koran. And until you do, you will be trapped in the age it was written, never to progress, never to advance, and *never* to succeed in your mission, a perverted literal interpretation that has an entirely different figurative meaning.

"You misinterpret your own holy book, sir, and it discredits you, and your cause. You and others like you should open your eyes to the loving God we have embraced, and cast aside this notion that killing will bring you closer to Him." She paused, taking another step toward the man. "But I can see by looking into your eyes that you are not a man of reason, but a man filled with hate, consumed with a lust for death that no words could sway." She stepped back then took several steps toward her chair in front of her makeup table and sat down, her knees together and to the side, her hands resting on them.

Dignified to the end.

William's eyes glassed over as he looked at her.

If only her detractors could see her now.

During the entire speech, there had been no rebuttal, no comment whatsoever from the man, except an increasingly tightening jaw. The battle for the hallway was much closer now, and he wondered if this anonymous man was remotely aware of what was happening behind him.

Suddenly the man raised his weapon, swinging it toward the Queen.

"No!" yelled William as he dove toward his grandmother, his eyes focused on the trigger as it was slowly squeezed. A shot rang out and he felt a jolt then a searing pain in his shoulder. As he hit the ground a rapid series of shots rang out. William felt his stomach flip and he spun toward his grandmother, but saw she remained unscathed. His weapon still gripped in his hand, he spun toward the gunfire, raising it, but found no one to shoot at, only his brother standing, weapon raised, and the bodies of six dead terrorists on the floor, those tours in Afghanistan apparently paying off.

Gunfire from the hall ripped at the rug in front of the bed and Harry jumped to the side, rolling to a kneeling position, weapon raised. The servants had hit the ground and scrambled away from the line of fire. William pointed at the two on the same side of the room as his grandmother. "Protect Her Majesty."

They nodded and rose, positioning themselves between their monarch and the door, just out of the line of fire. William and Harry approached either side as the gunfire continued in sustained bursts, tearing apart the floor and bed.

Something metal bounced on the floor of the hallway, then there was a hissing sound, a sound William recognized from Initial Officer Training. *Smoke grenade.* He risked a quick glance into the hall to confirm that smoke was now billowing from a canister not twenty feet from the door. Another canister hit with a heavier thud, the tone different from the first. He caught a glimpse and immediately recognized it. Shoving the door closed, he yelled, "Flash bang!"

Harry's eyes widened as he too began to push the other side of the door closed. A terrific explosion from the hall was followed by screams of pain as their attackers' senses were overwhelmed. Even William's ears pounded from the intense noise and he turned to check on his grandmother, and almost laughed when he saw her primping herself in the mirror, as if nothing but a stray hair were amiss.

There were shouts outside, authoritative, and in English, then heavy knocking on the door.

"Is there anyone inside there?" asked the voice. "Your Majesty, are you okay?"

William looked at the bodies on the floor, his grandmother rising from the mirror, her servants, shoulders squared, in position at the center of the room, the two doormen already prepared to take over their duties at the doors now manned by the two brothers.

Harry stepped back as did William, both positioning themselves in front of their grandmother, weapons aimed at the door just in case this was a ruse.

"We are secure in here, and are armed. We are opening the doors now."

William nodded at the doormen, who opened the doors a little more slowly than they probably normally did. Smoke filled the corridor from the grenade tossed only moments before, and William squinted to try and see through it. Red laser beams sliced through the smoke as several black forms advanced. The first stepped through the smoke and into the room, his weapon raised, and immediately lowered it upon sight of his monarch and her heirs, instead training it on the bodies on the floor. He activated his comm.

"We have Redfern, I say again, we have Redfern, over."

Several more men entered the room and William lowered his weapon, as did Harry, both audibly sighing in relief.

"Is everyone alright?" asked the first man.

William was about to answer when his grandmother cleared her throat. William looked back then smiled, stepping aside as he recognized her expression, which was one of command. The two brothers stepped back and the Queen stepped forward.

"We are all unharmed." She nodded at the men on the floor. "Do what you must with them, I trust you can have this room restored to order before bed." She looked at Harry, then at William.

"Dinner?"

William and Harry exchanged grins, then followed their grandmother as she stepped around the bodies littering her bed chamber, and out into the hallway, two of the servants bringing up the rear as the family went for their evening meal as if nothing were amiss.

Nothing but dignity.

Nubian Desert, Egypt, University College London Dig Site

Professor James Acton stood amongst a throng that consisted of the entire population of the camp, all eagerly listening in on his conversation with his friend and boss, Gregory "Corky" Milton, Dean of Saint Paul's University. The camp had two satellite phones, one the official phone for the camp, so it was not being used at the moment in the event they were to receive a call about the current situation, and the other, Laura's private satellite phone, which was pressed to his ear now as he repeated the parts of the conversation he knew the others would be interested in.

"When did it happen?"

"About two hours ago, I think. I'm just getting up to speed on it now. They hit it late morning."

"Late morning. How?"

"Details are sketchy, but reports are saying boats might have been involved."

"Boats?" Acton resisted back chair quarterbacking, and instead tried to focus on the facts. "Is she—" His voice cracked, and he couldn't bring himself to say the words.

"Yes. Destroyed pretty much." His friend paused, and Acton knew he was trying to control his emotions. "God, Jim, it's the saddest thing I've seen since the towers fell, and this time there's nowhere near the casualties, but, there's something about it being *her* that makes it so hard to look at."

Acton felt a lump form in his throat, and he squeezed his free hand into a fist, his fingernails digging into his palm as he struggled to maintain control.

"Casualties?"

"They've pulled at least fifty bodies out so far, they expect a lot more."

"At least fifty dead," he said to the gathered group, which was greeted with gasps and some cries. "What else is going on?"

"They hit Buckingham Palace at exactly the same time, late afternoon there."

"And?"

"A lot of casualties, but apparently the royal family is okay. Prince William was shot saving the Queen, but he'll be fine."

Acton turned to Laura, then looked at her cadre of British students. "They attacked Buckingham Palace. There were a lot of casualties"—more gasps and cries—"but the royal family is okay. Prince William was shot saving his grandmother"—one girl collapsed, as did Terrence—"but he'll be okay."

"There's more," came Greg's voice over the phone.

"More?"

"Much more. They hit the Eiffel Tower but it's still standing, and they took out the Christ the Redeemer statue in Rio."

Acton's heart leapt into his throat as he pictured the mammoth statue of Jesus that overlooked the mighty Brazilian city.

"My God!" He quickly related what he had heard, and he joined the group now choosing to sit in the sand, rather than risk collapsing. "Is there more?"

"It's sketchy. There's random reports of some Hollywood types being targeted, musicians, and other famous people. This was extremely well organized."

Greg continued for a few minutes, but Acton had stopped listening as his mind pieced together what had happened, and why.

"They're targeting idols."

"What was that?"

Acton looked at Laura, gripping her hand. "They're targeting idols. Everything they've hit is something or someone important to us, that our culture worships in some way."

He heard the dawn of realization in Greg's voice. "My God, I think you're right."

"And we're sitting on one of the biggest icons of them all."

"Jesus, Jim, you've got to get out of there."

"We'll get right on it. I'll call you back in one hour."

"Be safe."

Acton ended the call. Laura had already jumped to her feet.

"Okay, we're getting out of here," she said, slapping her hands together. "We'll grieve later, but right now, we're in danger. Pack only what you need to reach Cairo. That means food and water, pretty much nothing else. Shutdown all of our equipment, pack up what needs to be protected from the elements, then we're out of here in thirty minutes." She clapped again. "Let's move!"

The students scrambled, and Leather motioned for his men to begin packing up their equipment, then approached the two professors.

"Mum, one little problem."

"What's that?"

"We don't have room enough for everyone. The workers took our transport truck. We've got a jeep and a small lorry. We can fit the students in those, but there won't be room for the, shall we say, adults?"

Acton quickly ran the numbers in his head as he stared at the two vehicles, both suddenly appearing very small, especially considering they needed to carry ten hours of food and water as well as gasoline.

He looked at Laura.

"What do you think?"

She frowned, looking at Leather then Reading and Chaney, and finally Acton.

"The students are our priority."

"Agreed," said Reading. "Get the students out of here now. We've called for help and it should be here by the end of the day. But get the students out of here now."

"I'm good with that," said Chaney.

"Me too," replied Acton.

"Should we arm them?" asked Leather.

"Absolutely not," replied Laura. "They're more likely to get killed if they start brandishing weapons. Unarmed, well documented. Hopefully they only run into regular military, or no one at all."

"Agreed," said Acton, turning to Leather. "Have your men make sure the vehicles are fueled up, get enough water and food on there, plus gas if needed, for the trip. I want those kids gone by the bottom of the hour."

Leather looked to Laura, and Acton smiled slightly as he realized Laura was in effect the commanding officer here, not him. Laura nodded and Leather snapped to a brief attention, then joined his men, barking orders.

Acton turned to Laura, her hand still squeezing his.

"You okay?"

She nodded.

"I will be." She sighed. "What a mad mad world we live in."

Acton put his arm around her.

"And I'm afraid it may always be this way."

At least until Islam has its own Enlightenment.

Nubian Desert, Egypt, University College London Dig Site

"Is everybody in?"

Terrence's heart was slamming against his ribcage, and he didn't do too good a job trying to hide the fact he was terrified. His hands shook, and it had been some effort to even start the jeep, his hand unable to grasp the key. It wasn't until Jenny had gently placed her hand on his, and with a reassuring smile, guided his hand to the key.

Her attentions had calmed him until somebody barked an order from behind, and the two professors were suddenly at his side.

He jumped.

"You know the way?"

"Yes, mum. There's pretty much only one way to Cairo, and then we've got a map for the city itself."

"Straight to the embassy, got it?"

Terrence nodded.

"You can count on me, mum."

He didn't sound very convincing, but if she had any doubts, she hid them well, instead smiling broadly and giving him a hug, then touching each student on their head or shoulder, saying goodbye to each. Tears were flowing freely from the passengers, and he gritted his teeth to block the tears from breaking free and flowing down his face.

"Take this," said Laura, handing Terrence one of the satellite phones. "Check in with us every hour, speed dial one."

Terrence nodded, putting the phone in his pocket.

"Okay, off you go. We'll see you in Cairo, hopefully tomorrow."

Terrence nodded, not trusting himself to reply verbally, and instead putting the vehicle in first and popping the clutch as he gave it gas. The vehicle lurched forward and he managed to keep it from stalling out, quickly giving it more gas then shifting into second. In his rearview mirror he saw the others all looking back at the camp as Professor Palmer said goodbye to the second vehicle of students.

A tear escaped and he felt a hand on his shoulder, gently squeezing.

"They'll be okay," said Jenny quietly, leaning toward him. "And you'll do great."

He had always had a thing for Jenny, but had never had the brass to ask her out. And now here she was, making the first move.

Or was she?

How was he supposed to know if she was making her feelings known in a romantic way, or simply a terrified friend trying to reassure another terrified friend?

The hand gently caressing his shoulders and back of his neck suggested to him that this was more than a friendly reassurance. He felt Little Terrence stir.

Are you daft you little bastard? We might be about to get killed and you decide to cast an eye on the situation?

He chuckled to himself, and Jenny looked at him.

"What is it?" she asked, smiling wryly.

Terrence blushed.

"Nothing," he stammered, then looking at her, smiled. "It's just—" He stopped, then shook his head, looking back at the road. "It's nothing."

Jenny said nothing, then suddenly leaned over and gave him a kiss on the cheek.

Terrence flushed crimson, Little Terrence demanded to see what was going on, and there were giggles from the back seat.

"Would you two get a room?"

"Hey, eyes on the road!"

"Can I have a kiss too?"

Jenny pulled away and turned to their four friends crammed in the back seat.

"Grow up!" she yelled in mock anger.

There was more laughter than somebody yelled, "Look!"

Terrence didn't need to look to see what was being pointed at, he had already spotted it and jerked the wheel to the right, taking them off the road and moments later behind a massive rock outcropping. He stood up in his seat and sighed in relief when he saw the second vehicle pull up beside him, both engines immediately cut.

"What is it? What's going on?" asked Jenny.

"I saw what looked like army vehicles coming down the road."

"Did they see us?"

"I don't know. They were at an angle to us, so they'd have to have been looking our way to spot us."

The grinding of gears and the roar of several engines cut off the conversation. Everybody ducked, and Terrence sucked in his breath, holding it as if trying to quiet a heart he was certain the world could hear pounding.

The sounds grew closer, and he felt Jenny gripping his arm. He clasped his hand over hers, and listened. The roar of the engines seemed to fill the area, and suddenly the rock they were hiding behind seemed small. He looked back the way they had come and his heart leapt into his throat.

The tire tracks!

There was no way they could miss those. But would they make the connection as to what they were? Or worse, how new they were?

But there was no change in the engines, no evidence they were slowing down, and within minutes, the sounds were gone, and they were all breathing easier.

"What should we do?" asked Jenny.

Terrence thought for a minute, his mind a jumble. If they were army, were they "good" army? He had heard the army could be pretty much trusted by foreigners in Egypt, it was the police you needed to worry about. Could they be there to evacuate them? Evacuation by the military would be far safer than driving by themselves.

But what if they weren't "good" military? What if they were there to loot the camp or worse, kill everyone in some mad religious fervor? What if they weren't military at all?

"We have to go back," said Terrence.

"Are you daft!" exclaimed half the back seat.

"If they're here to evacuate us, then it's safer to go with them."

"And what if they're not?"

"Then we should help the others."

"How?" asked Jenny, far gentler than the others.

"We might be able to warn them, or get them in the jeep and off to safety." He turned to the backseat. "You get out here and stay with the truck."

"But there isn't room!" protested Stephen, the second oldest in the group.

"We'll leave most of the water and food. If we're not back in one hour, jam yourselves into that truck and go. It will be uncomfortable, but you'll be alive. We'll try to catch up if we manage to get the others. If it's a proper evacuation, then the army will radio ahead to have you stopped, and you'll be safe. If it isn't, then you know it wasn't an evacuation, and we're all probably dead."

Jenny grabbed his arm tightly.

"I'm going with you."

Terrence shook his head.

"No, it's too dangerous."

"If it's too dangerous for me, then it's too dangerous for you."

Terrence frowned, then smiled, fishing the phone from his pocket. "I completely forgot I had this!"

There were groans from the jam packed truck as they began to pile out, Terrence hitting speed dial #1. He pressed the phone to his ear and after a few moments, heard the voice mail message. He hurriedly tried it again, and again was sent to voicemail.

He flipped the phone closed, looking at Jenny.

"What's wrong?" she asked.

"They're not answering."

Nubian Desert, Egypt, University College London Dig Site

Laura smiled and waved at a departing camera crew calling for a shot, then ducked into her tent. She paused a moment between the double doors, already beginning to feel the cool air that awaited her on the other side.

They're vultures!

She had never liked the press. Beyond interviews related to her position as the head of archeology at the British Museum, her first real exposure was when her brother died on a dig site in Jordan. Normally it wouldn't garner much attention, but he had been silly rich from selling his Internet startup, that it had created a sensation for several days in the tabloids, then died off when the next celebrity's boob popped out in public.

She hated the British press.

It was so uncivilized, so tacky, so brazen. But the readers seemed to love it, otherwise the papers wouldn't sell. Though James didn't have much respect for his press back home, at least those that engaged in the methods used by most British newspapers were not considered mainstream press— they were rags or cable shows that nobody respected.

But in the UK?

She shook her head, wishing those that were just leaving had room for everyone but they didn't, and they had all agreed it was all or none. She pushed through the second door and into the chilled interior of the tent, spotting Reading propped up rather indecently.

She cleared her throat.

He nearly hit the floor.

"Didn't see you there," he mumbled, straightening himself out. He nodded at the air conditioner. "I was just cooling off."

"I see." She pointed with her chin at the satellite phone. "Any luck?"

Reading nodded. "Rahim and his men won't be here until tonight. Probably four hours, maybe more. He said they're going as fast as they can, but there're roadblocks and livestock slowing them down."

"Livestock?"

Reading shrugged.

"Egypt."

Laura chewed on her cheek for a moment, then they both jumped as the phone rang. Reading flipped it open.

"Hello?"

He listened for a moment then held it out for Laura.

"It's for you."

Nubian Desert, Egypt, Five miles from the University College London Dig Site

Terrence hadn't recognized the copper's voice at first, but once he realized he hadn't misdialed, he managed a weak request for Professor Palmer, and moments later was relieved to hear her voice.

"This is Professor Palmer."

"Professor, this is Terrence."

"Terrence, are you okay?"

He could hear the concern in her voice, and it touched him how much she genuinely cared about them. It made a lump form in his throat.

I'm too damned emotional!

"We're fine, but several army trucks just went by us, heading your way."

"How long ago?"

"A couple of minutes. They'll probably be at the camp any minute now."

There was a pause, then when she finally replied, her tone had changed, and if he wasn't mistaken, there was a hint of fear in her voice.

"I'll call you in thirty minutes to let you know everything is okay. In the meantime, you keep heading for Cairo."

Terrence frowned. "Okay, mum, thirty minutes." He hung up then turned back to the group. "She will call us back in thirty minutes, but wants us to keep heading to Cairo."

"Then what are we waiting for?" asked Stephen. "Let's go!"

Terrence shook his head. "I'm going to wait for the phone call, just in case there's a problem. I might be able to get some of them out in the jeep."

"Are you daft? There were three lorries full of men that drove by. How are *you* going to help?"

Terrence realized it *was* useless. But his loyalty to his professor ran deep, and he realized the rest were right. He sighed.

"Okay, we'll keep going, but if I don't hear back from the professor in thirty minutes, I'm going back."

There were mumbled agreements, and Terrence wasn't naïve enough to not know they were just humoring him. He could see the fear in their eyes, and knew the right thing to do was to put as much distance as he could between them and the camp.

He also knew if the men on their way to the dig site now were hostile, there was absolutely nothing he or anybody else could do about it.

Nubian Desert, Egypt, University College London Dig Site

Reading's head spun as the sound of grinding gears echoed across the sunbaked landscape. There was nothing to see at first, then suddenly the front of a lorry emerged from behind a dune, two more in tow, and he felt his heart skip a beat as the military camouflage spelled either doom or rescue.

"They're here!" called Chaney, stating the obvious, as everyone who remained was now staring at the arriving vehicles, including the lone remaining reporter that had stayed behind after the attacks had been discovered, the rest all recalled to cover the bigger story.

He felt bad for his friends; this was the discovery of a lifetime. It would put them on the map forever, like that bloke who discovered King Tut whose name escaped him now. He grinned to himself how he had just disproven his previous thought.

Well, they'll be legends in their community, that's for certain.

And they deserved it. Good, honest people, who worked hard, cared about their families, friends and students, and never hesitated to do the right thing. When the decision had to be made on who would leave the camp, there was no hesitation. It was the students. Laura had approached him but before she could open her mouth, he had cut her off. "Students first. If there's room left, then we'll have the debate."

But they had both known full well that getting the students into the two remaining vehicles would be challenge enough.

If only we had one more vehicle.

He eyed the motorcycle and sidecar the young reporter had arrived in. The sidecar was filled with supplies, and the young man it belonged to, a reporter with one of the Cairo papers, stood next to it, watching the vehicles round the final bend and pull up to the dig site.

Troops piled out of two of the trucks, the one in the middle apparently empty save two men in the front. They quickly rushed forward, weapons held at waist level, pointing at the few remaining souls, orders being barked by a man who exited the lead vehicle's passenger side door.

Reading looked from the corner of his eye and noted that the four ex-SAS guards had already backed off, their weapons lowered but ready, each now behind an innocent looking barrier, ready to drop and engage their new arrivals should it become necessary.

He casually walked over to where Laura and Jim were standing, Jim already having placed himself between the soldiers and Laura, ready to die a human shield if necessary.

If this turns to shite, I just pray my other message got through.

Nubian Desert, Egypt, Thirty-two miles from the University College London Dig Site

Terrence looked at his watch for the umpteenth time.

"It's less than a minute since the last time," chastised Jenny with a smile. "They'll be okay. Stop worrying."

Terrence nodded, her words going in one ear and out the other. There was no way he was going to stop worrying until they were all safely back in London, behind a desk in her classroom. This entire idea of going into Middle Eastern countries, digging for trinkets, was insane. What were they thinking?

He gripped the steering wheel harder, his knuckles turning white, then with a conscious effort, he relaxed his grip, extending one finger at a time to let the muscles rest, then suddenly his fingers gripped the steering wheel tighter than ever before, jerking the vehicle to the right as he hit the accelerator.

Jenny screamed, and he found himself instinctively closing his eyes to avoid the impact of the lorry that had just sped around the corner, directly at them. With his eyes closed, he jammed on the brakes and felt something slam into the back of them, eliciting more screams.

Terrence forced his eyes open and saw three trucks drive by, catching only a good look at the final vehicle, the other two already past them while his eyelids had been clamped shut.

It was filled with men in army uniforms.

One of them grinned at him.

And bad teeth.

If they're the army, then who were the first blokes?

THE ARAB FALL

All their eyes were glued to the television, report after report of attacks, almost all successful to one degree or another, kept rolling in, then updates to the previous reports.

It's 9/11 all over again.

The death toll continued to rise, in the hundreds now, but it was expected to level off soon. This time the body count wasn't the goal, it was shock and awe. The civilized world's monuments to greatness were being destroyed, our icons and idols targeted. Never again would we feel safe visiting a national landmark, never again would tourists feel safe visiting the proud landmarks of foreign countries, never again would our celebrities and national heroes feel secure.

A ticker rolled the list of attacks, leading off of course with the one foremost on his mind.

The Statue of Liberty, New York, USA – Dozens of casualties, statue destroyed

Buckingham Palace, London, England – Dozens of casualties, royal family safe

Eiffel Tower, Paris, France – Dozens of casualties, tower severely damaged

CN Tower, Toronto, Canada – Hundreds of casualties, tower collapsed

Christ the Redeemer, Rio de Janeiro, Brazil – Dozens of casualties, sculpture destroyed

Mount Rushmore, South Dakota, USA – Dozens of casualties, sculpture severely damaged

Then there were the attacks on celebrities and sports figures. Seemingly random attacks, but all coordinated around the world to happen at the same time. And now that the word was out, not only was there dancing in the streets of many Muslim nations, there were additional attacks on anything that seemed blasphemous to Islam.

And non-Muslims were retaliating.

Reports were already coming in from Paris and London of tens of thousands marching on the Muslim quarters of the cities, setting fire to anything thought to be Muslim, beating those who got in their way. The police were too busy securing their leadership and other national monuments to have sufficient personnel to engage the rioters.

"Things are going to go to hell, fast," murmured Niner.

"They're going to have to declare martial law and put troops on the streets until things calm down."

Dawson looked at Atlas and nodded.

"I'm afraid you're right. Good thing so far is there aren't any reports of retaliation back home yet."

"It'll come," said Red, his eyes glued to the television. "How can't it? They destroyed the Statue of Liberty, for fuck's sake. They have to pay." He sighed, waving his hand in the air. "You know what I mean."

Dawson gave his friend a weak smile. He knew exactly what he meant, for he had the conflicting emotions too. He realized it was a minority, but right now, at this very instant, he wanted them all dead. It was the same way he had felt on 9/11. He wanted all Muslims everywhere dead so it could never happen again. But the emotions had subsided, and he had done his duty, protecting the innocent and killing those truly responsible. And the coming weeks and months would be no different. Those responsible, who would never have the courage to actually be one of those who sacrificed themselves, would be at large, would be identified, would be found, and would be killed.

By people like him.

The door to the common area opened, and Dawson looked up to see the Executive Officer beckoning him. Dawson pushed himself from the couch and followed the man into the hallway.

"Feel up for some action?"

Dawson's teeth clenched.

"After what I just saw, absofuckinlutely."

The XO nodded, his face one of understanding.

"We've got a group of British nationals in Egypt that need evac along with an American citizen. Should be a cakewalk, but you never know after today. You up for it?"

As soon as Dawson had heard the mission, his stomach had leapt.

"Archeological dig?"

The XO's eyebrows shot up.

"How'd you guess?"

Dawson shook his head.

"Just a hunch."

Those two are always involved.

Nubian Desert, Egypt, University College London Dig Site

Acton eyed the man approaching them, the smile being displayed clearly designed to put them at ease, yet there was something wrong that he couldn't put his finger on. The uniforms seemed in order, the vehicles as well, but there was something off.

Leather stepped up behind them and Acton turned his head slightly as the man began to speak quietly, his lips barely moving.

"These aren't Egyptian army."

"How can you tell," asked Reading.

"Their unit patches don't match, probably stolen or retired uniforms. And their weapons aren't standard issue, just a mishmash of Kalashnikov's."

Acton's eyes flashed to the shoulders of the men, suddenly realizing what it was that wasn't right.

"Who do you think they are?"

"If they were here to kill us, they would have already," said Leather. "I'm guessing these are the guys who were watching us."

"Recommendations."

"Play along. If they want us to leave, let's politely refuse and see what they do. If they insist, we insist on keeping our weapons. If that fails, I've got a contingency plan."

"What contingency plan?" asked Acton.

"I am Colonel Soliman of the First Field Army, Third Corps, Eighth Mechanized Division. Whom may I ask is in charge?"

The man's English was impeccable, probably American educated, and his interruption left Acton wondering what contingency plan Leather might have planned. He glanced over his shoulder to see that Leather was gone.

How the hell did he do that?

Laura stepped forward.

"I'm Professor Laura Palmer, University College London. We're here on a dig authorized by your government. Would you like to see the paperwork?"

The man's smile broadened and he waved his hands.

"Professor Palmer, that's not necessary at all. I'm well aware of your dig, and its legality. We're here to evacuate you, only temporarily."

"Why's that?" asked Acton, stepping to Laura's side.

"Have you not heard the news?" The man shook his head. "Perhaps you have not. There have been many attacks across the world today, terrorist attacks."

"We've heard," replied Laura. "How does that impact us?"

"Hopefully it doesn't, however word of your discovery has spread across the world, and, well"—the man shrugged his shoulders, displaying his palms—"I have my orders to evacuate you until we can be assured of your safety."

"Why not station a guard here instead, that way we can continue our work?"

It was Reading who suggested it, and it was a brilliant test in Acton's mind. It seemed to catch the man off guard, and his eyes darted between the small group until he finally found words.

"I have my orders. To disobey them in today's Egypt is not a good idea, I'm sure you'll understand." He motioned to the second, apparently empty vehicle. "There are supplies in the back, and plenty of room. Come, we have a long journey ahead of us."

"May we keep our weapons? We don't want to just leave them lying around."

Colonel Soliman thought for a moment, then nodded. "I don't see why not."

Acton heard the phone ring in Laura's pocket, but she didn't answer. It stopped ringing after three tries, then went to voicemail. *Probably Terrence checking in.* Acton's heart thudded a little harder.

Or somebody calling to warn us these guys are here to kill us.

"How many of you are there?" asked the Colonel.

"Just eight," replied Laura.

"So few?"

"Our students evacuated hours ago."

It in fact had been less than an hour, but Acton knew Laura was hoping their "rescuers" would think they were too far ahead to bother trying to catch. The Colonel smiled. "Good, I hope they will reach safety soon."

He stepped closer and extended his hand. Laura reached forward to take it, then suddenly grabbed the man by the shirt cuff, ripping it open, revealing a tattoo.

A tattoo of a king cobra, coiled around the hieroglyph representing Death.

The same design as on the inside of Cleopatra's tomb!

"Who the bloody hell are you?" exclaimed Reading as they all stared at the tattoo.

The Colonel simply smiled, continuing to hold Laura's hand, slowly turning his wrist up, exposing his lower arm for all to see.

"I am with The Brotherhood, and your actions here have been blasphemous."

One of the "soldiers" yelled something, pointing, causing the Colonel to break his grip of Laura's hand, and his eyes to bulge in shock. Acton spun around to see all four of their security team racing over the ridge and out of sight.

Acton just hoped the contingency plan Leather had referred to was not to save their own asses.

Nubian Desert, Egypt, Approaching the Egyptian Army Checkpoint

"I'm really worried."

"I know you are," soothed Jenny. "We all are."

"Why wouldn't she answer?"

"Perhaps they were busy loading the vehicles."

Terrence knew he was being patronized, but it still felt good to have someone like Jenny doing it.

"What's that?" asked Stephen, pointing as they rounded a bend.

"Shit!" exclaimed Terrence, taking his foot off the accelerator and gently applying the brakes so as not to have a repeat of just a few minutes ago. "What the hell is that?"

Jenny stood up and pointed. "Are those bodies?"

Terrence wasn't certain, but what was certain is there had been an accident or incident recently. Several vehicles were smoldering, and nothing seemed to be moving at what appeared to have been some sort of roadblock. Terrence took his foot off the brake, easing the clutch up as he gave it some gas, rolling slowly forward, toward what he didn't know.

As they neared it became clear that there were indeed bodies strewn about, and the stench of at least one burning corpse filled the air. As they rounded the shell of a vehicle and through what had been the roadblock, Terrence nearly yelped when he saw a man jump out in front of them, waving his arms.

Terrence hit the brakes, and the man was at his window within seconds, babbling in Arabic.

Terrence shook his head.

"I'm sorry, I don't speak Arabic. Do you speak English?"

"A little." The man sucked in a breath, then deliberately pronouncing each word, said, "Get. Me. The. Fuck. Out. Of. Here." He smiled. "Understand?"

Terrence couldn't help but laugh, as did the rest of the occupants.

"What happened here?"

"Bad men, army men, attack. Kill everyone."

"Why not you?"

The man pointed beyond a ridge. "I over there. Bathroom."

Terrence looked to where the man was pointing. *Lucky bastard.*

"Was it three trucks?" asked Jenny.

The man nodded. "Three. Very bad men." He grabbed Terrence by the shoulder. "Get. Me. The—"

Terrence held up his hand, nodding. "I got you. Give me a minute, okay?"

The man nodded and Terrence pulled out the satellite phone, hitting the speed dial. It rang several times, then answered, but all he heard was gunfire and shouting. He put it on speaker so the rest could hear, both vehicles of students surrounding the phone, listening in horror as their guardians died.

Tears streaked the faces of them all as they stood helpless to do anything.

Nubian Desert, Egypt, Within Sight of University College London Dig Site

Adel lay on the ground, his chest still heaving from the sprint of several miles he had just completed. His Imam had requested that he go ahead to survey the archeologists' camp before the attack, and what he had seen was of no comfort. There appeared to be at least two dozen armed Egyptian troops, along with half a dozen Westerners. Where the students were, he had no idea. He had run back to the convoy to report this, and had been ordered to return and report when the troops left.

Three trips, with a fourth in his future, had left him exhausted and thirsty. Why no one had thought to bring radios was beyond him, and their cellphones wouldn't work out here in the desert. It wasn't his place to question the wisdom of his Imam, but sometimes he had to wonder.

And why the delay?

All over the world their brothers were sacrificing themselves, willingly, to strike at the infidels who would prevent the return of the Caliphate, yet here, today, his Imam and his followers sat, waiting for the enemy to leave? Why? Why not simply charge in and kill them all, then destroy the blasphemous idols that had just been discovered?

It suddenly occurred to him that his Imam had waited in the truck during the assault on the checkpoint. He hadn't risked his life at all. Was it because he was more important than them? It had to be. Adel sighed, satisfying himself with that explanation, rather than the one that had been nibbling its way forward in the back of his mind.

He's a coward!

There were no cowards amongst the true believers. A true believer knew what awaited him on the other side in paradise, in Jannah, if he died in service to Allah. Seventy two virgins, there to please him for eternity.

I wonder what women get?

He shrugged his shoulders.

As long as I get my virgins, I'm happy.

He peered through the binoculars, surveying the camp, and nearly jumped up to shout a warning when he noticed four of those from the camp strolling up an embankment to the south.

And that's when he noticed what appeared to be a pulley system set up.

That must be where the blasphemous idols are!

Gunfire erupted and he watched as the four men scrambled over the ridge and out of range. He felt his heart slam into his chest as nearly half the soldiers ran in pursuit. Adrenaline surged through his veins, his hands beginning to shake with liquid courage as he damned his orders from the coward who would claim to be their better, and instead rose to his feet, Kalashnikov at the ready, and charged down the hill, unnoticed.

I do this in your name, Allah, please reward me should I die!

"Allahu Akbar!"

Nubian Desert, Egypt, University College London Dig Site

Acton was still staring at the ridge where their supposed security team had fled, debating whether or not he hoped the men chasing him were successful or not, when the all too familiar scream of "Allahu Akbar" rang out from behind him. He spun around to see a man charging over a dune and rushing toward them, his weapon belching lead. Several of the imposters dropped, two crying out in pain, the third silent, the hole in his head explaining why.

The "colonel", if he could be called that, raised his weapon and calmly fired, dropping the man less than fifty feet from the first truck. He continued to writhe on the ground, his shouts of "God is great" in Arabic muted, but continuous. Several of the imposters rushed over to him, the first kicking his weapon away, the rest aiming their weapons at his chest as the colonel approached.

Acton, unable to resist, and unhindered by the preoccupied force, walked over to see who the man was. His uniform matched the others, but his weapon seemed old and well-worn, suggesting he too was an imposter.

He muttered something while glaring at Acton, and the colonel looked over his shoulder at the archeologist.

"What did he say?" asked Acton.

"He said 'many more are coming'."

Acton shuddered.

"Who is he?"

"I don't know. He's not army."

"Neither are you."

It was Laura, now standing by his side, who challenged the man with the hypocrisy of his statement.

The man nodded. "You are correct, neither are we." He pointed at the man who began to shake on the ground, then stop breathing with a gurgle, the hole in his stomach finally doing its job. "But if there are more like him coming, then like the proverb said, 'The enemy of my enemy is my friend.' And we must become friends, if we stand a chance."

"Why would we help you?" asked Acton, exasperated at this sudden turn. "And who the hell *are* you?"

The colonel motioned for the body to be moved away, then he led Acton and Laura back toward the camp, where Chaney and Reading were standing with the lone reporter. The colonel pointed at the reporter.

"You are?"

"Naser Khattab. Al Ahram newspaper, Cairo."

The colonel nodded. "I know you. I've read your work. It is very good." He leaned in. "At times."

Naser stammered, not sure what to say to the qualified compliment.

"Umm, thank you?"

"You will report nothing of what I say, or I shall have you killed."

Before Naser could respond, the colonel turned to Laura.

"You have discovered the tomb of Cleopatra."

"Yes. And Antony."

The man nodded toward the pulley on the ridge to the south.

"Over there."

"Yes."

"And what are your intentions?"

"To document the find, and should the Supreme Council of Antiquities wish it, remove the artifacts so they can be shown to the world."

"Are you not aware that it is blasphemous to touch the tomb of a pharaoh?"

"I understand that there are those in the past who held those beliefs."

"In the past?" The colonel seemed slightly exasperated at this. "I can assure you it is true in the present as well."

"By some, I'll grant you. However I think a proper, respectful cataloging of the find should satisfy even those people."

The colonel seemed to pause a moment, then looked at the four Westerners.

"I am happy to see I was right about you. Your intentions are good, your motivations are good, only your ignorance is at fault here. Which is why I did not order your immediate execution."

Acton instinctively placed his shoulder ahead of his fiancée.

"And again, we ask, who are you?"

"I am Mohammad Soliman, Eldest of The Brotherhood."

"The Brotherhood?"

"We are the male descendants of a family sworn to protect the tomb of Cleopatra, and of other Pharaohs, from blasphemers who would desecrate their final resting places."

Acton squinted slightly. *Another two thousand year old organization?* If he didn't know of several others, he'd be inclined to dismiss the man's claims, but with the knowledge he had gleaned over the years, nothing surprised him anymore.

"So you're not a colonel in the army?" asked Reading.

"Actually, I was. Recently retired. I find the uniform and title come in handy at times."

"How many are you?" asked Acton.

"Enough."

"But didn't you desecrate the remains yourself?"

Acton cringed at Laura's question.

Don't antagonize the man with the gun, Dear!

The man nodded, a slight smile of respect emerging from the corners of his mouth.

"Indeed we did, but from necessity. The founders of our group discovered Queen Cleopatra's tomb violated within mere weeks of it being sealed. We took matters into our own hands and moved her tomb here, onto lands my family once owned millennia ago. We have kept her secret ever since."

"You mentioned others." This time it was Reading who had been paying attention.

"We have moved several tombs into the area. At least our ancestors had. We merely guard those already moved from people looting them."

"And why are you here?"

"To evacuate you."

"Why?"

The colonel motioned at the corpse now resting behind a nearby boulder.

"Because of fanatics like him."

"And why should we help you?"

"You have no other choice."

"How's that?"

"We possess the only vehicles, and they leave with us. You may walk across the Nubian Desert of course, this after all is, or rather *was*, a free country."

Several of his men chuckled, then one pointed. They all turned to see the men who had left in pursuit of the SAS guard returning, empty handed. There was a quick exchange in Arabic, and Laura translated under her breath.

"They got away."

It was Reading who quietly asked the question on all their minds. "But where did they go? Were they saving their own hides, or positioning to save ours?"

The colonel returned.

"What is your decision?"

Laura looked from man to man, each nodding in turn, then looked at the colonel.

"We stay, but this is my camp, and our dig site has to be respected."

"Of course."

"And when this is all over, we are allowed to document the find."

"Of that, I can make no promises."

Laura frowned.

"We'll discuss it later."

The man bowed slightly, and if he were wearing traditional Bedouin robes, Acton could picture him flaring them slightly in respect. Laura turned to Acton.

"Recommendations?"

"Hide the find, set up a decoy, fortify the camp, kill anything that tries to get past us, hope our security returns and Reading's friend Rahim gets here sooner rather than later."

Laura nodded, then looked at the gathered men.

"Then let's do it."

And with those words, the final battle for Cleopatra and Antony's resting place was to begin.

Nubian Desert, Egypt, Egyptian Army Checkpoint

Terrence nearly leapt at the phone as it vibrated. Taking a deep breath, he hit the button to take the call as everyone gathered around to hear.

"Terrence here."

"Terrence, it's Professor Palmer. Are you okay?"

"Are we okay?" asked Terrence, incredulity left unhidden. "Of course we're okay, are you okay?"

"We are. Where are you?"

"We're at some sort of military checkpoint. Professor, everyone here is dead!"

"Hey!" piped up the civilian bystander they had found.

"Dead? What happened?"

"Some sort of ambush would be my guess. Professor, we saw a second set of vehicles heading your way, army. They didn't look friendly."

"We've heard."

"What are you going to do? Will the army evacuate you?"

"They're not the army."

"Who? The first group or second?"

"Both from what I understand." There was a pause. "Listen, the first group claim to be some sort of brotherhood sworn to protect the tomb of Cleopatra. Now that they know about the second group, probably on their way here to destroy the tomb, they've decided to stay and defend the site."

"What about you and the others?"

"We have no choice but to stay."

"Nonsense!" cried Terrence. "Evacuate with one of their vehicles, get out of their while you can."

"Not possible. They won't give us one of their vehicles." There was a pause. "Listen, Terrence. Don't worry about us. Your one job is to get those students to safety. We'll take care of ourselves."

Terrence didn't say anything.

"Understood?"

"Understood," mumbled Terrence.

"Okay, we'll check back within thirty minutes. Good luck."

"Good luck," said Terrence, the conversation already ended. He slipped the phone in his pocket, then marched over to a jeep, one of its rear tires flat, several holes torn though the upholstery. He looked and smiled when he spotted the keys in the ignition. He climbed inside and had the engine purring moments later.

"I'm going to change this tire and go back to the camp, see if I can get the others out. You lot take the trucks and return to Cairo. We'll reunite as soon as we can."

"But you'll get yourself killed!" cried Stephen. "We should stick together; do what the professor said!"

There were nods of agreement.

Terrence shook his head. "No, they have no transportation. If we had a third vehicle, they would be with us now." He pointed at the jeep. "We now have a third vehicle. I'll go in the back way, and with a little luck, I'll be able to get to the camp, load our people in, and get out."

"I'm coming with you."

Terrence looked at Jenny.

"Not bloody likely."

"If you go, I go. Otherwise, you're going nowhere."

Terrence looked at her, frowning. But inside, he was jubilant. He was terrified, and having someone with him to share the fear would make his idiotic decision easier to live with.

"Fine. Let's get moving then."

USS Arleigh Burke, Flight Deck

Dawson pushed the last of his men aboard the MH-60S Knighthawk helicopter and was about to climb aboard when a figure ran toward them, dressed head to toe in black.

Kane!

"Care for some company?" asked Kane as he came to a halt at the side door of the helicopter.

Dawson shrugged his shoulders, smiling.

"My orders say nothing about giving lifts to those who don't exist, so why the hell not?"

Kane grinned and jumped aboard, the parachute he was sporting not going unnoticed by Dawson. Dawson climbed aboard, closing the door, then signaling the pilot to lift off.

Dawson hit the parachute with his hand.

"Don't trust our flight crew?"

"Not for a second!"

Kane settled back and closed his eyes, as Dawson gave the mission brief.

"We have an archeological team of mostly British nationals located in southern Egypt. I think you're familiar with a few of them."

Atlas laughed. "Don't tell me. Our two favorite professors?"

Dawson nodded.

"It would have been kinder if we had killed them in London. The shit they've been through since can't have been worth it."

There was a round of laughter, and Dawson cut it off with a wave of his hand over his throat.

"Since my DeLorean is in the shop, changing history isn't an option, so we're going in to provide security until an evac team arrives later tonight."

"ETA?" asked Niner.

"Three hours."

"Why the eagerness to get out?"

"They just discovered Cleopatra's tomb, probably the biggest archeological find of all time, and one of the biggest icons in ancient Egyptian history, on the same damned day a group of nutbars are destroying icons around the world."

"Ahhh, I see," said Niner in an exaggerated oriental accent, his own English perfect mid-West. "You want I should use brain more, mouth less."

Atlas elbowed him, his massive bulk knocking Niner into the lap of Spock who shoved Niner's head back at Atlas, Stooges style.

"Settle in, gentlemen. It'll be a long ride with a couple of midair refuelings. Let's just hope we get there in time."

Dawson settled back, looking across at Kane, who appeared to already be in a heavy sleep.

A spy with a clear conscience?

Dawson closed his eyes to rest, his conscience instead replaying the assault from earlier on the back of his eyelids.

I definitely need a vacation.

Nubian Desert, Egypt, Three miles from University College London Dig Site

Terrence pulled around the bend, almost inching his way, terrified he might run into the back of one of the trucks they had seen earlier. It had been the same routine for the entire return trip. Inch around the blind corners, then race forward when they had a clear line of sight. It was nerve-racking. It was slow.

It had kept them alive so far.

But for all he knew, the "bad guys" were already at the dig, killing everyone.

He pressed a little harder on the accelerator then slammed his breaks on as Jenny screamed, a man having stepped out from behind a large boulder, a weapon pointed directly at their windshield. As the vehicle skidded to a halt, two more men appeared, rushing toward the jeep before Terrence could react. Terrence pushed on the accelerator and was about to pop the clutch when a gun barrel was pressed against his temple.

"Please shut off the engine, Mr. Mitchell."

Terrence's eyebrows shot up as he did what he was told. With the engine quiet, the gun was removed from his head, and his head spun around to see Colonel Leather staring down at him, weapon now draped across his chest.

"What are you doing here?" asked Leather, the frown that seemed permanently etched on his face a little deeper than Terrence remembered.

"We're coming to rescue you guys!"

As soon as it was out of Terrence's mouth he regretted it. It sounded as stupid as it was futile, and his shoulders sank. And Leather's frown seemed to ease slightly but never quite make it into a smile.

The others however had no problem chuckling.

"Hey, he's here, isn't he?" snapped Jenny, putting her arm around Terrence's shoulders.

This elicited the hint of a smile from half of Leather's mouth.

"Indeed he is." He twirled his hand around his head and jumped in the back of the jeep. "We've got wheels, gents." The rest piled in or jumped on the back bumper. Leather pointed ahead, between the front seats. "Half a mile ahead, take a left. We'll come around the back of the camp."

Terrence started the engine and they jerked forward, his nerves getting the better of his shifting abilities, then after one false start, they were moving again.

"What are you doing here?" asked Jenny. "Why aren't you at the camp with the others?"

"Once we knew they weren't Egyptian Army, we beat it, holed up in a blind I had set up a few weeks ago, then when the coast was clear, left one sniper and made our way to the road to scout it. There's a second set of troops just ahead, about one mile, just sitting there. We're not sure if they're with the first group that arrived or not."

"I don't think they are," said Terrence as he turned off the road as indicated by Leather. "We saw two distinct groups of trucks heading toward the dig site, and came upon an army checkpoint where everyone had been killed."

"So we have at least one group of hostiles, perhaps two."

"Red Leader, this is Red Two, come in, over."

Leather grabbed the mike off his hip and activated it.

"Red Two, Red Leader, go ahead, over."

"An unknown hostile showed up, was taken out by the previous arrivals, and now it appears it's all hugs and kisses between our people and the new arrivals. They're working together to fortify the camp by the looks of it, over."

"Interesting," muttered Leather. He activated his mike. "Hold position, ETA five minutes, over and out."

"So what does that mean?" asked Terrence as they rounded a rock outcropping, revealing a smooth level surface devoid of any hiding places for about one mile. He pressed a little harder on the accelerator.

"It means that things aren't exactly as they seem."

Jenny turned to look at Leather.

"Is that good?"

Terrence watched Leather shrug in the rearview mirror.

"Rarely."

Nubian Desert, Egypt, Three miles from University College London Dig Site

Imam Khalil tried to hide his impatience. He knew his men were beginning to wonder why they were waiting, and why they hadn't simply attacked like they had at the checkpoint. The answer was something he wasn't proud of.

He was never supposed to be here.

It was a rash decision to come with his men, for it put him at risk. The original mission these men were supposed to be on was an attack on the pyramids, something with a very small likelihood of success. But the Cleopatra mission? There was every indication they could succeed, and some of them would survive, as there was no one left around to kill, or be killed by, once finished with the students and their teachers.

An easy, survivable attack, despite it being a suicide mission, like all the others. If anyone were to survive the initial attack, their orders were simple.

Keep killing until killed.

When they had encountered the checkpoint, its elimination was a routine matter. They outnumbered the outpost three to one, and had the element of surprise. Minimal risk, so he had simply remained in his truck, and prayed he wasn't hit by a stray bullet.

But when they neared their final destination, he realized what they were walking into was a complete unknown. What if the army had arrived first? What if they had security? Police? He had ordered the convoy to halt, and sent a man ahead to perform a recon.

Which led to the unfortunate discovery they had no communications equipment.

But then no one was supposed to survive, and no coordination should be needed. This was a simple head on assault. Kill everything in sight.

When word had returned of approximately two dozen army personnel, his heart had leapt into his throat. His initial instinct was to order the convoy back to Cairo, but he could think of no way to actually give the order without losing face.

But now with their recon volunteer overdue, and dusk beginning to fall, a decision had to be made, and there was only one decision that could be made.

He barked his order at the driver, and the engine fired up to cheers from the back.

Khalil closed his eyes, and prayed to Allah he survived the rest of the day.

Nubian Desert, Egypt, University College London Dig Site

Laura had been hidden away in their tent, furiously working on her computer from the moment they had decided to make a stand. She wasn't self-centered enough to believe she could do the work the men outside were doing. She simply wasn't physically strong enough. And she had no problem with that.

So she did something else that she felt was completely necessary, then forced each of her three remaining comrades to do the same.

Write a letter home.

Chaney took less than five minutes, but emerged from the tent teary eyed, Reading took even less time, his face stoic but flushed. James took longer, as she expected, he being so close to his parents, and if she knew him, he'd write her a letter, and his students.

He showed no shame of having red eyes when he emerged fifteen minutes later.

Hers had flowed freely.

She compressed the letters, along with some housekeeping matters for the museum and the school, then sent them via satellite to her email account.

She still held out hope that their attackers, if that's what they even were, may change their minds and turn around when they found themselves facing dozens of men, all armed, all equally willing to die, rather than a bunch of students and their teachers.

But her experience with fanatics told her otherwise.

She sighed and snapped the laptop shut, locking it in its metal case, then wiped the tears from her eyes as she stepped outside. Dusk had fallen. She could see a group of men working on the south ridge where the tomb had been found, the pulley system gone, and to the north, on another ridge, she saw James, Reading and Chaney returning, the decoy complete.

The Brotherhood had positioned themselves in the prepared positions her security team had previously set up, expanding several of them and positioning one of the trucks to the rear of the camp as a final fallback position and escape route, which she was certain none of the new arrivals would make use of if it truly were a suicide mission.

The gnashing of gears and the sound of an engine echoing across the desert had her frozen in place for a moment, then rushing toward the secure position near the center of the camp she, James, Reading and Chaney would occupy, their weapons already in place with plenty of ammo.

Her weapon readied, she pulled out the satellite phone as the headlights of the first truck sliced through the encroaching darkness.

Nubian Desert, Egypt, Seventy miles from University College London Dig Site

Stephen, unlike Terrence, had wasted no time in continuing their journey. He felt bad for Terrence, even a little proud of the bastard. His going off to "fight" certainly seemed completely out of character for the egghead, and it had attracted the gorgeous Jenny.

Perhaps that's why he was mad.

He was jealous.

He had had his eye on her for over a year, and his advances had been rebuffed, though politely. She was beautiful, smart, and apparently smitten with Terrence.

Smitten with Terrence!

It was ridiculous.

He growled.

"You okay?"

It was Naomi that asked, her perch in the passenger seat once occupied by Jenny giving her full view of the emotions playing over his face.

He gave her a quick glance, his eyes glued to the darkening road, the headlights doing little at this time of the evening.

"Just frustrated at the situation, that's all."

"Worried about Jenny?"

Am I that obvious? And shouldn't I be worried about her, rather than mad at Terrence?

"Worried about everybody. I just want to get us all to Cairo, then back to London. *All* of us. What Terrence did was stupid and selfish, and now he's got Jenny mixed up in his foolhardiness."

"It was her choice." Naomi slid closer and patted him on his right hand, his fingers sore from the constant grip. "They'll be okay. We'll be okay. You'll see."

She beamed him a smile that could melt some things and harden others, though Stephen wasn't certain he was reading her signals correctly. Most likely her smile was innocent, and he was just horny from three months in the desert without a moment of privacy to "read a magazine".

Damn I'm pent up!

The phone ringing in his pocket made him jump and swerve slightly on the road, protests from the back seat forcing him to apologize. He fished out the phone as he pulled over to the side of the road, not willing to risk talking and driving.

"Hello?"

"Stephen?"

"Yes? Is that you Professor Palmer?"

"Yes it is. Where's Terrence?"

Stephen felt a hint of glee in being able to tell his teacher how Terrence had disobeyed her orders. *Pathetic. What? Do you expect him to get sent to the corner with a dunce cap?*

"He's not here. Umm…" Stephen searched for the words, then realized there was no getting around the truth. "He and Jenny took a jeep we found at the checkpoint and came back to evacuate you." Then he suddenly realized something that had his heart slamming against his chest. "Aren't they there yet?"

"No." There was a pause and he could hear the professor saying something with the mouthpiece covered, then an exclamation from what had to be Professor Acton.

He sounds pissed.

"Listen, whoever the second group is has arrived. I've sent an email to my account that has some letters and instructions zipped up. Should we not make it, open that email and follow the instructions, understood?"

Stephen's voice cracked as the lump in his throat threatened to burst forth.

"Yes, mum. I'll take care of it personally."

"I know you will. Hopefully all will go well—" There was a burst of static, then the distinct sound of gunfire and shouting.

"Professor! Are you there!" cried Stephen, the second vehicle now emptied, everyone huddled around the phone. He turned to Naomi. "I can hear gunfire and screams," he said, his shoulders shaking as he tried not to cry out in horror. "Professor!"

"We're under attack!" came the voice finally. "Under *no* circumstances are you to return. Get yourselves to Cairo and the British Embassy. They'll take care of you. Good bye."

The phone went silent, and Stephen's head dropped onto the steering wheel, his shoulders heaving as he sobbed at the horror of what he had just heard. He felt several sets of hands trying to comfort him, as the others too joined in his mourning, for in all of their minds, their mentors were already dead.

Somewhere over Egyptian Airspace

A particularly rough bit of turbulence caused the chopper to shake, rousing Dawson from the stupor he had managed shortly after takeoff. He looked around and saw most of the men either sleeping or resting, a couple of them entertaining themselves with their phones or various other electronic devices.

Spock was reading on his eReader, a device Dawson had just picked up and had to admit loved. He kicked himself now for leaving it at home, it so new it didn't yet occur to him to bring it on missions for the downtime.

He looked at Kane, still apparently sleeping across from him.

I'd kill to hear some of his stories.

Dawson once had a chance to go CIA, but had turned it down. The idea of being a lone wolf didn't appeal to him. The army was a family. You counted on each other, you socialized with each other, you fought and cried with each other. When someone lost a friend, you all lost a friend. It was a bond that most could never fathom, and it was something he could never give up.

Bravo Team was his life, and he couldn't imagine doing a one man op, knowing that after it was done, the next op would be one man as well, with no one to talk to about it, no one to celebrate its success with.

And no one to watch your back.

But Kane had been different. A bit of a loner from what he remembered. He had been consumed by 9/11, signed up to fight those responsible. Dawson remembered during training the young man seemed like he was on a mission to secure the country himself.

There was a slight smile on Kane's face.

He seems happy.

But Dawson knew *he* wouldn't be. When he had been approached, he had turned them down cold, refusing to even sign the non-disclosure agreement that would tell him what job he was being offered. For he had known already. When two suits approach you in a parking lot, flash Company credentials, and ask you to come with them, you say no.

Especially when you know you can kick their asses.

They had insisted, and when he had said, "You're here to offer me a job in Special Ops, right? Well I'm not interested," they had quickly backed off. He never heard from them again after he told Colonel Clancy, his boss, about the incident, and told him in no uncertain terms to get them to back off.

But Kane had apparently jumped at it the first chance he got.

One of the flight crew entered their compartment, hunched over as he made his way toward him. He gave Dawson a nod, then shook Kane by the shoulder.

Kane immediately awoke, looking up.

"It's time, sir."

Kane nodded then rose as the crewman turned and to Dawson's surprise, opened the side door. Wind whipped through the cabin, waking the rest, and Kane stood up, checking his equipment and chute. Dawson rose, and spun Kane around, checking the chute himself, then smacking him on the back.

"Tired of our company?" he asked.

Kane smiled. "Consider me the first salvo in America's retaliation." He winked then stepped out the door without a moment's hesitation. The crewmember closed the door as Dawson sat down and glanced at his watch. He did a quick calculation in his head.

Somewhere near Cairo?

Nubian Desert, Egypt, Just outside University College London Dig Site

Terrence felt like they were inching forward, but no one was complaining. Leather had refused to let him put on his headlights, and at first he had wondered why, then realized they must be extremely close to the camp. Any light in this environment would be seen for miles, and the element of surprise was obviously critical to any plan Leather may have.

He just hoped that plan included him and Jenny surviving the night.

And it was night, or almost. Dusk had settled firmly in, and the stars were making their appearances, crisp and white against an unblemished night sky free of clouds and pollution.

It was one of his favorite things about the desert, and he found himself some nights lying out under the stars, staring up for hours at a view this city boy had never experienced until his first archeological dig with Professor Palmer.

A dig that had ended in tragedy. He had been a freshman, an eager, promising archeologist according to a letter the Professor had shown him years later. First years weren't allowed on expeditions, but an exception had been made for him as the professor had apparently taken a liking to him.

It had been thrilling, exciting, terrifying and in the end, deadly.

They were in Jordan, working on a well-established dig site with students and professionals from all around the world, when on their second last day, there was a cave in that nearly killed him. He was buried alive, nearly out of breath when he had felt hands on his ankles, pulling at him. He had wiggled his body, and within minutes was freed, greeted by none other than Professor Palmer's brother, who made sure he was okay, then sent him toward the surface as he clawed desperately at the rocks in search of another student.

The final collapse was massive. And unsurvivable.

He felt his chest tighten at the memory. Professor Palmer's scream had been heart wrenching, a sound he had never forgotten, and the only time he could recall ever seeing true grief, true horror, in his life. It was nothing he hoped to ever see again, to hear again, the one experience enough. Part of him had wondered if she blamed him for her brother dying. After all, if he hadn't rescued him, and stayed to search the rubble for others, he would be alive today.

But his mind was set at ease over the years as she continued to mentor him, continued to invite him on her expeditions, and continued to confide in him, sometimes talking of her brother, sometimes of her work, as she would an old friend.

Until Professor Acton had come along. Terrence had to admit he had been jealous at first, her attentions turned to this new man in their lives, his boyish fantasy of he and her together dashed. But he quickly realized that his fantasies were just that, and he was pleased to see the Professor so happy these past couple of years.

And Professor Acton had turned out to be one of the coolest men he had ever met, a father figure to them all when needed, and a blast around the campfire, his stories legendary.

"Stop here and turn off the engine. Leave the keys in the ignition."

Leather's voice cut through his reverie, snapping him back to the horror of the moment. He stopped the jeep and did as he was told, the security team exiting, he and Jenny climbing out, following them as they walked into the darkness. Jenny took his hand and squeezed. He returned the silent comfort, and wondered just what he had gotten them into.

That's when the gunfire began.

Nubian Desert, Egypt, University College London Dig Site

Colonel Soliman looked across the camp at the Westerners on the other ridge setting up the decoy, and nodded with approval. They appeared to be done, beginning their return to the camp. He looked back at his own men who had returned the thick canvas over the crevice, then repositioned the rocks. They were now smoothing out the sand, removing any evidence of the tomb.

The sound of approaching trucks, and the beams of headlights had him sprinting back toward the camp, shouting at his men to follow before they were seen. As he hit the valley floor the first truck had already come to a halt, the second and third pulling up beside it as men began to jump out from the backs, spreading to the left and right, their weapons trained on the camp, but the near complete darkness would be to everyone's disadvantage.

There appeared to him to be three trucks, each with a dozen men, the headlights slicing across the camp, revealing little, everyone within the beams huddled behind their reinforced positions. The man he had killed earlier had no radio, only a cellphone that didn't work here. He wondered if there had been others that reported their strength.

He had to assume yes.

And the fact that nobody had yet fired a shot, had him wondering if those who had just arrived were indeed regular army, or the zealots causing chaos around the world. If it were regular army, they would probably face arrest for impersonating military personnel, which would mean there would be no one to protect the tomb.

He took up position behind a pile of dirt that had been dug out of the desert floor by the archeologists during the course of their work, readying his weapon along with four of his men, all close relatives.

He glanced back at the rise to the south, and save the footprints he had just left, visible only from the moonlight, there was no evidence of the tomb. A glance to the north and the decoy was prominent in its singularity, silhouetted against the night sky for all to see.

The question was, if they were all killed, how long would these fanatics continue to search once they discovered it was indeed a decoy. He kicked himself for not having had the time to disguise the footprints he and his men had just left, and made a mental note that should he need to retreat, he would retreat up the rise to try and provide an alternate explanation for the prints.

He glanced over at the Westerners' location and saw the female on a phone, talking to someone, the other three men now having joined her, and for a moment admired her bravery. He admired independent women, and was proud that a once secular Egypt had given many rights to its women. Though by no means perfect, it had been far better for women in Mubarak's Egypt than it was in countries like Saudi Arabia or Yemen.

But now with the Muslim Brotherhood in charge, things were regressing rapidly. Already quotas for women representatives in the election had been completely ignored, their share of the parliament dropping from twelve percent to less than two, but it was the day to day actions that truly sickened him, with those women who still tried to assert their independence being harassed on the streets, sometimes verbally, sometimes physically, and all too often sexually. And it was coming from not only men of his age, but boys, barely old enough to have hair on their faces, using the new found acceptance of this behavior to assault women and girls alike.

His Egypt now disgusted him, and if it weren't for his sworn duty to protect the tomb and lead The Brotherhood, he would take his family to America or Canada, and leave this place, and the hatred, far behind.

There were several shots, and they all looked up as flares lit the night sky, then hit the dirt as dozens of guns opened fire on them to the fanatic screams of "Allahu Akbar!".

Allah protect us from those who would corrupt your teachings.

Imam Khalil tried to remain calm as they rounded the bend, the camp revealed below them. His eyes immediately took in the sight. A group of men running from the south down into the camp, disappearing behind a pile of dirt, another group running from the north and hiding behind something near the center of the camp.

His eyes immediately looked to the north and saw something silhouetted against the sky, and smiled.

That must be it!

He stepped out of the truck as his men spread themselves out in front of him, he remaining with one foot on the running board, his body behind the metal door of the truck, his shaking hands gripping the frame where the rolled down window would be.

Flares fired into the night sky, lit up the landscape, and to the shouts of "Allahu Akbar" his men opened fire, and he found himself filled with pride and power, his adrenaline beginning to flow, his flight instinct giving way to his fight instinct.

As he surveyed the well-lit scene below, he noticed the hill to the south again.

Why had they been there?

His mind raced, and it occurred to him that there might be reinforcements behind that hill, or something hidden that these infidels didn't want found. He made a mental note to check the south of the camp thoroughly once they were victorious.

Watching his men pour their fire on the camp, so far completely unopposed, he began to wonder why he had been scared at all. Perhaps his fears had been unwarranted, and they were facing cowards who wouldn't fight back. It would be in typical apologist Western fashion.

But why weren't the army troops firing back? Could they be unarmed? It made no sense. He tried to remember what Adel had said after his first report. He was sure the boy had said they were armed.

Of course they're armed!

It was just wishful thinking that they weren't. But why weren't they firing back?

Acton sat with his back against the dirt dugout, Laura huddled beside him, Chaney and Reading next to her, all crouching to avoid being hit, but so far their defensive position had proven itself. The only problem was they had no way of knowing what has happening without someone literally sticking their neck out.

We have to know.

He flipped around, and crawled on his knees slightly away from the pile of dirt, much to the shock and horror of Laura.

"What are you doing!" she hissed, loud enough for him to hear over the gunshots.

"Checking to see what's happening."

He looked to his left, and could see no movement, then to his right, more of the same revealed. He scampered back to the safety of the dirt as a few shots he was convinced were unaimed tore at the dirt several feet away. He then poked his head up for a split second, then dropped, repeating it and looking at the attackers' position, then again dropping down.

"What did you see?" asked Reading, apparently not at all upset with his antics.

"Not much. Our attackers don't seem to be moving in, but The Brotherhood doesn't seem to be fighting back."

"What do you mean?" asked Laura, her voice slightly incredulous. "You mean all that gunfire is from the bad guys?"

Acton nodded. "Seems so. The Brotherhood doesn't appear to be firing a shot."

"Could they be dead?" wondered Chaney aloud.

"Can't see that. It's too soon."

"It doesn't make sense," said Acton, "unless they're trying to get the nutbars to use up all their ammo."

"That's mighty presumptuous," replied Reading. "For all we know they could have a truck full of ammo. However, there is something to be said for keeping your head down and letting the enemy waste some of it, as long as they're not advancing, and not picking you off slowly."

"I haven't heard anybody get hit yet," said Laura. "At least wounded, I mean. I'm sure we would have heard something if somebody was wounded."

"Agreed. But what do we do?" said Reading. "Do we fight back?"

Acton shook his head. "No, this isn't our fight. We were forced into this. We'll fight to defend ourselves so we can make our escape, but right now, let's keep our heads down, and see what happens."

The flares suddenly sputtered out, and the gunfire stopped.

As did Acton's heart as he heard the shouts of "Allahu Akbar", and boots pounding on the rock and sand.

"Here they come!"

Colonel Soliman hid behind a pile of stakes with four of The Brotherhood, all with their heads down, flinching as each bullet hit the wood. He had half a mind to start digging a hole to hide in, but instead gripped his weapon tightly, wondering if any of them had any real combat experience. Most had been in the army at one point or another, something The Brotherhood encouraged to get some self-defense training, then once out, they would go about their daily lives. They were shopkeepers, teachers, artisans and public servants.

The only difference between these men and any others in Egypt were that they were all moderates, and they were all descendant from the same line of brothers who had founded The Brotherhood two thousand years ago with the aim of protecting Cleopatra's tomb.

He was proud of his fellow brothers tonight, resisting the temptation to fire back, knowing the shots would be wasted. Their orders were to fire once the enemy was advancing, and to conserve their ammo, for all they had were two clips each for their Kalashnikovs, and whatever bullets they had in their handguns, *if* they had them.

He cursed himself for not having arrived better armed, but the reality was they were supposed to scare a group of kids and teachers into getting on a truck and leaving, not engage a well-armed group of fanatics.

He looked up as the flares spurted their last gasp of light, then the area went dark, his eyes slowly adjusting to the near darkness, moon and starlight, with a hint of light from the western horizon, all that was left.

And against that horizon were dozens of men jumping to their feet, storming toward them, screaming "Allahu Akbar!"

And Soliman agreed. He just wondered whose side Allah was on today.

Terrence and Jenny were lying on their stomachs, looking down at the dig site. A steady stream of gunfire was being poured onto the camp from a line of what appeared to be dozens of individual weapons. Leather and one of his men were with them, surveying the situation, while the two others had left a few minutes ago.

"Why aren't they fighting back?" asked Jenny, a question that was echoing in his own mind.

"They're not advancing, so let them waste their ammo. I'd estimate each of the opposition has expended at least three clips so far, and the fact we haven't seen anything heavier like grenades or fifty cals tells me they don't have them. We're dealing with a lightly armed unit, most likely not very well trained."

"But they're fanatics, right? They'll die before they fail?"

Leather looked at Terrence.

"So it's our job to make sure they not only die, but fail as well."

"How?"

Leather pointed behind them.

"Grab a weapon, and follow me."

Jenny scrambled over to a stockpile of weapons that Leather had apparently prepositioned for this very possibility, and grabbed a Glock and an MP5.

Terrence gulped. He had been training like the others, in fact, more than the others, but never in a million years would he have thought he'd actually have to use the training on real people.

Jenny looked at him and he quickly scrambled over to save face, selecting the Glock and MP5 as well, then filling his pockets with clips.

"Body armor!" hissed Leather, pointing at a pile to the right.

Terrence tossed a vest to Jenny, then slid his own over his head, quickly securing it in place. He felt a little better now, but not much. He looked about for a helmet, but found none. He and Jenny returned to Leather's position just as the flares died and shouts of the two words that were meant to provide comfort but now terrified the world over, "Allahu Akbar!", echoed across the desert.

"Here they come!" whispered Jenny, her voice filled with the terror that was gripping Terrence.

"And here we go," said Leather, jumping to his feet and rushing toward the camp with his comrade.

Terrence looked at Jenny. She gave him a quick kiss, then jumped to her feet, rushing after Leather. Terrence looked up at the heavens, said a silent prayer, then chased after the two, not sure if he felt safer alone on the ridge, or together with the others.

A huge hail of gunfire from below settled the question in his mind.

The ridge, alone.

Imam Khalil watched from his vantage point, behind the door of the truck, as his men rained lead on the infidels and their defenders. It was a beautiful sight, the night sky lit by the flares, the muzzle flashes accentuating the determined faces of his men, the glee in their eyes as they executed Allah's will.

He himself was caught up in the moment, the heroism of his men, the glory of Allah filling his chest, as they fired round after round at the blasphemers below.

Blasphemers who weren't fighting back.

It took him a minute to realize that they weren't returning fire, and another minute to ask himself why, rather than rejoice in their lack of response. But when he did finally realize he should be asking the question, his mind filled with a rush of possibilities. They could be dead already. They might be unarmed. They may have no ammo. They may simply be letting his men waste their ammo.

He frowned, then the flares sputtered out, and it was too late. His men jumped to their feet and roared "Allahu Akbar", charging forward, guns blazing yet again.

And he stepped out from behind the truck door, gun raised in the air, shouting with them. "Allahu Akbar!" His chest filled with the fighting spirit, adrenaline fueling his courage, Allah urging him into the fight. He rushed forward, after his men, shouting into the night sky, hoping his god was listening.

Then suddenly all hell broke loose.

The sound of their attackers charging forward was unmistakable, yet still no one returned fire. And if they didn't within the next few seconds, the camp would be overrun and their lives lost.

"To hell with it!" muttered Acton, jumping up to one knee and aiming his weapon at the first thing he saw. He squeezed the trigger then relaxed his finger, a short burst erupting from the end of this MP5, and the target dropping. He shifted his sight to the right, and repeated the short burst, taking out another.

Movement beside him then the ear ringing roar of weapons fire told him his friends had joined in, and as he watched, at least another half dozen of their attackers dropped.

Colonel Soliman yelled something to their left, and finally his men jumped up and opened fire, but it seemed too late, the enemy nearly at their positions. Another half dozen went down before gunfire was directed at the central position Acton occupied. They all dropped as sustained fire pounded on their earthen barrier.

"Wait until he has to reload!" yelled Reading, the only truly experienced soldier in the group. Acton looked over at Laura and could see the fear in her eyes. He tried to give her a reassuring look, but was certain he had failed miserably, he himself terrified. His heart was pounding so hard he felt like he was halfway through a marathon, and his adrenaline was pumping so freely, he could feel his hands shake.

He closed his eyes and sucked in a slow breath through his nose, counting to five and pushing it into his stomach, then holding it for a five count, he slowly let it out through his mouth over another five seconds. Repeating one more time, he felt himself begin to calm when the gunfire stopped.

"Now!" yelled Reading.

They all jumped up at the same time, which in retrospect turned out to be the wrong thing to do. The one who had been charging their position and was now reloading was dropped by Laura, but immediately behind him he had a friend, who was fully loaded, who returned the fire. There was a cry from somebody in their group, and Acton squeezed the trigger, taking the man out, his body dropping in an uncoordinated heap not ten feet from their position.

A quick glance to his right and he didn't see the rest of his comrades, but before he could look, a scream of "Allahu Akbar" to his right had him swinging to engage a lone attacker who had managed to break through their flank. His weapon belched lead at Acton, missing widely as the uncontrolled weapon bounced in the air. Acton took a bead and dropped him, then quickly scanned from left to right for any threats, but found the rest focusing on the positions held by The Brotherhood.

Acton dropped and automatically reloaded his weapon as he looked to see what was going on with his friends. Reading was applying pressure to a wound in Chaney's chest. Chaney, even in the moonlight and muzzle flashes, appeared ghostly pale.

"Is he going to be okay?" asked Acton, giving Laura a shake on the shoulder to see if she was okay. She looked up at him, tears in her eyes, but no look of physical pain. The relief he felt knowing she wasn't hurt spurred him to keep it that way, and he jumped back up to scan the area.

That's when the silent body of one of their attackers leapt through the air at him, no shout to Allah on his lips, merely hatred sneered across his face. Acton instinctively swung his weapon toward the man as he ducked back down, but it was too late. The barrel of his gun hit the man's shoulder, the shot blocked, the bullets blazing harmlessly into the night sky.

Laura screamed.

Colonel Soliman heard the cry of a man come from the archeologists' position, but he didn't have time to deal with it. He and his brothers were now fully engaged, and he knew within minutes their ammunition would be depleted, and they would be overrun if they couldn't turn the tide of this battle quickly.

But we're outnumbered almost two to one!

He jumped up and swept his Kalashnikov from left to right, his finger depressed on the trigger as precious lead erupted from the barrel, removing three more of their attackers from the long term picture, when two of his brothers went down beside him. He dropped to a knee and saw his two cousins Mohammad and Mahmoud down, and dead, their chests ripped open.

Another shout and his nephew Rahim dropped beside him. Tears filled Soliman's eyes as he saw the boy he had known from birth stare up at him with dead eyes. Rage filled his heart, and he jumped up, cover be damned, and shot at the first thing he saw, emptying his magazine into the one man, wasting those precious few last bullets he had.

He dropped, grabbing Rahim's weapon and yanking the clip.

Empty.

He began to check his cousins for ammo when a roar from overhead caused him to spin around, pulling his knife off his belt. On instinct he shoved it upward and into the man's belly, twisting it hard, scrambling his innards as he groaned, toppling forward, a dead weight that crushed Soliman under it. He hit the ground with a grunt, pushing the mass off him as the man's intestines flowed out onto Soliman's uniform. He scrambled backward, then in a blind rush, sprinted toward the center position where the archeologists were, just as the scream of a woman rang out.

Terrence watched the battle unfold below, passing the night vision goggles back and forth with Jenny, their stomachs glued to the ground Leather had told them to hug, he and the other guard having continued closer to the camp.

"Oh my God!" exclaimed Jenny, pushing her neck forward, as if the extra inch might give her a better view.

"What is it?" asked Terrence, desperate for his turn.

Jenny handed him the glasses. "I think that detective, Chaney, just got hit."

Terrence looked, the view racing across the desert, then the camp, then finally the foxhole, if it could be called that since it wasn't actually a hole, that protected the professors and their friends.

He gasped.

Somebody was down, of that there was no doubt. It was hard to tell who, the greenish hue he was looking at hard to distinguish facial details. He breathed a sigh of relief when he saw Professor Palmer moving about, her slight frame compared to the men easy to distinguish. And he was pretty sure it was Professor Acton that was on his feet firing at the approaching enemy.

The firing from the position stopped for a moment, then Terrence leapt to his feet and yelled, "Look out!" to no avail, as an attacker leapt over the pile of sand.

Terrence sprinted toward the camp, pulling his weapon into position, strapping the night vision goggles to his head, ignorant of the shouts from behind him as Jenny jumped to her feet to give chase.

I have to save the professor!

Acton's weapon bounced off the man uselessly as he continued to fly at him, the man's arms outstretched, one hand containing a knife Crocodile Dundee would have been proud of. Then suddenly the man jerked to his left, as if pulled by a cord ninety degrees from where he was headed, followed by a clap of thunder Acton recognized immediately from the incident in China.

But this time it was on their side.

He dropped, checking his weapon, and glancing at Chaney. Both Reading and Laura were working on him, but with the rapidness the blood seemed to be saturating the shirt Reading had ripped off himself, Acton had the sinking feeling their friend wouldn't make it.

A sound of footfalls to his left caused him to spin, weapon whipping up as his finger began to squeeze the trigger.

"It's me!" yelled the voice, a voice not yet familiar enough for Acton to think "It's me" was a sufficient enough greeting, but it at least caused a moment's hesitation that allowed him to recognize the colonel and temporary ally.

Acton lowered the weapon, returning his attention to their front, popping up and firing as another body was ripped from existence, skipping across the desert floor as their ex-SAS guards began their defense.

Sorry I ever doubted you, boys!

Another body skidded across the desert, this time in the opposite direction, Acton surmising they had set up two positions to protect both flanks. But what was also becoming too clear was that The Brotherhood positions were nearly completely overrun, and it was time to retreat. He looked at Reading.

"We need to fall back, now!"

Reading looked at Acton, then the battle.

"Give me sixty seconds."

He jumped up and raced toward the nearest tent before Acton could yell at him to get down, leaving him instead to provide cover fire long enough for Reading to reach the safety only canvas could provide.

"Weapon?" asked Soliman, now behind the mound of sand.

Acton motioned with his chin to Chaney's weapon lying on the ground. "Clips are stacked up here," he said.

Soliman quickly grabbed the weapon, reloaded and opened fire.

Acton decided footfalls behind him were Reading's, confirmed by the heavy grunt as the man hit the ground. Acton took a quick glance and saw he had retrieved a cot with a sleeping bag still on top.

Good man!

"Cover us," Acton said to Soliman, and Acton dropped his weapon, helping the others load Chaney onto the cot, the sleeping bag open. They then zipped up the back just as two forms came rushing out of the darkness.

Acton grabbed his weapon, raising it, when Laura yelled, "No!", reaching out and slapping the barrel of his weapon up as he squeezed the trigger.

But it was too late.

The first of the approaching figures dropped to the ground, the other crying out in a voice he recognized as one of Laura's students, Jenny.

"Terrence!" she cried.

Oh my God! Please no!

Acton jumped up and ran over to Terrence and flipped him over. He wasn't moving, and they were totally exposed. He grabbed him by the shirt and pulled him toward their cover, Jenny following as she sobbed uncontrollably.

Another shot from the sniper rifle rolled across the site, but as Acton quickly took stock of the situation, he could see their attackers were now all huddled behind protective barriers, pinned down, but still a threat as guns were held up blindly and fired.

And it appeared The Brotherhood was gone, all that remained was Colonel Soliman. Acton began to wonder whether or not he was the last of the entire Brotherhood, or if there were more in Egypt, when Terrence coughed. Acton let go of the boy's shirt, and gave him a quick look, then rapped on his chest, the hard feeling of body armor on his knuckles unmistakable.

Acton looked at Jenny.

"Check if any bullets went through," he ordered, then fired several shots at one of their attackers bold enough to reveal more than an arm. He ducked back behind the large rock.

"He's okay!" cried Jenny, the joy in her voice obvious.

"What the hell are you two doing here?" demanded Laura in about as angry a voice as he had ever heard from her.

"He insisted on coming back to save you guys."

"What?" It was Reading this time who exploded. "Of all the daft things to do!"

"We found another vehicle, the rest are half way to Cairo by now."

Acton's mind twigged. *Another vehicle?* Two of The Brotherhood trucks had already been overrun by the attackers, the other they had hoped to escape with now had a flat tire from a stray bullet.

"What kind of vehicle?"

"Jeep."

"How many will she hold?"

"Not a lot."

But enough, even if we're piled in there we could put some distance.

He did the mental math. There were seven of them here, one of them wounded, plus the four guards. Two in the front, four in the back, two on the rear, two on the sideboards, and Chaney's stretcher strapped on somehow.

It may just work.

He looked at Reading and Laura.

"You guys ready?"

Both nodded.

"Okay, when I signal, all of you head straight back, behind the main tent, then Jenny, you lead them to the Jeep. The Colonel and I will hold them off until you're out of sight, then join you."

"Who's going to cover you?" demanded Laura.

"Your friends," he smiled. He leaned over, gave her a quick kiss, holding her by the back of the head, pressing her hard against his lips, then letting go. "Now go!" he yelled, jumping up and pouring fire on the remaining positions. He heard grunting behind him as Reading and Laura picked up the cot containing Chaney, and Jenny hauled a still gasping Terrence to his feet.

Acton emptied his clip, then quickly reloaded, checking behind him as he did. He caught sight of Laura disappearing behind the tent, and Terrence just seeming to get his wind back, his pace picking up as he and Jenny rounded the canvas.

Acton opened fire again, several short bursts, in between bursts shouting directions. "Gather as much ammo as you can!" he said, firing, "then when I'm done this clip, we go!"

Soliman was immediately on the ground, loading his pockets with clips and stuffing Acton's as well, when the final shot rang out.

"Let's go!"

Acton jumped up, sprinting after his friends, Soliman on his heels. As they rounded the tent Acton heard a terrified yelp and spun around to find the reporter, Naser Khattab, huddled in the darkness, apparently not destined to be a war correspondent.

"Come with me if you want to live," said Acton, holding his hand out and beginning to smile at the coolness of having been able to actually deliver that line unintentionally in real life. The young man nodded, taking the proffered hand.

Acton hauled him to his feet, all too aware that the count had just increased to twelve people, but still one jeep. He wondered if the vehicle would even be able to move with so many people hanging off it.

One problem at a time.

Imam Khalil peered into the darkness, the tone of the battle having changed. There were new weapons involved, high powered weapons, that seemed to be picking his men off. He himself had retreated back to what he hoped was the safety of the trucks, but as man after man dropped, he began to even question that.

Then when the automatic weapons that had been firing back at them stopped, he climbed up on the running board, and saw several dark figures disappearing into the night.

"They're getting away!" he screamed, rage pushing aside the fear once again. "After them!"

His men hesitated at first, but one brave soul had courage enough to shout "Allahu Akbar!" and the rest joined in, reminded of the glorious orgy of lust that awaited them in paradise should they die today.

And several died within seconds of the charge, their bodies torn apart by what Khalil could only imagine to be some type of cannon. He found his feet carrying him forward, the cry of *God is Great!* on his lips, but as a body skidded to a halt in front of him, he stopped, then rushed back to the truck, jumping in the driver's side as his force of more than three dozen men continued to dwindle, now less than ten left.

The engine roared to life as he turned the key. Slamming it into reverse, he popped the clutch and gave it gas, the truck leaping backward as he tried to flee in his mad panic. The truck jerked to a halt as it slammed into something, the engine stalling out with a shake.

He turned the key, and the engine chugged as it tried to restart. The passenger side window shattered, and the back of the seat was torn apart, the hole the bullet left behind massive.

They're trying to kill me!

The gall of these infidels never ceased to amaze him. Did they give no thought to the fact he was an Imam, a servant of Allah himself? Did they not know they would be condemned to an eternity in Hell while he, should he die, would be blessed for eternity?

The engine roared to life, and as he slammed it into first, the truck leaping forward, he was saved from contemplating the answers. He risked turning the lights on, figuring a hasty, safe exit was better than a slow, blind one, and within moments was safely out of sight of the battle, his last glance through the rearview mirror of several of his men turning back to the trucks.

Cowards! You should be fighting to the death for Allah!

Leather slammed his fist into the ground as the first truck pulled away. Then he realized this wasn't a military operation, this was a civilian defensive one. If the enemy were to flee, that most likely meant they wouldn't have to worry about them again. Then his thoughts turned to the news reports. If these men were part of the worldwide attacks, then they *would* have to probably deal with them again at some point, whether it was men like him, or men like those that still remained in the active service.

Either way there was the chance of more innocent blood shed.

"Take out their remaining vehicles," he ordered over the comm. He heard his second-in-command begin to respond, then the distinct sound of gunfire and cries of pain. He looked up at the opposite ridge, his view through the hazy green flying rapidly by when it came upon the second position.

Two men were standing over his comrades, a third bent over doing something that involved his arm jerking up and down, then suddenly the man stood up, holding the head of Sergeant Hewlett high in the air, shouting something at the night sky.

"Sonofabitch!"

He took aim, eliminating the groin of the man holding the head, the gaping hole certain to kill him, but low enough to let him die an agonizing death over the coming minutes. Leather's partner took out the second target at the same time, removing his head chest and neck from existence, then Leather took out the third target as he fled, sending him flying out of sight.

Leather jumped to his feet.

"Get to the professors, provide whatever protection you can. I'm going after the first truck."

And with that he sprinted in the direction of the road he knew the vehicle would be forced to follow in the night, as his comrade rushed in the opposite direction.

Tonight they all die.

Terrence continued to stumble, his chest aching from the impact of having been shot by Professor Acton of all people. He thanked God that Leather had told him to put the body armor on, and though it had stopped the bullet, it hadn't prevented it from either bruising or breaking at least one rib.

But he was alive, and Jenny's reaction to his apparent death had been spectacularly romantic, if the bit of it he caught when he awoke was any indication.

He also knew the professor felt profoundly bad, practically carrying him over his shoulders, as some other man whom Terrence at first had thought to be one of the enemy, helped on the other side.

Jenny was ahead, night vision goggles on, leading the way back to their jeep, while the gunfire behind them had all but stopped. Which in his mind could mean only one of three things. One, which he knew he wasn't lucky enough to be true, was that the enemy was fleeing, the second was that they were all dead, another option he considered himself not lucky enough for, or third, they were in pursuit.

Which was the most likely.

And the fact the guards weren't firing any more had him terrified. Were they dead? Why weren't they engaging the enemy anymore?

Maybe they *are all dead?*

A nervous glance over his shoulder yielded little except the sight of the ex-cop Reading carrying a cot with his dying friend, Professor Palmer having switched positions with the young reporter. She was now covering their rear, and he felt a twinge of guilt for that, since if he didn't need help, Professor Acton and this colonel gent could be back there instead, and his mentor and former secret crush could be up here with him, perhaps not safe, but safer for certain.

Several shots rang out behind them, and he heard the professor shout, "They're coming!" as Acton extricated himself from Terrence, and rushed back to assist his fiancée.

And Terrence didn't blame him a bit, his entire being wishing it was him that were racing back to be the hero.

Instead, he focused on the beautiful Jenny in front of him, a consolation prize by no means, and smiled through the wheezes at how lucky he felt at this very moment.

Imam Khalil cranked the wheel, following the barely there road in the darkness. To call this anything but a trail would be ridiculous, how it had ever come to be beyond him, and he cursed then begged forgiveness every time a wheel perfectly found a hole in the ground that rattled his teeth and strained his arms as he braced himself from slamming into the steering wheel.

He rounded another corner and he caught something from the side of his eye as the beams from the headlights whipped around the corner. It was a man. Khalil instinctively ducked, flooring the truck, as gunshots tore apart his windshield, the rush of wind filling the cabin as he picked up speed. He risked a glance, straightening out the wheel as the truck whined, demanding a shift in gear, but his position preventing him from doing so.

Instead, he grabbed the weapon sitting on the passenger seat and raised it just as a figure jumped on the running board, shoving its own weapon into the cabin.

Khalil fired, the man flying backward just as he himself fired. Khalil felt a burning hot pain in his shoulder, the weapon dropping from his hand, coming to rest on the floor of the passenger side, hopelessly out of reach should he need it again. With a valiant effort, and a scream of pain and a prayer to Allah, he shifted from second to third, gaining speed, and minutes later, with no sign of pursuit, burst out onto the open highway.

Khalil tore the sleeve of his left arm off with his teeth, then, driving with his knees, tied a tourniquet over the wound, staunching, at least temporarily, the bleeding.

Now he just needed to hang on until he reached a town with people he could trust.

And Allah willing, I will be alive tomorrow to continue the fight.

"There it is!" yelled Jenny, pointing to the jeep that sat behind a large rock outcropping. The colonel hauled Terrence to the jeep, placing him in the passenger seat, then scrambled around to the other side, firing up the engine, the keys thoughtfully left in the ignition.

Jenny jumped in the back as the colonel turned the vehicle around, facing it toward the way Terrence had come earlier, the tracks still visible in the sand. The makeshift stretcher was placed across the rear doors, covering the back seat, then Professor Palmer and Reading jumped over the rear, placing their legs on the rear seats, and holding onto the cot with one hand, the jeep with the other.

"Let's go, let's go!" yelled Acton, waving at the colonel to get moving.

"What about the guards?" asked Laura.

"They'll have to catch up," said Acton as he grabbed the windshield and jumped on the running board, the reporter doing the same on the other side. "They can take care of themselves. Those guys"—Acton pointed at the men coming into sight—"aren't going to wait."

"Then we go!" said the colonel as he put the vehicle in gear and the jeep roared forward. Gunfire from behind rang out, and Acton spun, aiming his weapon one handed, and fired as they gained speed. Suddenly the colonel slammed on the brakes, sending Terrence and the others flying forward as one of their guards came into view. He leapt on the passenger side of the hood, then motioned for them to continue on.

The colonel stepped on it, and once again everyone was tossed about, but within minutes they were out of range of any hostiles, and on their way along a path Terrence wasn't sure he'd recognize at any time of day. In fact, after about fifteen minutes, Terrence was convinced they were lost, and said so.

"No, this is a back way. It will keep us off the main roads so we avoid any checkpoints."

"Why the hell would we want to *avoid* the authorities? Don't we want to go *to* them?" exploded Reading. "We've got a wounded man here, we need help!"

The colonel frowned in the moonlight, then nodded. "You are of course correct. I will take us to the main road, and from there, you will continue on yourselves."

"What about you?" asked Terrence, uncertain why he should concern himself with this man's wellbeing.

"I will be fine. My brothers will find me very quickly."

"So there are others?" asked Acton, still kneeling on the runner, his weapon slung over his shoulder, his head mostly behind the windshield.

The colonel nodded.

"Many others. What you saw today was a small group meant to scare some children and their teachers into leaving. Not engage an armed force."

"What are your intentions, now that we're gone?" asked Acton, the concern for their find evident in his voice.

How can you think about that now?

Terrence couldn't believe what he was hearing. They had barely escaped with their lives, half the world was on fire from madmen, and the professor was worried about the tomb of someone dead two thousand years previous.

But before the colonel could answer, the engine began to sputter and their speed quickly reduced, and less than a minute later, they rolled to a halt.

Out of gas.

In the middle of the Nubian Desert.

We're screwed.

Leather pushed himself up off the ground as the lorry roared around the corner and out of sight. He began to run after it but immediately stopped, his ribs roaring in protest.

Lucky damned shot!

But lucky or not, he was now officially compromised. He checked his vest and found his shirt torn open where the bullet had entered, then a gouge in the chest plate but no bullet, it apparently ricocheting off and back out his shirt, his last second twist when he saw the barrel of the gun probably saving his arse from meeting his maker.

He took several tentative breaths, then started to walk back toward where the rendezvous would be taking place, and after a minute, broke out into a gentle jog, each step painful, but bearable.

Nothing broken, just bruised.

Nothing a few days on the beach in Spain wouldn't cure.

Then again, with the amount of sun and heat he'd experienced on this job, perhaps someplace cold and wet would be better.

England. Home.

He smiled when he realized how much he missed the weather everyone loved to complain about. It had only been a couple of months since he'd been home, but he really did miss it. He wasn't married, no kids, but he did have family he was close to, friends he missed.

And football.

He missed football. It wasn't the same kicking a ball around on the desert sand for a few minutes. He needed an open field, grass, greenery, and a score of his mates to play with to really open up the lungs and enjoy it.

He winced, and his hand darted to his ribcage, pressing tenderly.

Football will have to wait.

It took almost ten minutes before he reached the rendezvous point, and as he expected, they were already gone.

Good. That's what they should have done!

At least he didn't have to worry about them. Roger was a good man, and the fact he wasn't milling about indicated he had made it in time. He would take care of them, getting them to safety.

Now as for himself...

He spun around, pulling his knife from his belt as a foot scraped on the rock behind him. The man, covered in blood, was complaining in Arabic about the impossibility of finding the tomb in the dark, which clinched the friend or foe question for Leather. The next moment the knife was buried in the man's chest. Leather rushed forward, dipping down to pull the knife from the still gasping man's ribs, then with a swift upward motion, begun before the man's partner came into sight, he shoved the dripping blade into the second man's stomach, shoving up hard, then twisting, the man's only response a muffled, gurgling cry as his innards ran down Leather's hand, half buried in the man's stomach.

Which was when the other two men with them reacted.

Leather yanked his hand out of the second man's stomach and held him by the back of the collar as the others opened fire, Leather's meat shield blocking the shots as he ducked behind the twice dead man.

When both stopped to reload, foolishly finishing their clips at the same time, Leather exploded from behind the bloody stump of a corpse, and to the surprise of the closest man, buried his knife in the man's neck, then drawing his sidearm, put two bullets in the final man's chest, then one in his head just in case he was wearing body armor.

Leather continued forward, around the large rock that had concealed his would be attackers, but found no one else. He dropped to his knees and quickly used the sand to wash his hands of the blood and innards, then flipped his night vision goggles down, scanning the area for any heat signatures or movement.

Nothing.

He crawled to the edge of the ridge and looked down at the camp below. There were several dim green forms, most likely dying or recently dead men, their body heat quickly dissipating into the cool night air, and three bright figures, wandering around the area where the professor had set up his decoy find.

Brilliant move, Professor!

He pushed himself to his feet and jogged to the far ridge where his two dead comrades would be, keeping low the entire time, behind dunes and ridges when possible. In the darkness of the night, he almost tripped over their bodies. Two of their killers were dead, and looking to the left he could see the third man about ten feet away, having rolled down the dune.

He knelt down, prying the sniper rifle from his dead mate, trying not to look at the bloody stump where his head once was, the uncivilized bastards beheading him for no other reason than to show they were as primitive as he thought they were.

And now it was time for pay back.

He set up the weapon, reloaded, and adjusted his sights to target the three remaining men on the opposite ridge, but not before scanning the area behind him once again for any surprise guests.

Nothing.

He took aim at the first target, the one closest to cover, and aiming for his head, the more difficult and selfish shot, he fired, immediately chambering another round and acquiring the second target who stood frozen, wondering apparently what to do.

Let me help you with that decision.

Leather fired, removing the man's head.

Stay put!

The third man ran toward the trucks as Leather reloaded. Now that his target was moving, he checked the urge to remove his head, instead aiming lower and fired, removing a significant portion of the man's left shoulder. He dropped, writhing on the ground. Leather reloaded, then put the man out of his misery, despite part of him wishing unending pain on one of those responsible for the death of his mates.

He scanned the camp and surrounding area again and found no one remaining. Rising, he strode into the dig site, then into the central tent, dropping on the nearest cot.

And fell asleep.

Nubian Desert, Egypt, Approaching the University College London Dig Site
90 minutes later

"Jesus Christ!" exclaimed the pilot over the comm. "It looks like a warzone down there!"

Dawson stood up and made his way forward, pushing his head into the cockpit. Before he could ask what the pilot was so excited over, he saw for himself and gasped, the beam from the searchlight darting from body to body, nobody moving.

"Is anybody alive down there?" he asked, his chest tightening as he thought of all those kids they were there to rescue.

"Nothing's moving. Infrared shows only one possible live target in the central tent, but it's not moving either. The rest are all long dead or recently dead."

"Drop us on the north ridge, right there," said Dawson, pointing to a level area about half a mile from the center of the camp. "Do a perimeter sweep and report back if you find anything."

"Roger that," said the pilot, lowering the chopper as Dawson returned to the rear.

"Suit up, boys, we're going in. Looks like we might have one target in the central tent, the rest are dead. There might be others in the vicinity, so keep your eyes open. Spock, Atlas, Stucco, you're with me at the tent, rest of you fan out, secure the perimeter."

The helicopter touched down with a bounce, and one of the flight crew pulled open the side door. Dawson jumped out, sprinting toward the central tent, the footfalls behind him telling him his men were in hot pursuit, the sound spreading out to the sides indicating the perimeter positions being taken. He reached the central tent, Spock right behind him, the younger Stucco at his side, probably having to hold back a little to not show up his comrades.

Using hand signals, Dawson outlined the plan, then flipped down his night vision goggles, pushing through the outer flap then the inner, his head scanning the room, coming to rest on a body lying on a cot. Dawson advanced, aiming his weapon at the armed man's chest as Spock and Stucco cleared the rest of the tent, then joined Dawson.

Dawson flicked his night vision goggles up and turned on a flashlight, shining it at the man's face. Stucco kicked the bottom of the cot and the man stirred, pushing himself up on his elbows, squinting at the flashlight.

"Bloody hell, can't a man get a good night's sleep without being disturbed."

Dawson chuckled, recognizing that style bravado anywhere.

"I'm Sergeant White, United States Military. And you are?"

"Colonel Cameron Leather, Retired, Special Air Services, and if you're name's White, I'll wear a Liverpool jersey all next season."

Dawson chuckled, lowering his weapon and extending a hand. Leather took it, pulling himself to his feet, wincing.

"Are you okay?"

"Ricochet off the body armor. Probably bruised a rib or two. I'll live."

"What happened here?"

"Mate, it was pretty crazy shit, as you might say."

Dawson then was given the rundown on a group of imposters ordering an evacuation, then a second group of terrorists, also imposters, who arrived and engaged everybody. The first group and the professors had fought side by side for a reason Leather didn't know as he and his men had bugged out to set up sniper positions to try and save their charges.

The students had apparently left earlier and were hopefully safe in Cairo by now, or soon to be, the professors and their guests, along with one of Leather's men and a reporter, were presumably safe having escaped in a commandeered jeep brought back by two students.

And everyone else, attackers and allies, were dead.

They exited the tent, and Red approached, nodding to Leather.

"BD, we've taken photos of all the bodies, at least those with heads."

"Sorry about that," interjected Leather.

"It looks like they're all in Egyptian military uniforms, but no consistent patching. I'm guessing they were all in disguise. From the positioning of the bodies, it looks like two different groups of imposters engaged each other. We also found two Caucasians on the ridge behind us." Red looked at Leather. "I'm guessing they're yours?"

Leather nodded.

"Sorry about that."

Leather shook his head. "They died doing what they loved."

"So no sign of our students or professors?" asked Dawson.

"Negative, it looks like they all got away."

Dawson pursed his lips.

Thank God. Now where the hell are they?

He turned to Leather.

"Any idea where they might be?"

Leather pointed to the ridge where the jeep had been hidden.

"I suggest we pick up their trail over there. We can follow their tracks on foot, the chopper can go on ahead and hopefully spot them."

Dawson nodded.

"It's as good a plan as any."

He pointed at the trucks. "See if one of these is working."

Leather pointed at the trucks near the front of the camp. "Don't bother with those, we took them out. This one back here," he jerked his thumb over his shoulder, "might still be functioning. Needs a tire change though."

Dawson jerked his head toward it and Red motioned to Niner to join him. Moments later the engine roared to life, Red giving the thumbs up Niner began to change the tire. Dawson stuck his head inside the cabin.

"Red, you take Colonel Leather and your squad, follow the trail as best you can. My squad will take the chopper and scout out ahead to see if we can spot them. It's been a couple of hours, so they could be anywhere by now, but I'm guessing they'll try to stick to the roads so maybe we'll get lucky."

"Roger that, BD. Good hunting."

Dawson jumped down from the running board and signaled the chopper to power up as the team split into two squads.

So far this mission was turning out far simpler than he was used to with this group.

And he'd be perfectly content if he got through the night without firing a single shot.

Nubian Desert, Egypt, Ten miles from the University College London Dig Site

Everyone was huddled around the front of the jeep, the headlights providing valuable psychological relief from the reality of their situation. They were stuck in the middle of nowhere, not certain where they were, and Laura's satellite phone had been crushed in her pocket during the attack.

The jeep had a jerry can of water, and rationing had already begun. Acton knew that Greg would be doing everything he could from the university to find them, Laura's bosses would be doing the same. Reading's friend Rahim was apparently on his way, and once the students arrived at the UK Embassy, they would be taking action as well.

But it could be days before they'd be found.

Acton and Reading had already decided they'd walk back to the camp at first light and see what was going on. Hopefully their attackers would have left already, and they might be able to salvage a vehicle. Even if they couldn't, those searching for them would start at the camp, so being there was the most logical choice.

But that would have to wait until morning, and would be several hard hours of walking.

Right now he was more concerned with Chaney. He was still on his cot, wrapped in the sleeping bag, but the bleeding still hadn't stopped. It had at least slowed, but he was drifting in and out of consciousness.

And there was nothing they could do about it.

They had no supplies, and Chaney was the only one amongst them with anything beyond basic first aid training. In the morning they had agreed they would try and remove the bullet if they could retrieve supplies from the camp, but right now, in the dark, with nothing but fading headlamps and precious little water, they were hopeless.

Chaney stirred, and Acton saw Reading squeeze the man's hand, the two having been partners at Scotland Yard for years. Acton felt for him. *It must be like losing a son.* Chaney was many years Reading's junior, and Reading had been mentor to the young man for most of his career. The bond formed would be tight, like family, like soldiers, and losing someone like this, while on vacation, a thousand miles away from civilization, was senseless.

"Jim, he wants to talk to you."

Acton looked over, his eyebrows rising a little. He patted Laura on her shoulder as he rounded the jeep and sat down beside Chaney.

"What is it, my friend?"

"I have something I need to tell you," gasped Chaney, the act of talking apparently excruciating.

"It can wait. Help will be here soon. Save your strength."

Chaney shook his head.

"No, it's the reason I'm here. The Triarii—" He coughed, blood sputtering from his mouth. Acton wiped it away, exchanging a concerned glance with Reading.

Chaney sucked in several rather loud breaths, then grabbed Acton by the shoulder, pulling him down.

"They have one last favor to ask of you."

Acton wanted to tell Chaney to tell the Triarii to go to hell, but there was no time for that. His friend was dying, of that there was no doubt, and the mere act of delivering this message was killing him quicker. Better to have the message delivered without interruption, so the poor man could rest.

"What is it?"

"You must see the—" Chaney winced then dropped back into the cot, still. Acton checked Chaney's pulse, then felt his chest, and sighed, looking at Reading.

"He's just passed out. Probably for the best."

Reading was about to say something when Acton held up his finger. He thought he had heard something, but couldn't be sure. Laughter from Terrence and Jenny filled the air.

"Quiet!" he shouted, cutting off all conversation.

He cocked an ear, and soon they were all listening. It was faint at first, but after a few seconds, the sound became unmistakable.

"It's a helicopter!" exclaimed Terrence, immediately wincing and grabbing his ribs.

"If anybody's got a flashlight, start shining it up!" ordered Acton, who jumped into the driver's seat and turned on the flashers and began turning the headlights on and off.

Leather's man, Jeffrey, held up a flashlight, waving it at the night sky as the pounding of the blades became louder, then suddenly roared over the area as the chopper came over a nearby ridge, their jeep in an ancient river bed. A searchlight raced across the desert floor and came to rest on them as they all waved, tears of joy and relief flowing as the chopper came to rest several hundred feet away.

Acton climbed from the jeep, walking toward the chopper with Jeffrey, Laura and Reading, as half a dozen men jumped out, running toward them. Acton didn't care who they were, he just assumed that if they were in a chopper, they were friendlies.

Otherwise they were all about to die.

"Professor Palmer? Professor Acton?"

The voice sounded familiar, and as the two groups met Acton smiled in relief.

"Sergeant, thank God it's you!" he exclaimed as the Delta Force leader extended a hand.

"Professor. Care for a lift?"

Acton laughed, then became immediately serious.

"We've got an injured man here. He needs immediate medical care."

Dawson motioned to two of his men who rushed by them, then activated his comm.

"Prep for immediate medical evac. Find the nearest safe harbor, over."

The rotors, which had begun to power down, immediately roared back to life as Chaney was carried toward the chopper under the care of two of the Delta Force team.

"Everybody on the chopper!" ordered Dawson.

Acton turned to make sure no one was left behind, doing a mental tally, when he noticed the Colonel was missing.

"Where's Soliman?" he asked, looking around.

"I don't know," said Laura, stopping beside him. "I haven't seen him in a while."

"Well, hopefully his people find him soon."

Acton took one last look, then jumped into the chopper, the door slamming shut behind him as it lifted off.

He put his arm around Laura who laid her head on his shoulder, and within minutes they were both asleep, the exhaustion of the past couple of days finally overcoming them.

Ahmed Ragheb Street, Garden City, Cairo, Egypt
One block from the British Embassy

Stephen poked his head out from the alleyway, the massive city still dark and mostly asleep, the only life at this hour seeming to be police and city workers. They had arrived in the city without incident over an hour ago, but at the first sign of a police checkpoint, Stephen had jerked the wheel to the right and down an alleyway, the other vehicle following. After driving for several minutes, taking random turns, but still following the GPS on his phone held by Naomi, he had stopped in an alley and shutoff the engine.

"Why did you do that?" demanded Naomi. "They were police!"

"Remember what the professors said? Trust the army, not the police."

Naomi huffed, but said nothing as Stephen climbed out and was joined by the others.

"What happened?" asked Joel. "Why are we stopping?"

Stephen held out his iPhone, showing their location on a map.

"We're about a block from the embassy. It should be just around that corner," he explained, pointing to the end of the alley. "I suggest we check it out first, and make sure it's safe to approach."

"Why wouldn't it be safe?"

"What are you, daft?" erupted Naomi. "It's a Western embassy in a Muslim country! There could be protestors in front for all we know!"

Stephen held out a hand to calm her down, but secretly appreciated her backing. "I'll check it out," he said, "you all stay here."

He had jogged as quietly as he could to the end of the alley and peered around the corner. Nothing. Not a soul in sight. The bright lights of the gate of the embassy were tantalizingly close, and he was about to signal to the others to join him when a police vehicle turned into the alleyway from the opposite end, and turned on its lights.

"Run!" he yelled, his friends at first frozen in place, then Naomi grabbed two of them and pushed, rushing after them. Screams broke out as the vehicle rushed toward them, then screeched to a halt, the alleyway blocked by the two vehicles Stephen and his friends had just arrived in.

Stephen watched in horror as four men jumped out, weapons at the ready. Naomi reached him first and he pointed toward the gate.

"Go!" he yelled, and she didn't hesitate, instead sprinting toward the gate, the rest of the students following. Gunfire erupted from the alleyway and Stephen ducked around the side as the slowest of them rounded the corner. They were now in the street, racing across it, a rag tag group of crying and screaming young adults, their yells incoherent to anyone. The guards on the other side of the gates raised their weapons, ordering them to halt, but no one heard.

They slammed into the bars, shaking them, pleads of "Let us in!" and "We're British!" falling on deaf ears as the police raced around the corner, their weapons in full view.

Stephen hit the gate, his passport extended and pushed it into view of one of the guards.

"We're British subjects who were victims of a terrorist attack. We require sanctuary!" he said in his calmest voice. The man activated his radio and a moment later the gate rolled open, the students rushing forward, the footfalls of the approaching police echoing through the empty streets.

Stephen pushed his friends through, waiting until the last one had made it before he himself stepped through and onto British soil. He felt a hand grab him from behind and begin to yank him back onto the street.

The sounds of weapons around him, their safeties being flicked off, filled the air as the world closed in around him. He stretched his arms out, grabbing onto the gate on either side as someone continued to drag him back to Egyptian soil.

"Halt!" yelled a voice. "This is British soil, and we are within our rights to engage you!"

The grip loosened, and Stephen yanked himself away as another set of hands pulled on his shirt, toppling him into the embassy grounds as the gates rumbled closed. He flipped over and saw the angry glare of the Egyptian police, the weapons of his countrymen still trained on them until the moment the gate slammed shut.

Heels on cobblestone clipped through the night as Stephen was helped to his feet. A woman rushed up to them, her arms extended, touching each of them as she arrived in their midst.

"I'm Lois MacLeod. Are you the students from University College London?" she asked finally, after seemingly confirming they weren't apparitions.

"Yes," replied Stephen. "Have you heard from Professor Palmer? Are they okay?"

She smiled at him, then cocked her head toward the embassy.

"Why don't you come with me, I have a phone call for you."

They quickly made their way to the embassy, and it wasn't until they were inside the building itself that Stephen began to feel safe. They entered a side office, everyone crowding inside, and Lois activated the speaker on the desk phone.

"I have someone who wants to talk to you," she said.

There was no reply, and Stephen tentatively leaned forward.

"Hello?"

"Stephen, is that you?"

Professor Palmer's voice was the sweetest thing he had ever heard. There were cries and cheers from everyone, and the next words were lost to history, but he didn't care. He just dropped into the nearest chair, and sobbed in relief, the job he hadn't wanted, the job meant for Terrence, now complete.

They were all safe.

USS James E. Williams, Red Sea
Medical Bay

Reading sat beside his friend and partner. It was hard to think of Chaney as his former partner at a time like this, despite it being a couple of years since they had officially worked a case together. But at this moment, with his friend clinging to life, he had never felt closer, and more desperate, for anyone to live.

It reminded him of the Falklands, the Battle of Mount Harriet, and the aftermath as he and his comrades mourned the death of two of their mates, and prayed for the recovery of the over two dozen wounded, some severely.

A doctor entered the room, and Reading looked up, waiting as vitals were checked, and charts read.

"What's the prognosis, Doc?"

"Looks like he'll live," said the greying Lt. Commander. "The question now is whether or not he'll come out of this coma. Just give him time. I've seen men far worse than this come out of these things, so there's lots of reason for optimism."

Reading nodded, looking back at his friend, when a Seaman rushed into the room.

"Sir, you have a phone call."

Reading pointed at himself. "Me?"

"Yes, sir." The young man grabbed a phone off the wall and hit a few buttons. "You can take it here, sir."

Reading stood up and took the phone.

Who in the blazes would be calling me here?

267

"Reading here."

"Hugh, my friend! This is Rahim! Where the bloody hell are you?"

Reading breathed a sigh of relief that it wasn't more bad news, a smile spreading across his face as the doctor and Seaman left the room.

"I'm on some American ship in the Red Sea. We were rescued by some—" He stopped himself before he broadcast the fact US forces had been on Egyptian soil, then realized it was pointless. The fact the chopper had to be refueled several times on the mission in mid-air meant clearances had been obtained. "—friends," he completed.

"Thank Allah, my friend. I thought the worst when we arrived. Everyone is dead, it is quite the horrible scene."

"Apparently there are two British citizens amongst the dead," said Reading, recalling Leather's debrief. "Please make certain they are treated with respect, and returned to the British Embassy as soon as possible."

"Absolutely, my friend, we have already found them. Are you okay? You are uninjured?"

"I'm fine, no need to worry about me."

"And your friends?"

Reading felt a lump form in his throat as he stared across the room at his friend.

"Chaney took a hit. He's in a coma. They think he'll make it."

"I will pray for him, my friend."

"Please do that."

"I must go, my friend, I will contact you when I return to Cairo."

"Do that, and thanks for coming for us."

"Any time!"

The call ended, and Reading hung the handset up on the wall, returning to Chaney's side.

And prayed harder than he ever had before.

USS James E. Williams, Red Sea
Segregated Common Area

Dawson sat with his squad as they all waited for Red's team to arrive, a second chopper having been dispatched to pick them up when they had had to do the emergency evac of the British cop. Nobody was worried, it was a routine retrieval, but until every boot that had hit the ground returned, they waited, saying nothing except watching the newsfeed of what had happened while they were away.

And it was disturbing.

The attacks were over, at least the large scale ones. Search and rescue operations were still underway in some cases, and the cleanup was beginning in others. Presidents and Prime Ministers the world over had taken to the air waves to urge calm, and to promise justice, but the people were furious.

They knew justice was impossible. The perpetrators were already mostly dead, the leadership protected behind the walls of silence of Muslim countries secretly pleased with the actions, though publicly condemning them, while couching things in terms suggesting the West had asked for it due to its overreaction to 9/11.

And this time, who would we attack?

There was no Taliban regime in power, providing training camps and funding to a specific group. Which was the problem with terrorism. It quite often wasn't state sponsored, and if it were, it was difficult to prove. There were no more easy targets to take out. And this time, the nationalities were mostly Egyptian as opposed to Saudi, a supposed ally in the Middle East. The US and its allies could hardly invade Egypt or bomb it in retaliation. All they could do was demand action by its government, a Muslim Brotherhood government that probably tacitly supported the terrorist actions.

This was the new Middle East, applauded at the outset by all, now feared by those who understood what had truly happened.

The frustrations of the populations in New York, Los Angeles, Paris, London, Toronto, Rio and others, was palpable, with random attacks on Muslims, fire bombings of mosques, and protests in the streets demanding the deportation of Muslims, reactions far worse than anything seen after 9/11.

Last time they killed people, turning the Twin Towers into symbols of America's loss. This time they killed our symbols, our history, our culture.

And this time none of the morons claiming it was an inside job had anything to cling to. Dawson only hoped the protests would calm down, the retaliations stop, and the discourse begin sooner rather than later. His greatest fear was troops on the street, and if law and order couldn't be maintained, martial law could be declared.

And once that slippery slope was started upon, Western democracies as we know them may become a thing of the past, the terrorists winning in the end.

The door opened and Red stepped in with a grin on his face.

"It's about fuckin' time!" exclaimed Niner, jumping up and giving each man a thumping hug as they came through the door. Dawson stood and gave his friend a firm handshake then pushed him onto the other side of the couch he had been occupying.

"Problems?"

"Nope. Just had to duck a group of Egyptian police that arrived at some point, but other than that, nothing."

Dawson nodded. "They were apparently friendlies, requested by that Interpol guy, Reading."

"See, you say it right all the time."

"What's that?"

"The Interpol guy. Every time I read a report I say 'Reading', but it's actually pronounced 'Redding'. How the hell do you keep that straight in your head?"

"Umm, I've got more than two neurons firing?"

Red booted him in the shoulder, Dawson unable to make the block in time.

"Didn't you ever play Monopoly?" asked Dawson, massaging his shoulder.

"Who didn't?"

"Well, it's pronounced 'Redding' Railroad."

Red's eyebrows narrowed.

"It is?"

Dawson nodded.

"Huh. I guess I shouldn't have corrected Bryson when he was calling it 'Redding'. He said he was at a friend's house and that's what they called it."

"What did you say?"

"I said his friend was an idiot."

"That's nice. Who was the friend?"

Red laughed.

"You."

Dawson chuckled and pulled his knife half way from the sheath when the door opened.

"Call for you, sir, you can take it here." The Seaman pointed at the wall and Dawson nodded. A few keys were pressed, and the phone handed over.

Must be the Colonel.

"Sergeant Dawson here."

"I thought it was Mr. White?"

Dawson smiled, immediately recognizing the voice of CIA Special Agent Dylan Kane.

"What can I do for you?"

"Oh, ask not what you can do for me, but ask what I can do for you."

"Okay, what can you do for me?"

"Care for a little payback?"

Dawson smiled, staring at the television screen showing the ruins of the Statue of Liberty.

"Absolutely."

Mahmoud Bassiouny Street, Cairo, Egypt

Two days later

Imam Khalil sat in the back of the black 1982 Mercedes 380SEL provided by one of his supporters, of whom today there were many more than last week. It was a poorly kept secret that he had been behind the coordinated attacks that had brought the infidels to their knees, but word was out, and accolades continued to pour in, even from various governments around the world, though through discrete backchannels.

Today, nobody could be seen in support of the attacks, as the Western militaries were desperate for a target to hammer into the stone age, but over time, when things had calmed, he would be a hero, acclaimed by over a billion of his brethren for his boldness. He would need to remain in hiding for the rest of his life, however that was a sacrifice he would be willing to make. Already he had been offered sanctuary in a palace in Saudi Arabia, where he would live out a life of pampered luxury, with all the modern conveniences available to the richest of the rich.

And women of all shapes, sizes and colors.

It would be paradise on earth, a gift for sure from Allah himself.

The driver slammed his fist into the steering wheel and looked in the rearview mirror.

"I'm sorry, Imam, but the traffic at this time of day, it is terrible!"

Khalil waved off the man's concerns with a flick of his wrist.

"It is of no concern. We have air conditioning, plenty of gasoline, and no set time for our arrival. Let the people enjoy their market."

"I think it is a little busier than usual, Imam," said the driver, looking at the bustling streets and sidewalks.

"Indeed," smiled Khalil. "There seems to be a spring in their step that was missing last week."

A motorcycle revved its engine behind them, Khalil ignoring it, the driver taking a glance in his rearview mirror, then side mirror. It pulled up beside them, the driver, his black helmet and visor completely blocking his face, stopping, then looking at the driver, then Khalil.

Khalil felt his chest tighten slightly, his left leg beginning to push himself away from the window when the motorcycle's engine revved again, and shot ahead into traffic, then out of sight.

He breathed a sigh.

Perhaps I should get to Saudi Arabia as soon as possible.

Red banked right, racing into the traffic circle and out of sight of Imam Khalil's vehicle, as he spoke into his comm. "Occupant confirmed. One driver, left hand side, one passenger, positively ID'd as Mahmoud Khalil, rear seat, left side. They're stuck in traffic, looks like they'll be there for at least a few minutes, over."

"Roger that," came Dawson's voice over the comm. "Proceed as planned."

Red pulled into an alleyway about half a mile from their target, and waited. His part of the plan was over, but he was to remain in the area for backup in case it was needed. This was a precision plan, devised by Big Dog and the CIA guy whose name he had never been told.

The intel had arrived quickly, the moron Khalil a little too vocal in his boasting, and using Echelon and various other tracking methods available to the CIA and the Pentagon, they had quickly found him in a well-secured compound, awaiting a transfer to a nonexistent palace in Saudi Arabia.

Pathetic hypocrite.

The man was willing to let his followers die for their cause in exchange for a paradise filled with virgins, but lacked the courage to die for his convictions here, instead jumping at the opportunity of living in decadence offered to him by a Sheik in the Saudi royal household, who owed a favor to the CIA, lest a certain set of photos of him with several young men should surface on the Internet.

Red lifted the visor slightly to scratch his nose, then flipped it back down with a smack as his anger grew. He recalled one of their briefings for a recon mission a few years back, where a terrorist was suspected of frequenting a rub and tug parlor run by Muslims in Detroit. But these were devout Muslims, and having sex outside of marriage was against the Koran, and an offense to Allah.

No problem!

There was an Imam on site to marry you to the girl, then you'd do your business, and then he'd divorce you on the way out.

Problem solved.

Hypocrisy intact.

Bigamy laws be damned.

Red sucked in a deep breath and let it out slowly, calming his racing heart.

"Moving in now," said Dawson over the comm.

Red gripped the handles of his bike a little harder.

Time for revenge.

Dawson gunned the engine, speeding along the left side of the cars, deftly avoiding the pedestrians, most seemingly oblivious to the dangers surrounding them, but also managing to somehow always avoid getting hit. Part of him thought it was a game between the traffic and the pedestrians, the latter pretending to not see the traffic, the former pretending to not see the pedestrians. And always, at the last moment, someone would lose the game of chicken, avoiding the collision, and smartly, that was almost always the pedestrian.

When Kane had called with the offer for some payback, he had jumped at it, receiving immediate clearance from Colonel Clancy, and insertion into Cairo the next day with several of his team. They knew where Khalil was, and thanks to their false offer, knew where he'd be heading. They just had to wait.

It was Red's shift that alerted them to the move, satellite imagery from several specially tasked birds, plus a UAV confirming the mass murderer entering the vehicle.

Within minutes they were in place, the plan simple, yet precise timing necessary. There were quite a few variables beyond their control, but the key to a good plan was minimizing those variables, and having contingencies in place should something unexpected happen.

But as expected, the Imam had become stuck in traffic, a completely expected, planned for, and indeed hoped for, occurrence.

"Approaching the vehicle now," said Dawson through his comm, slowing down as he approached. At the last second, he slowed down dramatically, almost coming to a stop, leaning the bike toward the vehicle. Niner, on the rear of the bike, leaned over and placed a magnetic shaped charge on the rear driver side door, patted Dawson on the shoulder, and Dawson gunned it toward the traffic circle that provided five separate means of escape.

It's like God's on our side today.

"Charge placed," he said as he banked into the mess of traffic.

"Roger that," came Spock's voice over the comm. "Stand by."

Spock, sitting on his motorcycle about fifty feet back, watched for an opening in the crowd, their aim to minimize, if not prevent entirely, civilian casualties. They had placed a shaped charge on the door which would direct the blast inward, reducing shrapnel and the concussive force that would be ejected toward the pedestrians.

But getting an opening where the civilians weren't right beside the car was proving a challenge.

Then he saw one point at the charge, waving over a friend.

"The charge has been spotted. I'm moving in."

He revved the engine, gunning the bike toward the pedestrians beginning to gather around, pressing the button for his horn as he gained speed. People began to jump out of his way, the time honored dance between pedestrian and vehicle forgotten. He laid on the horn, now reaching almost thirty miles per hour in this last ditch effort to save the op.

He reached the rear bumper and the crowd jumped back, shaking their fists at him, and he pressed the trigger.

There was a large roar behind him, then screams, as the charge blew a hole through the door, and in his side mirror, he could see those closest the blast laying on the ground, the traditional white robes appearing soiled, but not bloody.

"Explosive triggered," he reported needlessly as he turned into the traffic circle, the few who had given chase left behind as he raced through traffic and to his exchange point where he'd dump the motorcycle, and switch to a diplomatic vehicle.

"Moving in," came the voice of the CIA operator over his comm.

Payback's a bitch.

CIA Special Agent Dylan Kane rushed forward, pushing aside the gathering crowd. He had been following the vehicle on his own motorcycle when it had been trapped in traffic and the plan set in motion. He had passed Khalil's vehicle, parking his bike near the entrance to the traffic circle, then quickly made his way back to the Mercedes as it crawled through traffic. Keeping pace with it had been easy, and his gentle manipulations of the crowds had helped keep their casualties to simple cuts and bruises.

But now it was time for the money shot.

He raced around a group of bystanders, most pushing back from the vehicle in fear of another explosion. Kane jumped inside, drawing his weapon, suppressor in place. The driver, still in shock, spun around at the new arrival, and Kane put a bullet in his head, splattering his brains across the shattered windshield.

He grabbed Khalil, pulling him upright, the moaning man covered in blood, but still alive. Kane grabbed him by the face, shaking his head back and forth until he had his attention.

"Who are you?" asked Khalil in Arabic.

"I'm a messenger," replied Kane in perfect Arabic.

"From who?"

"From the American people. They say hi."

Kane fired a shot into each knee cap, then one into the groin, another into Khalil's stomach, then his neck, each shot eliciting a cry of pain. Though he'd like to prolong the torture, he didn't have time, the crowd outside getting louder.

He pulled the man's face closer and placed his Glock against the man's temple.

"See you in hell."

He squeezed, and Khalil's eyes widened as the bullet sped through his skull, turning his brain matter into mush, then exploding out the other side. Kane threw him down on the seat, took a quick photo with his phone, then jumped out the other side of the car, walking with purpose through the crowds as if he belonged there, some nearby looking and pointing at him. He ducked into an alleyway and climbed on his bike, roaring away from the gridlocked street as he pushed the helmet on his head.

"Mission accomplished," he said through the comm, marking the end of America's first counterstrike against the horror struck against it and its allies.

Cairo International Airport, Cairo, Egypt
Later that day

James Acton sat in the international passengers' waiting area, Laura on one side, Reading on the other, their students spread out across several rows. It had been a grueling several days. Chaney had been airlifted back to England, and was still in a coma, leaving Acton to wonder what the message was he had tried to deliver, and leaving his friend, Hugh, to wonder whether or not his partner was going to make it or not.

Apparently there had been complications on the flight, and Chaney had nearly died. They had managed to save him, but the coma they had been optimistic he would recover from, was now thought worse.

Again, only time would tell.

Acton looked at his friend and could see the worry on his face, his stare already in London. Laura's head was on his shoulder, herself in a deep sleep at the relief all her students were safe.

He himself was wired. He was exhausted, but couldn't sleep. His mind was preoccupied with the dig site, and what they had left behind. The world had forgotten the discovery, side tracked by the terrorist attacks and its aftermath, but he was left wondering if their discovery was still intact, or had it been destroyed.

And it was driving him nuts.

He had told Laura they should return immediately, at least he himself, and she had called him daft.

And she was right.

If it was destroyed, there was nothing he could do. And if it wasn't, the chances of anyone finding it again were slim. Then his heart leapt into his throat as he remembered the reporters, and the fact they had footage of where the tomb actually was.

He gripped the arms of the chair he was in, his shoulders tensing.

"What's wrong?" mumbled Laura, awakening.

"Nothing, go back to sleep."

Laura sat up, looking at her watch.

"When are we boarding?"

"Any minute now," he replied, looking at the board in front of them.

"Okay, I'm going to let everybody know. There's no way I'm letting anybody get left behind."

She stood up and Acton watched as she made the rounds then he froze, standing up suddenly.

"What is it?" asked Reading, snapped from his reverie.

"I thought—"

But Acton stopped himself as his suspicion was confirmed. Walking past their seating area was his former student, now CIA operative, Dylan Kane, his secret life revealed to him only recently when Kane had paid him a visit at the university. It was a reunion, and a conversation, Acton would never forget, the secret shame confessed to him filling his own dreams with horror filled images.

I can only imagine what the poor kid is going through.

Kane made momentary eye contact with him, his left eye almost imperceptibly winking, and continued on. Acton immediately realized he must be undercover, and dropped back down into his seat.

Word had hit the newswires that the Imam responsible for the attacks, some guy named Khalil, had been assassinated earlier this morning. They had all rejoiced at the news, and now Acton, resisting with all his might the urge to look behind him, wondered if his former student had been that assassin.

And if he was, he would be sure to congratulate him, should he ever see him again.

Reading sighed, causing Acton to return his attention to his friend.

"What's wrong?"

"Hmm?"

"You sighed audibly, my friend. That's never a good sign."

Reading gave a weak smile, still staring ahead, his arms crossed over his chest, feet stretched out in front of him.

"I've been thinking of retiring."

Acton's eyebrows shot up. *Retiring?* It had never occurred to him that Reading would be the type.

"Really?"

"Yeah, I'm getting too old for this shite."

"Bullshit. You're what, fifty?"

"Fifty three."

"Fifty three, you've still got a good six, maybe eight months left in you!"

Reading glanced at him, cocking an eyebrow.

"Piss off."

Acton laughed and elbowed him.

"In all seriousness. Fifty three isn't old. Besides, you're doing desk duty now."

Reading unfolded his arms and twisted to face Acton.

"You do realize that my job may be officially behind a desk, but since I've met you two, I've seen more action that I did in the Falklands? And that was a bloody war!"

Acton feigned being hurt, grabbing his chest.

"What are you saying? You don't want to be friends anymore?"

Reading huffed, straightening himself in the chair.

"It would make life easier."

"But not as exciting. And you know damned well you'll come charging to our rescue if you hear we're in trouble. You're not the type to sit back."

Reading grunted again.

"Always been my damned problem."

"What, having a conscience?"

He nodded, crossing his arms again.

"Fucking conscience." He sighed. "Maybe I'll stick it out a little longer." He turned back to face Acton. "But the next time you invite me to the fucking desert, I'm saying no. And if I *ever* figure out how the hell you manipulated me into going this time, I'll put out an international arrest warrant on you if you try it again!"

Acton raised his hands in mock surrender.

"How's my dig in the Andes sound?" he asked out of the corner of his mouth.

"Bloody cold."

Nubian Desert, Egypt, University College London Dig Site
Several months later

James Acton jumped down from the truck, then held out his hand for Laura. She took it, and far more gracefully than him, stepped down from the running board. They stepped forward, hand in hand, as they surveyed the remains of the dig site together. Laura's hand was on her mouth, her eyes glassed over at what she saw, and he had to admit, it was hard for him to look at.

It was a wreck.

A warzone.

The shot-up vehicles were still here, their tents were in various states of standing, most having blown down or away with no one left to mind the stakes, and their dig site was covered in sand, the desert quick to reclaim all it had once possessed.

Their defensive positions still showed some signs of the attack, bullet casings visible here and there, but the blood was gone, the bodies taken away, and as they stepped forward, the excited shouts of their students, every one of which had insisted on returning with them, filled the air as they rushed forward to see the state of all their hard work.

Four tents stood alone, well maintained, its occupants all sitting out front in chairs. Acton smiled and waved at Leather and his men as they got up and walked toward them, having arrived two days before to scout the site and confirm its safety.

Leather shook their hands, then turned to face the dig site with them.

"What do you think?" he asked.

"We'll rebuild it, and start again. It won't take long," replied Laura.

"We didn't touch anything, figured you'd want to catalog everything."

Acton blurted out the question he was dying to ask.

"What about the tomb? Cleopatra's tomb?"

Leather frowned.

"That we did check out." He pointed toward the hill. "You'll want to see this."

He strode out ahead, briskly walking toward the ridge containing the tomb's entrance, Acton and Laura, then the students, following. It had been months and Acton was dying to know what had happened. It was a career making find, and all they had were photos and video, but nothing to prove what they had found was real.

The archeology community was desperate for news as well, and everyone feared that grave robbers would loot the find. The Egyptian police had agreed to place guards there, but after a few weeks of no activity, they had abandoned the post without telling anyone.

They reached the site and Acton saw the canvas had been moved aside, and several ropes lay nearby.

"Lower me," he said, and Leather nodded, grabbing one of the ropes and tossing one end into the hole. He and several students held the rope tight as Acton stepped over the edge, dangling in midair. He lowered himself quickly, then snapped on his flashlight and was about to head toward the tomb when Laura called down.

"Don't you dare look without me!"

He stopped and steadied the rope as she scrambled down. Turning on her own flashlight, they aimed their beams at the massive cover stone they had moved out of place, and found it still laying on its side. As they rounded the massive piece of rock, their lights played into the tomb, and Laura cried out.

Acton stifled his own cry, a pit cleaved from his stomach that almost made him vomit right then and there, he instead managing to stumble into the tomb they had discovered that fateful day.

A tomb that was completely empty, save a piece of paper sitting in the center of the room.

Acton leaned over and picked it up, then breathed a sigh of relief.

"What is it?" asked Laura.

He turned the paper so she could see, shining his flashlight on it, revealing the symbol for The Brotherhood, and a handwritten note.

There's nothing you Westerners love more than a good conspiracy. Enjoy. S.

Laura began to laugh, and Acton hugged her, he himself getting caught up in the moment, as relief, disappointment and anger washed over them all at once. Their find was gone, they were left with no proof it had ever really existed, they would be called frauds, and perhaps laughed out of their profession.

But the mystery of Antony and Cleopatra, one of the greatest love stories in history, would go on, their whereabouts unknown, their bodies interred together in peace, and undisturbed.

Under the watchful eye of The Brotherhood.

THE END

ACKNOWLEDGEMENTS

As usual I had a blast writing this book. Professor James Acton and his friends become more and more familiar with each adventure, and more is revealed about their characters and pasts as they evolve. Introducing new characters is also a treat, especially if they are to become recurring. Terrence had a small part in Brass Monkey, yet in this one he takes a more prominent role, and since I didn't kill him, there's a good chance he'll appear again.

And Dylan Kane makes his first appearance in an Acton novel, which was fun to work in. If you want to read more about him, check out Rogue Operator, the first installment in the new Special Agent Dylan Kane Thrillers that is set in the James Acton universe, and has become a huge hit.

The idea for discovering Cleopatra's tomb once again comes back to one of those spitballing sessions, and from the research that comes with these novels. I knew I wanted the book to take place in Egypt, and to involve the discovery of something "cool". The idea of finding a pharaoh's tomb came up for discussion, and I sent my researcher (my retired dad!) off to look for a "cool sounding" Pharaoh.

That's when he came back with the stunner that Cleopatra's tomb had never been found. As we dug deeper, we realized her story, and that of Antony's, was fascinating, and their deaths marked the end of Ancient Egypt as we know it.

And left a tantalizing mystery behind.

A mystery that demanded to be solved by Professor Acton.

As usual there are people to thank. My wife, daughter, friends and parents, especially my dad who did a huge amount of research for this one. Other names to mention are Ian Kennedy for researching the effects of high explosive blasts on the human body, as well as Richard Jenner.

And of course to you, thanks for reading!

ABOUT THE AUTHOR

 J. Robert Kennedy is the author of eleven international best sellers, including the smash hit James Acton Thrillers series, the first installment of which, The Protocol, has been on the best sellers list since its release, including a three month run at number one. In addition to the other novels from this series, Brass Monkey, Broken Dove, The Templar's Relic (also a number one best seller), Flags of Sin and The Arab Fall, he has written the international best sellers Rogue Operator, Depraved Difference, Tick Tock, The Redeemer and The Turned. Robert spends his time in Ontario, Canada with his family.

Visit Robert's website at www.jrobertkennedy.com for the latest news and contact information.

The Protocol
A James Acton Thriller
Book #1

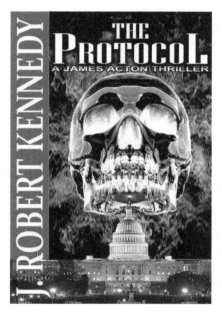

For two thousand years the Triarii have protected us, influencing history from the crusades to the discovery of America. Descendent from the Roman Empire, they pervade every level of society, and are now in a race with our own government to retrieve an ancient artifact thought to have been lost forever.

Caught in the middle is archaeology professor James Acton, relentlessly hunted by the elite Delta Force, under orders to stop at nothing to possess what he has found, and the Triarii, equally determined to prevent the discovery from falling into the wrong hands.

With his students and friends dying around him, Acton flees to find the one person who might be able to help him, but little does he know he may actually be racing directly into the hands of an organization he knows nothing about...

J. ROBERT KENNEDY

Brass Monkey

A James Acton Thriller

Book #2

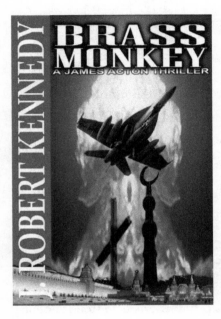

A nuclear missile, lost during the Cold War, is now in play--the most public spy swap in history, with a gorgeous agent the center of international attention, triggers the end-game of a corrupt Soviet Colonel's twenty five year plan. Pursued across the globe by the Russian authorities, including a brutal Spetsnaz unit, those involved will stop at nothing to deliver their weapon, and ensure their pay day, regardless of the terrifying consequences.

When Laura Palmer confronts a UNICEF group for trespassing on her Egyptian archaeological dig site, she unwittingly stumbles upon the ultimate weapons deal, and becomes entangled in an international conspiracy that sends her lover, archeology Professor James Acton, racing to Egypt with the most unlikely of allies, not only to rescue her, but to prevent the start of a holy war that could result in Islam and Christianity wiping each other out.

From the bestselling author of Depraved Difference and The Protocol comes Brass Monkey, a thriller international in scope, certain to offend some, and stimulate debate in others. Brass Monkey pulls no punches in confronting the conflict between two of the world's most powerful, and divergent, religions, and the terrifying possibilities the future may hold if left unchecked.

Broken Dove

A James Acton Thriller

Book #3

With the Triarii in control of the Roman Catholic Church, an organization founded by Saint Peter himself takes action, murdering one of the new Pope's operatives. Detective Chaney, called in by the Pope to investigate, disappears, and, to the horror of the Papal staff sent to inform His Holiness, they find him missing too, the only clue a secret chest, presented to each new pope on the eve of their election, since the beginning of the Church.

Interpol Agent Reading, determined to find his friend, calls Professors James Acton and Laura Palmer to Rome to examine the chest and its forbidden contents, but before they can arrive, they are intercepted by an organization older than the Church, demanding the professors retrieve an item stolen in ancient Judea in exchange for the lives of their friends.

All of your favorite characters from The Protocol return to solve the most infamous kidnapping in history, against the backdrop of a two thousand year old battle pitting ancient foes with diametrically opposed agendas.

From the internationally bestselling author of Depraved Difference and The Protocol comes Broken Dove, the third entry in the smash hit James Acton Thrillers series, where J. Robert Kennedy reveals a secret concealed by the Church for almost 1200 years, and a fascinating interpretation of what the real reason behind the denials might be.

The Templar's Relic

A James Acton Thriller

Book #4

The Church Helped Destroy the Templars. Will a twist of fate let them get their revenge 700 years later?

The Vault must be sealed, but a construction accident leads to a miraculous discovery--an ancient tomb containing four Templar Knights, long forgotten, on the grounds of the Vatican. Not knowing who they can trust, the Vatican requests Professors James Acton and Laura Palmer examine the find, but what they discover, a precious Islamic relic, lost during the Crusades, triggers a set of events that shake the entire world, pitting the two greatest religions against each other.

Join Professors James Acton and Laura Palmer, INTERPOL Agent Hugh Reading, Scotland Yard DI Martin Chaney, and the Delta Force Bravo Team as they race against time to defuse a worldwide crisis that could quickly devolve into all-out war.

At risk is nothing less than the Vatican itself, and the rock upon which it was built.

From J. Robert Kennedy, the author of six international bestsellers including Depraved Difference and The Protocol, comes The Templar's Relic, the fourth entry in the smash hit James Acton Thrillers series, where once again Kennedy takes history and twists it to his own ends, resulting in a heart pounding thrill ride filled with action, suspense, humor and heartbreak.

Flags of Sin
A James Acton Thriller
Book #5

Archaeology Professor James Acton simply wants to get away from everything, and relax. A trip to China seems just the answer, and he and his fiancée, Professor Laura Palmer, are soon on a flight to Beijing.

But while boarding, they bump into an old friend, Delta Force Command Sergeant Major Burt Dawson, who surreptitiously delivers a message that they must meet the next day, for Dawson knows something they don't.

China is about to erupt into chaos.

Foreign tourists and diplomats are being targeted by unknown forces, and if they don't get out of China in time, they could be caught up in events no one had seen coming.

J. Robert Kennedy, the author of eight international best sellers, including the smash hit James Acton Thrillers, takes history once again and turns it on its head, sending his reluctant heroes James Acton and Laura Palmer into harm's way, to not only save themselves, but to try and save a country from a century old conspiracy it knew nothing about.

The Arab Fall
A James Acton Thriller
Book #6

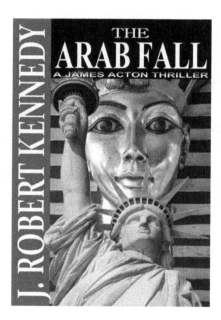

THE GREATEST ARCHEOLOGICAL DISCOVERY SINCE KING TUT'S TOMB IS ABOUT TO BE DESTROYED!

The Arab Spring has happened and Egypt has yet to calm down, but with the dig site on the edge of the Nubian Desert, a thousand miles from the excitement, Professor Laura Palmer and her fiancé Professor James Acton return with a group of students, and two friends: Interpol Special Agent Hugh Reading, and Scotland Yard Detective Inspector Martin Chaney. It's work for the professors and their students, and a vacation for the two law enforcement officers, but as Reading quickly discovers, he and the desert don't mix, and Chaney is preoccupied with a message he has been asked to deliver to the professor by his masters in the Triarii.

But an accidental find by Chaney may lead to the greatest archaeological discovery since the tomb of King Tutankhamen, perhaps even greater. And when news of it spreads, it reaches the ears of a group hell-bent on the destruction of all idols and icons, their mere existence considered blasphemous to Islam.

As chaos hits the major cities of the world in a coordinated attack, unbeknownst to the professors, students and friends, they are about to be faced with one of the most difficult decisions of their lives.

Stay and protect the greatest archaeological find of our times, or save themselves and their students from harm, leaving the find to be destroyed by fanatics determined to wipe it from the history books.

From J. Robert Kennedy, the author of eleven international bestsellers including Rogue Operator and The Protocol, comes The Arab Fall, the sixth entry in the smash hit James Acton Thrillers series, where Kennedy once again takes events from history and today's headlines, and twists them into a heart pounding adventure filled with humor and heartbreak, as one of their own is left severely wounded, fighting for their life.

The Turned

Zander Varga, Vampire Detective

Book #1

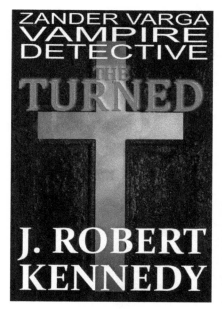

Zander has relived his wife's death at the hands of vampires every day for almost three hundred years, his perfect memory a curse of becoming one of The Turned—infecting him their final heinous act after her murder.

Nineteen year-old Sydney Winter knows Zander's secret, a secret preserved by the women in her family for four generations. But with her mother in a coma, she's thrust into the front lines, ahead of her time, to fight side-by-side with Zander.

And she wouldn't change a thing.

She loves the excitement, she loves the danger.

And she loves Zander.

But it's a love that will have to go unrequited, because Zander has only one thing on his mind. And it's been the same thing for over two hundred years.

Revenge.

But today, revenge will have to wait, because Zander Varga, Private Detective, has a new case. A woman's husband is missing. The police aren't interested. But Zander is. Something doesn't smell right, and he's determined to find out why.

From J. Robert Kennedy, the internationally bestselling author of The Protocol and Depraved Difference, comes his sixth novel, The Turned, a terrifying story that in true Kennedy fashion takes a completely new twist on the origin of vampires, tying it directly to a well-known moment in history. Told from the perspective of Zander Varga and his assistant, Sydney Winter, The Turned is loaded with action, humor, terror and a centuries long love that must eventually be let go.

Depraved Difference

A Detective Shakespeare Mystery

Book #1

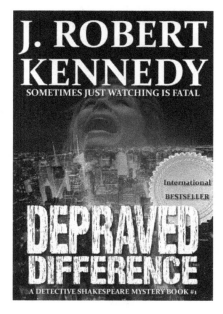

Would you help, would you run, or would you just watch?

When a young woman is brutally assaulted by two men on the subway, her cries for help fall on the deaf ears of onlookers too terrified to get involved, her misery ended with the crushing stomp of a steel-toed boot. A cellphone video of her vicious murder, callously released on the Internet, its popularity a testament to today's depraved society, serves as a trigger, pulled a year later, for a killer.

Emailed a video documenting the final moments of a woman's life, entertainment reporter Aynslee Kai, rather than ask why the killer chose her to tell the story, decides to capitalize on the opportunity to further her career. Assigned to the case is Hayden Eldridge, a detective left to learn the ropes by a disgraced partner, and as videos continue to follow victims, he discovers they were all witnesses to the vicious subway murder a year earlier, proving sometimes just watching is fatal.

From the author of The Protocol and Brass Monkey, Depraved Difference is a fast-paced murder suspense novel with enough laughs, heartbreak, terror and twists to keep you on the edge of your seat, then knock you flat on the floor with an ending so shocking, you'll read it again just to pick up the clues.

Tick Tock

A Detective Shakespeare Mystery

Book #2

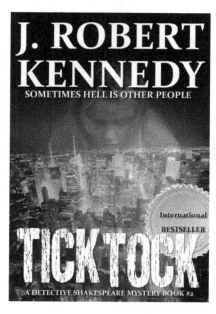

Crime Scene tech Frank Brata digs deep and finds the courage to ask his colleague, Sarah, out for coffee after work. Their good time turns into a nightmare when Frank wakes up the next morning covered in blood, with no recollection of what happened, and Sarah's body floating in the tub. Determined not to go to prison for a crime he's horrified he may have committed, he scrubs the crime scene clean, and, tormented by text messages from the real killer, begins a race against the clock to solve the murder before his own co-workers, his own friends, solve it first, and find him guilty.

Billionaire Richard Tate is the toast of the town, loved by everyone but his wife. His plans for a romantic weekend with his mistress ends in disaster, waking the next morning to find her murdered, floating in the tub. After fleeing in a panic, he returns to find the hotel room spotless, and no sign of the body. An envelope found at the scene contains not the expected blackmail note, but something far more sinister.

Two murders, with the same MO, targeting both the average working man, and the richest of society, sets a rejuvenated Detective Shakespeare, and his new reluctant partner, Amber Trace, after a murderer whose motivations are a mystery, and who appears to be aided by the very people they would least expect—their own.

Tick Tock, Book #2 in the internationally bestselling Detective Shakespeare Mysteries series, picks up right where Depraved Difference left off, and asks a simple question: What would you do? What would you do if you couldn't prove your innocence, but knew you weren't capable of murder? Would you hide the very evidence that might clear you, or would you turn yourself in and trust the system to work?

From the internationally bestselling author of The Protocol and Brass Monkey comes the highly anticipated sequel to the smash hit Depraved Difference, Tick Tock. Filled with heart pounding terror and suspense, along with a healthy dose of humor, Tick Tock's twists will keep you guessing right up to the terrifying end.

The Redeemer

A Detective Shakespeare Mystery

Book #3

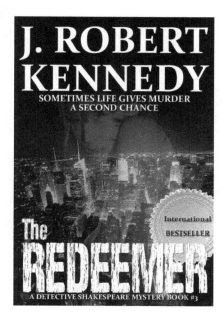

Sometimes Life Gives Murder a Second Chance

It was the case that destroyed Detective Justin Shakespeare's career, beginning a downward spiral of self-loathing and self-destruction lasting half a decade. And today things are only going to get worse. The Widow Rapist is free on a technicality, and it is up to Detective Shakespeare and his partner Amber Trace to find the evidence, five years cold, to put him back in prison before he strikes again.

But Shakespeare and Trace aren't alone in their desire for justice. The Seven are the survivors, avowed to not let the memories of their loved ones be forgotten. And with the release of the Widow Rapist, they are determined to take justice into their own hands, restoring balance to a flawed system.

At stake is a second chance, a chance at redemption, a chance to salvage a career destroyed, a reputation tarnished, and a life diminished.

A chance brought to Detective Shakespeare whether he wants it or not.

A chance brought to him by The Redeemer.

From J. Robert Kennedy, the author of seven international bestsellers including Depraved Difference and The Protocol, comes the third entry in the acclaimed Detective Shakespeare Mysteries series, The Redeemer, a dark tale exploring the psyches of the serial killer, the victim, and the police, as they all try to achieve the same goals.

Balance. And redemption.

Printed in the USA
CPSIA information can be obtained
at www.ICGtesting.com
LVHW042152210724
786130LV00025B/137